Dave Cameron's Schooldays

Dave Cameron's Schooldays

A Novel, as told to
Bill Coles

Legend ▌Press
Independent Book Publisher

Legend Press Ltd, 2 London Wall Buildings,
London EC2M 5UU
info@legend-paperbooks.co.uk
www.legendpress.co.uk

British Library Cataloguing in Publication Data available.

ISBN 978-1-9074611-7-0

Set in Times
Printed by JF Print Ltd., Sparkford.

Cover designed by Tim Bremner
Illustration by: Alan McGowan

Legend ⅂ Press

Independent Book Publisher

For Toby, my brother

Chapter 1

Spread evenly over my backside are four white stripes, each of them about six inches long. Sometimes when I come out of the shower, I catch a glimpse of those stripes in the mirror. The scars are slightly discoloured now, like old war wounds.

Those stripes are a memento of my education at Eton. I earned them within my first few days at the school, and the caning was so severe that I needed a full fortnight of treatment before the wounds had even begun to heal. But what a treatment! What a nurse! She alone was worth every second of the agony.

When I see those stripes today, they evoke so many memories for me. I only have to close my eyes and I can almost taste the leather belt being stuffed into my mouth; can feel my arms being pinned down to the table; the sound of running footsteps before I hear this very odd noise – like a wet fish being slapped onto a slab. Then, a tingling in my bottom that quickly grows to the most burning throb. Each stroke is counted off and, at the end of it all, the dismal offer of a handshake to show that I have taken my beating like a gentleman.

That was the manner in which I came by those stripes, and there has not been one single girlfriend who has not gasped in amazement when she's seen them. How they loved to hear the story of that caning; none of them could ever quite believe that sort of barbarity was still occurring at Eton in 1979. But it was, indeed it was, and my scars are the living proof of it.

The caning though was only the start of it. For what then followed in my first year at Eton was some of the most systematic bullying that a 14 year old boy has ever been subjected to. At least Tom Brown, during his legendary schooldays, only had Flashman to contend with. For myself, it sometimes felt like almost every senior boy in the house was intent on grinding me into the dust.

But I would not change it; would not change a single moment from my first year at school. For although the caning and all that came after it were beyond horrific, they were to set into motion the most extraordinary chain of events. And who knows where that chain will lead me – with luck and a following wind, I may even be in 10 Downing Street before my 45th birthday.

So this story is an explanation of how I became a Conservative. For the truth is that when I arrived at Eton as a callow 14-year-old, I could not have cared one jot for the Tories.

Most people tend to think that, because I'm from a family of blue-bloods, I've always been a Conservative. But this was not the case. And, as for politics itself, I cannot recall a single subject in my curriculum that was quite so monumentally tedious as 'political science'. As far as I was concerned the whole of Westminster could have drowned in its own ordure: I detested the lot of them.

What a sea-change I was to undergo. By the end of my first year, I had become the most diehard Conservative that you've ever met; Christ, I must have been insufferable. There's nothing on God's earth that's quite so repellent as a young Conservative who's seen the light.

And the catalyst was that first caning when I was to experience the most savage pain that had ever been inflicted on me. So: a brutal caning helps turn an Etonian into a Tory – who ever would have thought it?

Chapter 2

Mind you, at least my first caning was only witnessed by a handful of people – unlike the poor old 'School Dunces'.

This was the formal name for … now how can I put this politely, since I know that at least one junior Royal has borne the title? The School Dunces, as they were formally known, were basically the thickest boys in Eton. The title was awarded each year to the ten boys who had achieved the worst O-Level results during the previous summer's exams.

I'd heard all about it – and was greatly looking forward to the show. It was like they were putting on a special circus just to make us all feel welcome. All the new boys filed into Upper School, gawking about us at the busts of the old boys on the wall. Quite a few Prime Ministers up there too, you know – 18 as I remember it, but fingers crossed that figure may imminently need some slight amendment.

All the new boys – the F-tits as we were known because we were all Effing useless – were dressed up in jacket and tie. Behind us were well over a hundred Beaks, including the unmistakable bald dome of my Tutor, Tam Maguire. They were drumming their feet in unison as the Senior Master downed a yard of Theakston's Old Peculier. The Headman, togged up in gown and mortarboard, came on to give some dreary speech. But he knew – and we knew – that he was only the warm-up act. We couldn't wait!

Finally, he drifted to an end and bawled those four memorable words that have been declaimed at the Thrashing of the Dunces for nigh on 400 years: "*Pour encourager les autres!*" ['To encourage the others!' Voltaire pinched the line for *Candide*.]

The ten Dunces, dressed up in Eton tails, were escorted the length of Upper School by four gnarled Watchmen. What an extraordinary snapshot of Eton life: some proud, some cocky, some even with carefree smiles on their faces. But the one that I particularly noted was the tail-end Charlie, who was white and shivering with terror; even then I thought that he was putting on a pretty poor show. It was only a bloody beating, after all.

I wormed my way through to the front to get a good view of the flogging. The Eton beating block, black with age, was brought onto the stage. The electric frisson rippled through the assembled new boys as we let out a collective gasp! "Cooeee!"

One by one the Dunces were led onto the podium. They would be offered the choice of the Wad or the Bullet – of which more later – and would adopt the position, bending over the block. I was fascinated.

I had seen many beatings before at my prep school, but nothing to touch the wonderful stoicism of those 16-year-old Etonians.

All save the last. He had been getting more and more nervous as the nine other Dunces were thrashed in front of him. When it came to his turn, he was wriggling like a ferret. The Watch had no option but to hold him – actually hold him! – down on the block. The ignominy of it. He was screaming so much that they just shoved the Wad straight into his mouth.

The Caner selected a fresh cane from the rack and gave it a few practice swishes in the air. "Oooo!" we all cried. This was going to be fun.

"Tails up!" called the Keeper of the Watch, and the terrified Dunce's tails were flicked over his head. The Caner counted off his paces along the rostrum, like a bowler measuring his run-up. After a nod from the Keeper of the Watch, he turned, took six smart steps and delivered the most thundering crack to the Dunce's bottom. I was there, right up close to him. It looked like his bulging eyes were going to pop out of his head. "One!" cried the Keeper of the Watch.

Six blows he had in all and by the end you could practically see the steam coming off his trousers.

"I can see blood!" squeaked one boy.

"He's blubbing!" squealed another.

The Dunce shook the Caner's hand but – shamefully – did not even thank the man for his pains.

What an introduction to Eton. Talk about living history! There it all was, being acted out right in front of our very eyes. As we wandered back to our houses, even the narkiest new boys were beginning to appreciate the awesome spectacle they had just experienced.

My Tutor Tam Maguire was all eagerness to discuss the thrashing when he visited my room in Farrer House that evening.

Now, as Maguire has some small bearing on my story, I suppose I should give him the benefit of a little descriptive detail. He shaved his head every morning and was as bald as an egg. He liked to tell us that his pasty white pate "shone with the light of the wisdom of the ages", though for myself I always thought he looked like a skinhead at a funeral, having somehow managed to strap himself into a dark suit, wing-collar and white bowtie.

Because Maguire had no hair, his head never changed from one year to the next. If he'd had a bit of botox, he'd have looked exactly the same even 30 years later; especially if he were dead. Bulbous shining eyes that seemed to bulge out of their sockets when he became excited; snaggly teeth that were always in need of repair; and, now that I think of it, a rather queeny manner – not that there's anything wrong with that.

"Did you like the… the Thrashing of the Dunces, David?" he said, as he patted the space next to him on my fold-down bed. "I love a good Thrashing! I have not missed a single one in 20 years! Not one! I think there could be no better start to the school year. But 'twas a very poor show indeed from the last Dunce and he should be not a little ashamed of himself. Ashamed!"

He patted the bed again, a little tetchily this time. "David, come join me!" Pat-a-pat-pat, went his wrinkly old hand. And – isn't it funny how these delicious details come back to you? – it was said that he had more hairs on the backs of his two hands than on the *entire* rest of his body.

"Now we – we are going to get to know each other very, very well indeed over the next five years. I might even get to know you better than your own sister; think on that, David!" Then he said something that I have never heard uttered from another human's lips – not before and not since either. It was, I suppose, one of his catchphrases. "Hooo-hooo-hooo, David," he cried, eyes starting to bulge a little with excitement. "Hooo-hooo-hooo!"

"Yes Sir." I sat down next to him on the bed, and for a while he just sat there, this big grin on his face as he nodded and nodded his head – looking for the life of him like a starved mongrel that's been presented with the most enormous bone.

"Now before I flit, I fly, I wish to raise two small matters which have, for some unaccountable reason, not been covered in the school rules." He clapped his hairy old hand on my knee. "The first is on the matter of choking the chicken."

"I'm sorry?"

Maguire furrowed his brow a little, pulling at his lower lip. "Ah, well – perhaps you know it by another name, David. It is also called Onanism. Dancing with Mrs Palm and her five daughters – have you heard of that? Beating your bologna? Dancing the two-fisted tango?"

I looked at the man in utter incomprehension.

"Umm," he said, eye-lashes fluttering. "It has other names too – now let me see. Draining the vats? Firming the worm? A hand shandy? Jerking the turkey? Ahhh … Perhaps you know it as making the piggy squeal? Or even pulling the pork stick?"

"Oh yes, Sir!" I piped. "You mean wanking?"

"Ahh, er, yes," he said, perhaps a little taken aback by my obvious eagerness. "Well, what I would like to make clear, David, is that, ahh, wanking, as you call it, is nothing less than an abomination! An *abomination*! It is a sin against nature! It saps your life force. And, worse than that, it is such a waste of your delicate little botty!" (A slip of the tongue, I'm sure of it.)

"Yes Sir!" I said, eager to pledge my delicate little botty to the cause.

Maguire nodded his pleasure, delighted to have found such a willing disciple. "I have done my best, David, to root out this abomination from the House. Root it out! Root, Root, Root, that's what I do! And while I am still its Tutor, there shall be no masturbation in Farrer Houser! It was rife – rife! – before I took over the running of Farrer, but now I believe that we are a masturbatory-free zone. My fight against it is ceaseless and I will not – I will not! – tolerate the new boys bringing any of their filthy prep school habits into Farrer!"

Here he sniffed the air deep into his lungs. His eyelids flickered shut and his tongue tipped out over his thin lower lip, like an old snake scenting the air. "I always know when it's about!" he shrieked. "I can smell it! I can smell it out with my own nose!"

I goggled at him for a bit. He'd somehow latched his hand onto my knee and was pummelling my leg like a piece of dough.

"But what I shall have instead in this house, David, is honour. Honour!" Maguire suddenly left off my leg to start prowling round my room. He went over to my burry and sniffed; sniffed at my ottoman; and then started sniffing at all the posters I'd tacked up on the wall. Satisfied that my room still remained a wank-free zone, he stood before me, hands behind his back, legs astride.

"Now on the matter of honour, David." His Adam's Apple started to wobble, and I suddenly realised he was choking up. "Some people deride honour as a dead thing. A thing of the past! I, however, know that it is very much of the present! And I believe, David, that there are two kinds of honour. There is the honour of your own person. And, over and above that, there is the honour of the school. I like to call it your Eton honour."

Maguire did a little skip on the spot before prancing six steps over to the window. "In this house, I operate what I like to call the Maguire Code of Honour. I take things on trust. If a boy pledges his Honour, or indeed his Eton Honour, then I will believe him. 'Tis a small matter for some, but for myself I believe that, above all else, Honour is the paramount virtue of an Eton schoolboy!"

"Yes Sir!" I piped with gusto; if Maguire wanted to take

things on trust that sounded pretty all right by me.

"Some boys, however, they are without honour. Even boys in my own house!" He opened the door and wistfully shook his head. "There is one boy, BJ – I fear he has no honour; in fact, I very much doubt he ever had it."

Chapter 3

BJ. Nowadays, of course, he's known as something rather different. But when I first met him, he was simply BJ, and that – despite all his various other titles – is how he will always be to me.

It's so funny to see this man, this great golden bear, today and to compare him to the wild firebrand that he was 30 years ago. How different we were. For me, there has been this gradual metamorphosis over the past 30 years as I have emerged into a political player. But BJ: he always had it, had it right from his very first year at Eton.

Sometimes I see him looking at me across the room and I know that he would do anything to swap places. For here I am on the verge of having the job that was his destiny and BJ knows that he has been slightly sidelined. Without doubt, he has power and he has influence and he has crammed more into his 45-odd years than most people could fill in five lifetimes. And yet in all my dealings with him, I am aware of this slight air of melancholy and envy. Although it has never been stated, we both of us know that I am about to win the job for which he had always seemed preternaturally destined.

Maybe one day, after I'm long gone from the political scene, he'll have one final hurrah – like Churchill when his career as a politician seemed dead and buried. I'm not sure how good he'd be. BJ does have an astonishing talent for putting his foot in it.

Anyway, it is to BJ that I owe so much of my life. It was BJ who was to set me on the path of modern Conservatism. And it was thanks to BJ that I came within a whisker – an absolute whisker – of being killed. Mind you, he nearly got me expelled from Eton, so compared to that, death was relatively small beer.

We laugh about it now, when we are in our cups and there is nobody about to overhear our tall tales. For the moment, it is my turn in the sun. But then, when I was 14-years-old, BJ wasn't just basking in the sun's rays; he was the sun itself, around whom the whole of Eton's firmament revolved.

Of course none of us know how things will turn out: which events in our lives turned out to be pivotal, and which were nothing more than bumps along the track. But if there'd been no BJ, my first year at Eton would have been much more mundane. I would not have lost at least two of my nine lives and, but for BJ, I would not now be on track to be the first Old Etonian Prime Minister in over 40 years.

What an extraordinary introduction I was to have to this man-mountain, this sizzling fire-cracker of a human being, this enormous, unquenchable, unstoppable force of nature.

The first I heard of it was not just a shout, but a roar. It was the day after Maguire's lecture on the dangers of wanking. I was sitting lonely in my room thinking that I'd much rather be at home – home at Peasemore with my parents and with Caroline, the local girl whom I was sweet on.

It was quite dark outside and nothing could be heard but the steady drum of the rain on the windows. Then this extraordinary bellow, a war-cry, shattering in its suddenness, as if a Mongol horde had erupted from the very bowels of the house.

I was on the ground floor but could hear the screaming continue as the horde thundered upstairs to the senior boys' rooms on the second floor.

More shouting and the sound of a window being smashed overhead. Then: one of the more surreal moments of my life. An old-style gramophone whistled past my window and exploded into the ground. A rain of plant-pots and books follow. I thought I could make out a cry: "Where is he?" Well, not in his room, obviously. Soon the rain of plant pots had stopped and the screaming horde was tearing downstairs – down to my floor.

I opened the door a crack to peep out. I had never seen anything like it. I'd heard about them, all right. but never seen them *en masse*. Hooray Henrys to the last man; it was much like the coronation of a Tory leader, now that I think of it.

The Poppers were the school's prefects; self-elected and with a host of perks, of which the best by far was to be in possession of the world's most stunning school uniform. Oh, even now, even now that I am on the verge of becoming Prime Minister, I still feel a prickle of envy at the thought of those gorgeously clad boys. For my entire five years at Eton, I longed to be a Popper. But I never quite made the grade. And I daresay that it's thanks to not being elected into Pop that I was so desperate to join the bloody Bullingdon Club. (And hasn't that picture, with me trying to look like Tony Hadley from Spandau Ballet, just come back to haunt me?) Looking back, I think if I'd made it into Pop, I might have been weaned off my desire for flashy uniforms and in consequence might have been slightly more chary about joining those chinless wonders at the Bullingdon. If, if, if … and if Nanny Irish had wheels she'd be a bloody tea-trolley.

To continue. This screaming horde of Poppers was charging

onto the F-tits' corridor. They erupted from the stairwell into the middle of the corridor and at first they charged off in the other direction. A great shriek, as if a pack of hounds had finally seized their prey. I peeped out through the chink in the door.

The next moment, the mob was coming back the other way. One Popper had run ahead into the communal bathroom next to my room. I could hear the thunder of running water as one of the baths was filled. Then came a cluster of about 10 Poppers who were carrying over their heads a naked man – looking for all the world like a sacrificial victim. But this man was no victim – he was singing, bellowing, at the very top of his voice. He seemed to writhe on this quilt of hands in an absolute orgasm of ecstasy. A glimpse of wild blonde hair and a look of perfect happiness on the man's face – a man whose dream was that very moment becoming a reality.

More Poppers followed. They had raided several food cupboards and were carrying everything from eggs to coffee jars and loaves of sliced white. More ululating, more screaming before a final wolf-howl. It all stopped as suddenly as it had started. One after the other, the Poppers darted down the F-tits' passageway and out of our lives.

I waited until the last Popper had left before going into the bathroom. Total and utter carnage – eggs smeared across the walls, dripping down the mirrors, a carpet of coffee granules on the floor. Oh, and I may as well correct one minor fallacy that people have about Eton. The taps are not all made of solid gold. The bathroom was just a regulation school bathroom that you could see anywhere in Britain, with maybe ten sinks and a couple of bath cubicles. (And, now that I'm on the subject of correcting minor fallacies about Eton, we didn't wear top hats either. Frottage and blowjobs, on the other hand… well of course there was a little bit of that. An absolutely tiny amount. But not to my personal knowledge.)

I pushed open the door to one of the bath cubicles – and there in all his naked glory was the blonde man I'd seen earlier. He was lying in a bathtub filled to the brim with water, baked beans and about eight loaves of bread. A couple of boxes of eggs had been cracked over his head, his blonde hair streaked orange and yellow. In his hand, nonchalantly on the edge of the bath, was a Magnum of Bollinger.

He'd been singing some ditty, in a world of his own. He looked up when he saw the door open.

"My name is Ozymandias, King of Kings!" he bellowed. "Look on my works Ye Mighty and Despair!"

"Sorry," I said nervously. "I think I've got the wrong room."

He thrust the bottle at me. "Have some!" he said. "Put hair on your chest!"

I wiped the top clear of some lingering egg yolk and took a sip. Not quite how I'd had champagne before.

"Easy, Tiger!" The man laughed and took the bottle. He seemed quite comfortable in his sea of beans. "Wondering what all that was about?"

"High-tea with your chums?"

He smirked and flicked a bean off his chest. "Who are you, anyway?"

"David," I replied. "And who might you be?"

"Aha!" he said. "That is the question on every girl's lips: who am I? I am a multitude of facets, twinkling like a diamond in this Eton shit-house. I am a scholar, domiciled in Farrer to bring some lustre to your tawdry lives; I am a rower, though I hate it; I am a footballer, though I have no skill; and above everything, I am a lover of all things beautiful." He held the bottle a few inches above his lips and let the Champagne cascade over his mouth and cheeks. "Especially women."

I goggled at him. "Is that it?"

"By no means!" He laughed, threw back his head and seemed to swallow half the bottle in a single draft. "I am a classicist. I can read Latin or Greek with the same fluency that you can read English. I am probably the untidiest human being you are ever likely to meet. And, as of tonight, I am this house's one and only member of Pop. I am, in short, a man with all the skills and reptilean talents to become a politician. Or possibly a journalist. But most likely I will have a shot at both. A man of my talents should not feel limited to a single profession."

I could not think of any suitable reply so I said what Nanny Irish always used to say when she was at a loss for words: "Oh really?"

"Yes, really." He sipped more champagne, before spurting it in a fountain across the bath.

"And do you have a name, Sir?"

"My friends and enemies alike, to all of them I answer to the name of BJ."

"BJ?" I said. "Why do they call you BJ?"

"Because, dear David, that is what I like."

Chapter 4

It's time I introduced you to another key ingredient from my Eton days: my Katy. You didn't think that I was going to turn Tory at 14 without at least one woman entering my tale?

I only knew her for but one single year, and how I would love to know what's happened to her. Katy, my Katy, where are you, my Katy?

Katy was one of the maids who served the food. There were others, and yet I cannot remember a thing about them. But even 30 years on, Katy has the most remarkable ability to stalk through my sleep and my daydreams. Perhaps it is that I am viewing that woman through the rosiest of tinted spectacles but, as I see her now, she seems to have a magnitude of beauty almost beyond human. I have known so many beautiful women in my life – and, by great good fortune, most of them biblically. But for me, Katy remains the most beautiful woman that I have ever seen in my life. She never changes; Katy is always stuck there in the amber of my first year at Eton.

I suppose she must have been in her early twenties, slim, with a long brown cascade of hair; full lips that always seemed to be one twitch away from breaking into the most beaming smile. Eyes of green, forest green, I remember that. She never really liked her eyes, but I think they suited her well, for they gave her this air of slight sadness. Even that first time I saw her, it was all rather intoxicating – the contrast of that most beautiful pearly smile and the underlying sadness of her eyes.

That day Katy was wearing, as I remember, a black skirt and a pristine white shirt, short-sleeved, with a frilly bit running down the middle. Although it was supposed to be a very formal look, she had contrived to look like a hoyden. Perhaps it was the heel-toe, heel-toe way that she walked, as if she were on a catwalk, accentuating the lovely roll of her rump. It might even have been the way she stood at the door, hand on one hip as she twirled a ringlet of hair. But, for me, my fondest memory of all, is the first time she came into my life. She leaned over me to take my plate. A wisp of hair fluttered in front of her face. A hint of perfume. A bare forearm, hands with long tapering fingers, and nails painted the most vivid red varnish.

"Thank you," I said, moving to the side as she leaned over me. I looked up at her and caught her eye. "Thank you so much."

"You're very welcome – David," she said, and smiled. Those lips, moist and scarlet, of a match with her fingernails.

David! She knew my name!

I was transfixed. This beauty was interested in me! But after all… why shouldn't she be interested in a 14-year-old boy who happened to be both short and flabby for his age?

I was a schoolboy in love.

I watched her as she went about her business, and gradually my hopes and dreams dwindled, like a piece of tinder that flashes for a moment before turning into a wisp of smoke.

I'd thought it was personal; I thought it was me she loved. But as I saw her weave about the room, I realised that she bestowed her favours on every boy in the house. She knew them all by name – smiled at them all, chatted, laughed, brushed her hair from her eyes; she'd have flayed them alive if she'd gone into politics.

But all that flirting with the other boys. It didn't really make any difference.

I still loved her all the same.

She'd met her match, though, with BJ. Katy had just served Maguire, and BJ was leaning back in his chair to give her some space. And as he leaned back, he stretched out his arm and draped it round her bum. Around her bum! And do you know what my Katy did next? The houri not only neglected to slap him in the face, but smiled at him.

After lunch, the F-tits had five minutes to prepare themselves for one of Eton's greatest traditions – The Running of the Fags.

Now that Health and Safety has done for fagging at Eton, I can only presume this age-old tradition has also gone to the wall. A shame. Like so many of Eton's activities, it was all useful preparation for life as an MP.

From outside the dining room came the echoing shout, "BoooyUppp!" and we charged out into the middle of this baying mob. Sort of like the Pamplona bull run, only in a tailcoat.

The entire house had formed a cordon all the way up the two flights of stairs to the top floor. We had to run the gauntlet as they pelted us with, of all things … cubes of ice and sugar. The sweet and the cool. It was supposed to be some sort of motto about the Eton way of life, though I'm damned if I can remember it. The worst of it, though, was the other fags – kicking, biting and gouging as we all hared to the top. The only thing that even compares is the first day of an Ashes Test at Lords: complete bedlam as the MCC members race to bag their seats in the pavilion.

What do I remember of the Running of the Fags? William M'Thwaite side-swiping me into a pillar; grabbing Mark

Davide by the ankle and, beautiful moment, watching his nose explode onto a banister; and arriving at the Library and having a lumpen Librarian, or prefect, hurl ice-cubes at me at point blank.

We then had about an hour or two to regroup before we were formally introduced to our fag-masters. Fags, in those days, had a number of general chores about the house, but their chief loyalty was to their 'fag-master', for whom they acted as a personal cook, cleaner and valet. Many outsiders like to believe that the fags acted as unpaid rent-boys. What is it with this total obsession with sex? Why does everyone – everyone! – seem to think that fags spent every waking moment pleasuring the older boys?

I mean, does everyone think that all the girls at Roedean, or St Mary's Ascot, were hopping in and out of bed with each other every night? Of course not. And yet for some reason, Eton has come to be perceived as this sort of hot-bed of boy-on-boy action. Now I'm sure that this sort of thing may very occasionally have occurred. But I would just like to reiterate – and I cannot say this enough – that I personally never witnessed any such sordidness.

My fag-master was – of course – BJ. Without him, I doubt whether I'd be even be in Westminster now: how happy that would make David Davis. And if I might just clarify one further point. That curmudgeon Davis currently believes that if it weren't for me, he'd now be leader of the Tory Party! Dream on!

I'd gone upstairs to the top floor to make my formal obeisances to BJ. Just before I arrived at his room, however, I somehow contrived to cause very slight offence to the House Captain; it rather tainted my first year at Eton.

A number of the senior boys were playing passage football,

and Henchman hammered the ball. It ricocheted off two walls before bouncing off down the stairs.

"Boy!" he screamed at me. Perhaps Henchman treated all the juniors like that; although I'm aware that I have a natural air of insolence that tends to vex. "Fetch that ball!"

Not even the courtesy of a "please". I stared at Henchman for a moment. "If you insist."

"I do insist," he said, perspiring in his shirt-sleeves. Our House Captain was tall, rake thin, with your usual Eton cowlick of hair plastered down his forehead. Most noticeably, he had a scar on his neck – long and thin, almost like a duelling scar – that pulsed when he was angry. There's a good story behind it too, but all in good time.

So, as eager to please as any Eton new boy, I set off down the stairs and retrieved the ball. "Here's your bally," I said.

"My bally?" he said. "My bally?"

I could see that a 'thank you' was probably not on the cards. But, as Nanny Irish always used to say, it never hurts to be polite. "My pleasure," I said.

Behind me I hear the sound of the ball being booted. Bonk-bonk-bonk as it drums down the stairs. "Boy!" screams Henchman. "Fetch that ball!"

Now that, that was unnecessary. Henchman stood glowering over me. Down the stairs I go and retrieve the ball. By now, the other boys have come over to see how this little stand-off will pan out.

Well, if it had riled him once, it was probably worth giving it a second crack. "Here's your bally."

I let the football roll out of my hands and it trickled to Henchman's feet. No prizes for guessing what he did next. A boot and off the ball bounces down the stairs again. Henchman is smirking now. Doesn't even speak, just nods at the staircase.

Not quite how I'd envisaged my entrance onto the Eton fagging scene. And yet, if I was not very much mistaken, I was now dead set on a collision course with the House Captain. What to do, what to do? "You know what my nanny used to say to me?" I said chattily.

Henchman pointed towards the staircase. "Fetch the ball." Definitely had the makings of a Labour frontbencher – you can probably see that.

"No – funnily enough, that's *not* what she used to say to me. And had she asked me to fetch her ball, I'm sure she'd have said 'Please'!" I shot my cuffs, well pleased with myself. "No – what Nanny Irish *did* use to say was this: first time funny; second time boring; third time, smack!"

I smiled my most pleasant, amenable smile. "Though, shall I tell you something else? Old Nanny Irish used to give us one hell of a sight more than a smack –"

"Fetch the ball!"

"I'd love to, I really would," I said, edging backwards. "But I have this most urgent appointment with BJ. It really wouldn't do to keep him waiting. Terribly sorry!"

"Fetch the ball!" he screamed. Talk about a scratched record – just what didn't he understand?

I sauntered off down the passage, a perky whistle on my heels – modelled not a little on Clint Eastwood in his early Spaghetti Westerns. Think of Clint gliding out of the saloon bar, though a little shorter and in a tailcoat and you'll just about be there. It was all going very well until I heard a bellow from behind and realised Henchman was out to scrag me so I tore off down the passage, *mit der Haus-Führer* screaming behind me.

I knew that BJ's room was directly above my own. I collided with his door, knocking and opening it in one single movement and leapt through the doorway just as Henchman's boot flailed in thin air behind me.

Henchman stood outside the door. Although he was the House Captain, he did not feel able to follow. I gave him a little wave of my fingers. "Ciao!"

I had entered not so much an Eton boy's room as a tented harem: purple silk hung in loops from the ceiling and across the walls; swagged silk curtains tied up by the windows; a luxurious shag pile carpet in magenta and gold that filled the entire room; and a wooden hat-stand in the shape of a large black bear. All fairly standard fare, of course, for a Tory MP – but it was a *little* precocious for an 18-year-old.

That wasn't even the half of it. None of those ratty beds on hinges for BJ, for instead he had a proper double bed with a black fur throw on top. Not just one burry, but two, side-by-side and overflowing with bits of paper. Then there were the two huge bunches of lilies in matching Chinese vases on either side of the mantelpiece. And as for the man himself, he was wearing a green smoking jacket and black monogrammed slippers, and was lying full-length on a brown leather sofa.

BJ was reading from a tatty first edition, while gesticulating with his free hand. "You are making rather a racket, you know David!"

"Henchman just tried to kick me up the arse!" My eyes wandered round the room. Propped against the fireplace was what appeared to be a Roman shield, emblazoned with the eagle of the imperial army. Above it were a pair of crossed Assegai and what looked like a genuine Magnum revolver.

"I'm sure you deserved it!" BJ took a sip of champagne before returning his cut-crystal rummer to an antique side-table. "Now you, David, are in the fortunate position of being my personal fag. You may even enjoy it!"

"Yes, BJ."

"In the morning at 7am precisely I desire to be woken with a pot of Lapsang Oulong, some sugar and a slice of lemon. Always bring two cups."

"Yes BJ!"

"After breakfast, my bed is to be made up. Fresh sheets in the cupboard, as and when required. Give the room an airing." He was counting the points off on his fingers. "Never touch any of the papers on my desks, though you can have your fill of the porn mags, which, just like every other Etonian, I keep underneath the mattress."

"Porn mags?"

"You may treat the room as your own. But I do not want you spanking your monkey in here. It's bad enough having Bouverie next door! Do you want champagne by the way? Help yourself – glasses above the fridge."

I poured myself a glass. The fizz bubbled over the side and onto the carpet.

"Watch it, you bloody tinker! Did your father teach you nothing at home?"

"Sorry, BJ."

The grandfather clock chimed by the door. "Christ, is that the time?" He leapt off the sofa and flung his smoking jacket onto the bear hat-stand. Kicking off his slippers, he tugged on some black cowboy boots that appeared to be made of ostrich skin. They slipped snugly under his hounds' tooth pop trousers.

"Hush now!" He put his finger to his lips. "What is that I hear from the distance? 'Tis my lady love. She is calling for her BJ."

He wrapped a silk scarf round his neck, before patting himself down. "A fly whisk!" he said. "Mustn't forget that!"

As I gaped on, he opened a beautiful tea-caddy on his burry

that was filled to the brim with condoms. He grabbed a handful and stuffed them into his pocket before giving me a cheery wave. "Eton's most dashing Popper has left the building!" He winked at me. "I never asked, by the way – do you enjoy extra-curricular activities?"

The door slammed, the pictures rattling on the walls.

Chapter 5

Extra-curricular activities? I only had to wait a few days to find out *precisely* what he meant.

I was tucked up in bed, fast asleep. At first I thought the tapping sound at the window was part of my dream, but then I groaned, woke up, listened. There was an erratic knocking, sounded like metal on glass. After a few seconds, I went to investigate. Was there someone outside?

I drew back the curtains, peered outside into the rain, and could see nothing at all. Then the tapping came again and I realised that what I was looking at was a small bunch of keys, attached to some string, which were being swung against the glass.

I opened the window, looked out, looked up – and there two floors above me was BJ, his wild hair outlined in silhouette.

"Thank God!" he called down to me. "Took your bloody time!"

"What do you want?" I called up to him.

"Yes!" he hissed down at me. "Set the fire alarm off! And quick!"

"What?" I couldn't quite believe my ears. "The fire alarm?"

"Quickly, quickly!" he called. "I can hear him! Set the fire-alarm off!"

"Now?"

"No – next week, you little idiot; when do you think I mean! Now, now, very now! An old black ram is tupping your white ewe!" (That's Shakespeare, by the way, though why on earth BJ was quoting *Othello* to me at a time like that, I have no idea.) "Just get on and do it!"

"OK, I'm going, I'm going!" Heaven knew why he wanted me to set the alarm off, but presumably he had his reasons. I felt like a young subaltern sent off on a covert mission by the brigadier – mine not to reason why, mine but to do or die.

I padded barefoot out of the room and out into the passage. It was lit overhead by a few dull emergency lights. I didn't remember ever seeing a fire alarm on the passage, but there had to be one somewhere – and there was, right at the very far end.

I inspected it gingerly. 'In emergency, smash glass'. Well, looked like I was going to have to take one for Team BJ.

One deep breath and I punched out the glass with the heel of my hand – idiotic way to do it. The glass jagged against my thumb. The house, so silent, suddenly exploded with noise. Hard as I could, I raced back to my room; it would have done me no good at all to have been caught anywhere near that smashed fire alarm. One of the Librarians, Tait, was out of his room in an instant, though I don't think he spotted me.

Slam the door, slip on my slippers and dressing gown, and then I'm blinking out of my room, yawning, and dutifully waking up my neighbours to prevent them from being roasted alive.

Then out the fire escape and onto Farrer's lawn, and by now it was absolutely pouring. There was BJ, the only one of us that was dressed for the rain. He had an umbrella and wore, as I remember, gumboots and an overcoat that was the colour of a banana-skin. He came over to me, happy as can be, and without a word gave me a thundering clap on the back.

Maguire, with the water streaming off his bald head, looked incandescent. He quickly rattled through the roll-call before cutting to the chase.

"Who," he asked, "set off the alarm?"

The 50 boys gawked at each other and I could do that with the best of them, so like the other F-tits, I stared about me in bemusement. "Not me, Guv!"

Nothing happened for about 10 seconds, before Maguire said querulously: "I repeat – who set off the alarm? I must have an answer! Who set off the alarm! And I tell you, it'll be the worse for you if you don't own up now!"

Well – do you think I stuck up my hand, like some village simpleton before piping up, "Please Sir! It was me!" Hah! You must be joking!

It is true that in America, schools operate what is known as 'the honour code', where the students are encouraged to own up to things, as if this is 'honourable' behaviour. They even consider it honourable to shop their mates. Ghastly!

Things are rather different in the British public schools, where only a complete noodle-head ever owns up to anything. And quite right too, as it's a much more practical training for life. What happens when the police arrest you for, say, some piffling kerb-crawling demeanour? Is it wise to immediately 'fess up and say, "Officer, I cannot tell a lie – I was lookin' for 'ookers." No – of course we don't. We keep our mouths shut, and tell the copper to do his worst and see if he can prove it.

All the boys continued to goop at each other, and Maguire had one more attempt at trying to browbeat us. "Better you confess now than I find out later!" he screeched. "If I have to find the boy who set off the alarm, then I will find him! And once I have found him, he will be punished! Severely!"

The boys trooped back into the house, but one thing I didn't like was that Maguire went into a huddle with several of the senior boys, including Tait. At one point, a pin seemed to have been thrust into him. Maguire goggled for a moment, scanned all the boys who were queued on the staircase – and who should his mad old eyes eventually come to rest on but little old me. I stoutly stared him down, the F-tit who aspires to a nobler, more gentle way of life.

Anyway – nothing to be done about it now. I went back to my poky little room. (Smallish: a window, fold-up bed, desk – or 'burry' in Eton-speak – rug, ottoman and armchair. The lap of luxury, it ain't.) I slipped off my dressing-gown and was just getting into bed, when I heard the rat-a-tat clip of footsteps in the passage. Some chums popping round for a visit?

A polite knock at the door and M'Tutor, Mr Maguire, still bedraggled from the rain, stepped in.

"Hello David," he started off, making a conscious effort to calm down. His grey suit was absolutely sodden. "Good evening. This is a rather difficult thing for me to ask, but I just wondered if you, if you, might know anything about the fire-alarm?"

"The fire-alarm, Sir?" I showed my sympathetic concern.

"Yes, David, the fire-alarm. I believe you might happen to know how it came to be set off?" His hands writhed like snakes as he dry-washed his fingers.

"Me, Sir?" I looked to left and right, scouring my brain to see if I could recollect anything that might be pertinent to the matter in hand. I looked him square in the eye, bluff John Bull at his most forthright. "No, Sir."

"Ahh," he said, not quite able to understand. "So … so you have no knowledge of how the fire-alarm was set off?"

I looked Maguire full in the face. "Sir – I find it shocking to hear that this fire-alarm has been set off as a mere prank. I, however, had nothing to do with it."

Maguire stared at his shoes, before turning those bulging eyeballs back to me. "On your honour, David? I'm sorry to ask you this. But can you assure me on your honour?"

Time for another earnest look to the eyes. "On my honour, Sir!"

Perhaps he'd expected me just to 'fess up immediately. Well he could carry on about his rotten fire-alarm till the cows came home; he wasn't going to get much change out of me.

For a moment, he looked almost confused. Could his sources be wrong? How was it possible for such a demure 14-year-old to be lying so brazenly? Perhaps he was mistaken…

"Very well, David. If you are telling me on your honour that you know nothing about the fire-alarm being set off, then I will believe you."

If you toss the ball up high enough, I can sock it out of the park like the best of them. "Yes Sir, absolutely, Sir. On my honour, I know nothing about the fire-alarm being set off." (So help me God.)

Maguire nodded his head, aware of the affront that had been caused to me. "Ye-yes," he said. "I'm sure that Tait must have been mistaken. After all… a mere boy of 14… David, I have been discourteous, and I… I would like to apologise."

I stood up. "Apology accepted, Sir."

He held out his hand, and I shook it manfully as I stared up into his watery oyster eyes.

He laughed, almost relieved that it had come to nothing. "I very much fear that Henchman and Tait were mistaken. I will go now and speak with them. Yes, I will have words with them."

That certainly sounded all right by me. "I am very hurt, Sir."

"I'm sure," he said, sniffing as he walked to the door, "I'm sure."

I'd got away with it, had got *clean* away with it, when there was a knock on the door and Tait – bloody Tait, the weasel, a Nicholas Coleridge mini-me even then – came in and messed the whole thing up.

"I've just been inspecting the broken glass, Sir," he said. "There's blood on it."

Maguire nodded at that, sniffed – and I felt this finger of ice trail up the middle of my back. "Blood, you say?" he said, that bald vulture head bobbing up and down. "Blood? Well!"

He turned to me, stroked his top lip. Could it possibly be? A dramatic Pinteresque pause, the three of us each locked into our positions, tension crackling in the air.

"I wondered …" he said, slowly gaining confidence. "I wondered David if I might see your hands, please."

"My hands, Sir." I squirmed. "Why would you want to see them?"

"Hands up, please," said Maguire. "Hands up! Let's have a look at them! Quickly now! Spit-spot!"

I didn't like the sound of this at all. I hadn't actually looked at my hand since I'd set the alarm off, but I was aware of a slight throb at the base of my thumb. I put my hands up, though with my thumb tight across my palm.

"Ahh," said Maguire, for a moment slightly disconcerted, before he smiled. "And thumbkin out please Mr Cameron."

Very slowly, I moved the thumb to the side. I didn't dare look.

"Hooo-hooo-hooo," tittered Maguire. "And what do we have here, Mr Cameron?" He came gliding over to inspect my hand more closely. "What do we have here? Why, we have one very small but bloody thumb! And look! Look at it, Mr Tait! There is even a piece of glass in there, too! I think, members of the jury, that we have found our smoking gun!"

Then – the very strangest thing of all – he just stood a couple of feet away from me, his head nodding up and down, up and down, with a smile on his varnished skin that split his face from ear to ear.

"I … I don't know how it got there, Sir –"

"Aha!" said Maguire. "Wait for it, wait for it! See, Mr Tait, how his evil mind works! See how he schemes and plots! And what will he say next! He will tell us, perhaps, that he nicked his hand while shaving in the dark. Hooo-hooo-hooo! Or did he perhaps cut himself on the fire escape as he scurried from the house?"

That was a bad one actually – because I'd been on the very verge of saying *exactly* that.

"Come on," Maguire said, a bit calmer now. "Admit it, boy, admit it now, and I will go easier on you. You've been caught red-handed – quite literally red-handed, as it happens – and all I wish to know is why you did it. So tell me boy, why did you set the alarm off?"

Looking back, I suppose I'd just given up the fight. There can't really be any excuse for what I did next. I think, perhaps, that I may just have been very tired. But anyway, like the idiot I was, I did it: I owned up.

"I might have done it while I was sleep-walking, Sir."

"Hooo-hooo-hooo!" Maguire was almost crying with delight, slapping his thighs as if I had said the very funniest thing he'd ever heard. "He did it sleep-walking! Of course he did. Dummkopf!" At that he smote his forehead with his hand. "How stupid of me not to think of that before!"

"I'm very sorry, Sir," I said. "I've always been prone to

sleep-walking."

"Well, I'm very sorry, too, Mr Cameron, because I no longer know whether to believe a single word you say! You squirm! You lie! In fact, it seems that every word you utter is a lie!"

"Honestly, Sir, I was unconscious when I did it! Is that a crime?"

"I am not prepared, Mr Cameron, to listen to any more of your insane lies for one moment longer! Not for one single moment! No – you will have to tell *them* to a different person entirely!"

And that, more or less, was how a legend was born. For that was how I started on the path to becoming the most notorious F-tit in Eton's history.

Quite a long stretch to becoming Prime Minister, ain't it now?

Chapter 6

You can imagine, perhaps, the degree of anticipation with which I went upstairs the next morning to make BJ his Lapsang Oulong.

Well, as it happened, I got my explanation without BJ even having to say a word. Maybe it's because it's now 30 years on, but looking back, I understand all, I forgive all. In that one instance I was more than happy to have taken one for Team BJ.

Still – it was quite a shocker. Left quite an unpleasant taste in the mouth which even months later had me wincing at the memory.

I made the tea, gave the Royal Doulton cups a polish, sliced up the lemon and got out the silver sugar tongs. And before I'd even gone into the room, I could hear something. Was it the sheets rustling? BJ thrashing about in his sleep?

A knock on the door, I enter – and the very oddest thing of all: there is no sound whatsoever. Complete silence. Not a single sound, not a snort, not a grunt from my slumbering fag-master.

I set the tea-things down, tugged open the curtains and, seeing as I was mildly peeved at what had happened the previous night, I immediately rounded on BJ. "Well, I hope you've got a bloody good reason for getting me to –"

The words died in my mouth. I just stood there gawking, in

such shock as if a freak surge had overloaded my synapses. My mouth may have moved up and down, but no word came out. I only have to close my eyes now and I can conjure up that image in an instant; as vivid now as when it first seared onto my eyeballs.

BJ had just rolled over. And there they both lay, without a stitch on, she nuzzling into his chest as he stroked her neck.

It was Katy! Katy, my Katy! My first love and now there she was! Bonking BJ – right in front of my eyes! It was one of the most revolting things I've ever seen – couldn't have been worse if I'd caught my dad at it with Nanny Irish. BJ had been bonking my Katy and now there they were, lying sated in each other's arms, and all the while smiling at me. Smiling at me! And not one of your nervy, embarrassed smiles, but your genuine cat-who's-had-the-cream grin.

I goggled a bit more. I could even see one of her breasts, which BJ was fondling with his grimy fingers. He looked, I have to say, absolutely delighted. Thrilled to have my Katy in bed with him. But was there not also a little delight in the shock that he had caused me?

And, as for my darling Katy, was she perhaps a little fearful that I had caught her in the very act of cuckolding me? Not a bit of it: the hoyden looked like a woman who had just spent the whole night being ravaged senseless. And, I have to admit it, there was perhaps about her the look of a woman in love.

For that was one of BJ's great charms. He may have been a sex-mad dog, but for the short time that a woman was in his arms, he loved them, he truly did.

"Morning, David!" he hollered, as if he were calling out to me from the far side of the cricket field. "Well, don't stand there like the village idiot! Get us some tea!"

Katy purred into BJ's flank. Her hair too, now that I think of it, was as wild as can be, a very Medusa with dark locks flayed all about her on the pillow. I could feel the blood draining from my face.

For a few moments, I was able to regroup. I busied myself with the tea, the lemon, the sugar, and took over a cup to Katy.

And I will never forget this, for as long as I live. She did the sweetest thing. "Good morning, David," she said, and then as I put down the cup and saucer on her side of the bed, she stretched up and kissed me on the cheek. I never really understood what it meant, but I like to think it was an acknowledgement, perhaps, that always in her heart there would be a small place for me. Well possibly. Maybe she was just an incorrigible little flirt.

"Morning, Katy," I said, all brisk assurance now, though I must admit my eyes did dart down from her face – both her boobs were now on full display, *both of them!* "Morning, BJ."

"Ta," said BJ, as he started slurping the tea down with his usual panache. "Oh, and thanks for last night. Life-saver."

"A, errr, a pleasure," I said.

"Bloody Maguire was spot-checking all the boys' rooms. He's got a nerve. The sheer effrontery of the man!"

Katy, sitting up now in the bed, breasts – *those breasts!* – now on full display, so brazen that she might have been sitting on a topless beach in Tenerife. And perhaps … I've just realised this, but is it possible that the minx *wanted* me to be feasting my little peepers on her ample curves? Missed opportunities: how I hate them.

"Might have been very nasty for you both," I said, picking up the clothes that were strewn all about the floor. Her knickers! Her bra! Lacy red satin! I had them – *held them* – in my very hands. Her black skirt, her white blouse: how I longed to bury my nose into the cotton and inhale her scent. And a garter belt. Black stockings. Teetering black stilettos! If I'd had the room to myself, I'd have clutched them to my face and howled like a dog!

"Anyway – thanks very much, David, and I think you can … you can be off now. No mishaps?"

I looked up from Katy's skirt, which I was so assiduously shaking out. And – I couldn't believe it – there was some rummaging going on in the bed. She was pawing at him underneath the blankets – in front of my very eyes!

"Well, not much of a mishap," I said, unable to take my eyes off what was occurring beneath the sheets. "'Fraid Maguire caught me. I think I might be on the bill."

"Caught you?" said BJ, looking up from kissing Katy's neck. "How the hell did he do that?"

"I cut myself on the fire-alarm. He had me…" I trailed off for the shame of it. I knew how weak it all sounded.

"You didn't bloody confess?! Have you taken leave of your senses?"

"He had me," I repeated. "I'd cut my thumb –"

"How many times!" he said. "How many times do I have to tell you, David? Deny, Deny, Deny! Of course he didn't have you. They've never, ever got you. Never! Until you've confessed, they can go hang themselves! Oh, for Christ's sake! Have you learned nothing? Well, you're going to get beaten – and frankly you deserve everything you get!"

Hah! There's sympathy for you – Eton-style.

"Sorry," I said, by now thoroughly ashamed of myself. "I was tired. There were two of them. I – I couldn't think of what… Look, I'm sorry! What more can I say?"

BJ lifted his head up from Katy's shoulder. "Tell it to your mother!" he said, and, with a disdainful flick of his hand, dismissed me from the room.

Chapter 7

The worst thing is never the punishment itself. It's the waiting. And at Eton they knew how to draw it out to the Nth degree. Two days I had to wait before I was called up to see the Lowerman. It was actually all very exciting – the F-tits in my Latin class had never seen anyone on the bill before. And BJ had somehow fixed it so that he was my harbinger of doom.

We were scribing away at some stultifyingly dull piece of Erasmus when the door boomed open – Poppers, as the messengers of the two senior masters, did not need to knock.

BJ strutted into the room in all his gorgeousness – let me give you a taster: sponge-bag trousers, slightly flared at the bottom; black winkle pickers narrowing to a stiletto point so sharp he could have pronged a cocktail sausage; a black tailcoat, piped with braid – it's all in the detail, you see; starched wing-collar and tie; and, to cap it all off, a Union Jack waistcoat that seemed to be made of fur. Oh – and one more thing, while I remember it. His hair. I never fathomed why, but BJ always, always took *especial* care of his blonde thatch, ensuring that at all times he looked like a Wurzel fresh from the hedge.

"Is Cameron in this class?" BJ bellowed. Wasn't he just the showman, shoulders squared, patrician face proudly surveying the room before he spied me at the back.

He gave me a wink.

"He's here," said the dusty old beak.

"Cameron is to appear before the Lowermaster on the bill. There is every likelihood he will be thrashed. Thrashed!" He stared about the schoolroom, nodding his head as he caught the eye of every single gaping schoolboy. "There may be blood! The doctor has been notified! A certificate will be required!"

A thrill of delicious horror rippled through the room. The other boys gawked, nudged each other, before turning to leer at me.

I got up with my schoolbooks and followed BJ off to the Lowerman's rooms.

"I hope you've got a few extra pairs of pants on," said BJ, smiling with the most absurd delight. "There's a huge book been opened on this one. You wouldn't believe the interest you've caused."

"Really?" I said, as we mooched past that old ornate street-light, the Burning Bush.

"Let me see," he tugged at his chin. "A white ticket at five-to-two. Rustication at seven-to-one. Expulsion at ten-to-one. And coming in at evens is the runaway favourite, a sound six of the best."

"Jesus!" I said. "Could I stick a book down?"

"They'll spot it a mile off," he said gleefully. "Here, have a couple of handkerchiefs, my silky and my cotton. Shame I can't lend you a tape-recorder. I want to hear it!"

"I'll bet you would." We crossed the road and went past the school office.

"I mean, normally I have my ear pretty close to the door," said BJ. "But sometimes I miss the best bits. And here we are!"

Three other boys, E-blockers – (E for 'Even more Effing Useless') – were already queued up. More agony as I had to wait for them to be punished. I even heard one of them screaming in pain as he was beaten; this was considered to be very poor form at Eton, though for some reason they don't object nearly so much when it's from the Whips' office.

And finally it was my turn. The Lowerman did his level best to look forbidding. BJ smirking as he closed the door behind me; he even fluttered his fingers, as if waving a fond adieu. I took up position by the black beating block, which had been placed square in the middle of the room – the better for the Lowerman to have a run-up.

And, well – I made a pretty good fist of a lousy hand. I had to take him through the whole story: always been a sleep-walker, always have been, always will. Old Nanny Irish was so concerned she used to tie me to the bed.

The trickiest part was trying to explain the lying. "I just pan-icked, Sir!" I squealed. "I was so mortified, so ashamed, at what I'd done. I have dishonoured the good name of Eton. It was a mistake! I – I am sorry!"

The Lowerman – what do I remember of him? Built like a rugby player, broad beefy chest, and a sort of military-style haircut. He just stared at me from behind his desk. A very unnerving tactic, this one. You start wanting to fill the silence and the next thing you're babbling away and even deeper in the mire than you ever were before. But BJ had warned me all about it. I just stood there silently, hands behind my back.

At length, the Lowerman picked up a pencil and started tap-ping the end against his desk.

"I don't know," he said. "I was going to beat you. But I sup-pose it's possible, just possible, that you might be telling me the truth…"

Music to my ears! Moss-picking, that's all he gave me, ten hours of picking the moss from the cobbles on the schoolyard. But I'm afraid my backside was living on borrowed time.

Chapter 8

As you get older, you get better at spotting the disasters that loom on the horizon. Even if you can't spot them, very often you can sense them. And sometimes, you have such an acute sense of the disaster ahead of you that you can actually *dodge* the damn thing altogether! Fancy!

These days, I have developed a slight sense of intuition, though not as good as my wife Sam's. I'd always take her gut feelings over my logical, rational evaluations, any day of the week. A small example from my early political career: as Michael Howard was standing down as Tory leader, there were a number of people who advised me to bide my time. Get a few more years in Parliament under my belt, learn the game, make the contacts; and then, in five, ten, years' time, sweep in as the next Tory leader-but-one.

Well, it was a view. But even then – even though I'd only been an MP for four years – I felt that my time had come. I don't know what the instinct was, but it was yammering at me to make my move – and the rest is history.

Being the smart political operator that he was, I'm sure BJ must also have known that the tide was high: that if ever a man wanted to be a Tory Prime Minister, then that was his moment. I never found out why he funked it – but funk it he did, and that's him out now on the political sidelines, performing his extraordinary one-man show. How it irks him, I know it, to see me with the chalice almost to my lips.

Intuition, then: a wonderful gift which must be cultivated assiduously, especially if you want to have a tilt in politics. The gift of knowing when an ally is on the turn; the ability to know the strengths of your enemies – and the weaknesses of your friends; and that sense of timing that tells you, ultimately, whether you're onto a winner or a painful loser.

I only mention all this to heighten the contrast between now and my complete lack of intuition 30 years ago. With such an immense storm-cloud flickering overhead, you might have thought I'd have had some inkling ... but no. It didn't register a single flicker.

And, after a few days of pleasant duties looking after BJ, it all kicked off.

Over such a footling thing too, but its consequences were immense.

After two weeks at Eton, the new boys had to go through what was known as a Colours Test in the Library, where they'd be asked about various dull aspects of school life.

Learning the stuff out of the school fixtures – the colours of the Eight, the Eleven, the Strawberry, all that rubbish – was a chore. But not to worry. "I still feel bad how you landed yourself in it over the fire-alarm," said BJ, in one of his more affable moments. "So don't you worry about the Colours Test. Leave it to me. I'll sort it out."

Hmmm. If I heard those words now – "BJ said he'd sort it out" – then instantly alarm bells would start claxoning.

That's 30 years of experience speaking. But back in 1979, I thought that when BJ had said he'd "sort it out", the Colours Test was in the bag. Hah! If I could see the 14-year-old boy that was myself, there's nothing I'd like more than to give him a well-deserved kick up the backside.

The Colours Test was due to take place in the Library at 7pm on a Sunday – and half-an-hour beforehand I was wandering upstairs to present myself to my flighty Fag-master.

I found him racing down the stairs three at a time. "Late again! Late again!" he bawled as he barged past another F-tit. "Hello, David!"

He sailed past and I had no option but to follow.

"BJ!" I called. "What about the Colours Test?"

"Bugger the Colours Test! I'm off to the Cockpit for dinner."

We were now out the front door and he was striding along Judy's Passage in the spitting rain. "But … but you said you'd help me with the answers!" I piped. "You were going to get all the questions for me."

"Oh yes!" he said – but in the manner that he might shriek out Hallelujah! "So I did."

"Well – I was…" I had to trot to keep up with him. "I was hoping you might have some of the answers."

"Moi foi! It's going to pour. I don't have an umbrella!" He started patting at his pockets. "I don't even have my poncho."

"But –"

"David, you couldn't do me a favour. I'm late as it is – any chance you could collect my umbrella? I think, hmmm." He stopped in the middle of the pavement and scratching at his hair. "I think perhaps the silk one in black and white. It'll go very well with my waistcoat. Just drop it off at the Cockpit."

"But I've got the Colours Test in 20 minutes!"

At this, he stopped and turned to me. "Piffle."

"But –"

The conversation was so typical of so many of mine with BJ. He was for ever tearing off after the next flibbertigibbet hare to have taken his fancy, while I – for at least many years –

ploughed after him trying to catch up.

He looked down at me, with that great mop of sheepdog hair glimmering wet in the streetlights. "David. Don't worry." He pinched my cheek. "The umbrella's not a problem. I'll catch a cab."

BJ loped off into the night as I dismally trudged back to the house.

But I wasn't out for the count – not by any means. I'd just throw a sickie. How useful this little ruse had been over the years – the perfect method of skipping unpleasant exams and invidious excursions. The art of the sickie is even practised at the very highest level of politics. Remember Margaret Thatcher when she was at bay in 1991, her cabinet circling her like a wolf-pack? Time and again, John Major was called upon to endorse Thatcher's leadership. But where was the sly dog when his leader needed him most? Back home in Huntingdon, nursing 'a tooth-ache'. Well, he may have had tooth-ache, and he may not, but somehow he managed to get the illness to last for at least a week, by which time Thatcher was finished and Major was the only person who'd been left unsullied by the whole squalid coup.

That's us Tories: we love a good coup. It shows how even the mightiest in the land can be humbled. And I guess it will be a coup that eventually does for me. I shall fight it, with threats and blandishments, and all the other knavish tricks that are part and parcel of being the Tory leader. But when the end comes, I will take it with good grace. It was a fitting end for Thatcher and it will be more than good enough for me.

But on with the story. My plan was simple enough: skulk back to my room, get into my pyjamas, press my forehead against the radiator for as long as I could stand it, and then nip into bed and await the turn of events. I'd put on a croaky voice, call for the Dame. Not perfect, but it should buy me at least 24 hours. It was a reasonable enough plan.

But I think you may know of the best-laid plans of mice and men ... They have a tendency to unravel. And as for any sort of venture involving BJ – well, even when BJ had the most peripheral role – I can quite categorically state that things *always* went awry. Just like Errol Flynn, you could always rely on BJ – because he'd always let you down.

I'd only just stepped through Farrer's front door when Henchman bearded me on the stairs. "Ahh," he said, appraising me. "The Upstart. Time for your Colours Test."

If I'd had any sense I'd have feigned an illness then and there. But if – when – I failed the test, what could they do? They might scream or shout a bit, but I'd heard worse even from dear old Nanny Irish. They might give me some punishment; what? Fifty lines? Go on, be a devil, make it a hundred.

Ultimately, though, what was the worst they could do?

Funny thought, that. You think you've run through every possible worst-case scenario – and then up one pops that you hadn't even conceived of. Didn't even know existed! Imagine a batsman, really on top of his game; he's ready for anything that the bowler can hurl at him. And yet even he would be mightily surprised if, instead of throwing a ball, the bowler were to shy a cricket bat...

I hope I'm not labouring the point. I am merely trying to convey the complete unexpectedness of what happened next.

I followed Henchman up the stairs. The other F-tits were already queued up in a line outside the Library. No slouching on the floor for them. Every one of them, from Pierre to Ricky, was standing back to the wall; a few even had their Fixtures out for some last minute swatting. Pah!

I was last in the line of the ten F-tits, and you know what the feeling was like? It was like being at my first constituency count in Witney in 2001. I'd been to plenty of other counts in my time, but the Witney one, of course, was the one that was going to get me into parliament. And what I remember about both those events was that, while everyone else was flapping around, I was making a conscious effort to be cool and remain in control. Barack Obama – 'No Drama-Obama', they call him. The more excited his minions become, the more he ratchets things down. He speaks more softly, his eyes turn to gimlets. I've tried it myself in the mirror but it's difficult if you've got a doughy face.

The F-tits went in one by one. We could hear the occasional jeer or hoot of laughter through the thick door. Pierre came out after five minutes and gave me a high-five; Mark Davide, thick but affable, came out scowling after ten and gave a thumbs-down.

And so, after well over an hour, it came to my turn. The Library was decked out like a rather fusty gentleman's club, pictures of the Quorn hunt on the wall, and a knobbly black cane above the mantelpiece. Adorned about the room were nine of Farrer's ten Librarians, excluding of course BJ, who was doubtless at that very moment having at some local girl with his fly whisk. A fly whisk? How the hell does one turn a woman on with a fly whisk?

I can feel the bile rising in my gorge just at the memory of it all – you've never met such a spineless, shiftless, bunch as those Librarians. I can't recall their first names, but I know all of their surnames, every one of them.

Henchman, of course, lolling in an armchair trying to be smooth; that simpering shyster Sweet; Tait the weasel; Hamill, Cripps, Stenson, Bouverie and Evans, five of the ugliest bullies you've ever laid eyes on, a festering pond of spots and greasy hair; Hitchen, Bitchin' Hitchen as he was known – a yowling, snivelling blancmange of pettish wetness. And one other boy. One other, and by God if I'm Prime Minister and the head of the SAS ever comes over on Christmas Day and offers me a free shot, I know exactly the man who I want slotted. Ottley. I haven't seen him in 30 years, but what I remember of him is a huge boy, vast – at least a foot taller than me, with ape-like hands, Popeye forearms and the heaving shoulders of a navvy. He was a rower: thick as five short planks but strong as an ox. Tends to rather be the way with rowers, you know.

The nine Librarians had draped themselves artfully around the room – some on the sofas, legs cocked over the arm-rests, a couple leaning up against the mantelpiece, tailcoats pulled up as they warmed their arses by the fire. They were all trying to be terribly cool – and carried it off with about as much panache as myself in that bloody Bullingdon club picture.

The Librarians were sipping beer for the most part, though Hitchen seemed to be nursing a mug of Ovaltine. Ottley, over by the window had an enormous Stein of lager, two litres it must have held, though in his hands it looked like a pint pot. I can even recollect what he was doing: chewing his nails, but chomping industriously, as if he were trying to make a square meal out of the end of his thumb.

"Hands out of your pockets!" said Henchman. Didn't I bridle at that – not that you'd ever have known it. I'm always at my iciest when you touch me on the raw. "Stand in the middle of the room."

I stood on a dainty round carpet and was about to put my hands behind my back. Then I thought, 'Stuff it!' and jauntily stuck my thumbs into my waistcoat pockets (I can just about carry it off now at the dispatch box, but it's definitely a difficult look for a 14-year-old).

"So, Cameron, where are the copper balls?" said Henchman.

Copper balls? What the hell was he on about? Well, actually, there is a correct answer to this question. It's a little Eton riddle: where are the copper balls? Underneath the copper horse, a huge statue at the end of the Long Walk in Windsor of George III on his horse. Though now I think of it, we actually called it the Copper Cow...

Anyway, not knowing the answer to Henchman's riddle, I started laughing, perhaps out of nervousness. "On the founder's statue?"

Henchman acted as if he hadn't heard me and sipped his beer. "What goes up Judy's Passage?"

Another stupid Eton riddle. And the answer, which of course I didn't know, was Lupton's Tower, the clock tower in the schoolyard. It wasn't even funny the first time round.

"The boys from Farrer House?" I replied.

No response – that was the unnerving thing. Not even the flicker of a raised eyebrow.

Hitchen put his Ovaltine onto a coaster on a side-table and threw me a multi-coloured shirt. It was covered in dried mud and looked like a Harlequins shirt.

Hadn't the foggiest. Then: I don't know why – perhaps it was the sullen cool of the Librarians that tipped me over the edge – I decided to play it for laughs.

I inspected the shirt very carefully, brought it up to my nose; inhaled the stench of dried sweat. "I know this one!" I said. "It must be... the Tour de France! King of the Mountains! Tell me I'm wrong."

Two of the boys, Tait and Cripps I think, did snigger at that, but for the rest of them the silence echoed around the room.

A sock was hurled at me. I caught it deftly with one hand. "What's that?"

56

Mauve and black quarters. Not that I was aware of it but it happened to be the house colours. "Hmm," I said, working at the toes with my fingers. "I definitely know this one too. I saw one of these only just this morning. It's... it's a sock! Order of the Garter?"

No sniggers this time. No raised eyebrows. Just this deadly silence as the Librarians realised that a stripling F-tit was taking the mickey.

It was a performance that was definitely going to warrant some sort of punishment. But then I did something that tipped them over the edge.

Ottley, still growling away over his fingernails by the window, threw a blue shirt at me. For the first time, he spoke – deep, deep voice. "What's that?"

Now, had I thought about it, I could have worked this one out. The shirt was blue, massive and saturated with sweat.

"My tutor's vest?" I hazarded.

"That's from the Eight."

"Oh, I've heard of them," I replied, so past caring now. "They go in hard – and they come out wet. They only recognise their friends from the rear. And if they stroke their oars too much, they catch crabs!"

Ottley twitched. Hitchen patted at his hair. The other Librarians sniffed down their noses and turned to Henchman to take the lead.

For a while, Henchman sat there on the sofa, fingers drumming on his thighs as he stared at me. "Gentlemen," he said. "What we have here is a junior boy who not only has not bothered to learn his colours, but who has openly mocked every one of Eton's best-loved institutions. That he must be punished goes without saying. Our young upstart here must be taught the error of his ways. But what shall we inflict upon him?"

He eased his finger underneath his starched wing-collar, as if easing the pressure on the scar on his neck. "I feel that among the array of punishments at our disposal, there is nothing that fits the bill. They will not teach him the lessons that he so needs to learn. Suggestions, gentlemen?"

Silence as the Librarians pondered my fate. "Clean the lavatories for the rest of the year?" said Tait.

"Roast him?" said another.

They paused, sipping their beers as they pondered my fate.

Then. Very quietly, Hitchen spoke. "Library tan?"

A sharp intake of breath from two of the boys. Ottley downing his Stein in one. He liked that one, he did; his nail-chewing seemed to move up a gear.

Henchman raised his eyebrows, head tick-tocking from side-to-side as he stared at me with those glassy eyes. "A Library Tan? It's been so long. I can't even remember when we last had one of those. But ..." and he rubbed his hands with excitement as he briskly stood up. "I think a library tan would be just perfect."

He went over to the fireplace and snatched down the knobbly black cane. He was suddenly alive with energy, flexing it in his hands. "Right, you young upstart, coat off if you please and bend over the table."

"You can't do that." I was still reasonably confident.

"Coat off. Bend over the table. And quickly, please."

"I've just said – you can't cane me, Henchman."

"Aha – that is where I have the better of you. Not only can I cane you but I *will* cane you. And the other Librarians will cane you also, a single stroke from each of them, the better that you might learn some manners."

A boy was helping me remove my tailcoat, while another shepherded me to the oak table. I vaguely remember looking about me. Some of the boys were relishing it, but a few, like

Tait and Bouverie, seemed positively queasy.

"Give him a belt to bite on." Henchman took a few practice swishes on one of the armchairs.

I was forced over the table, arms stretched out to the side, and a thick loop of leather was stuffed into my mouth.

"Hold his arms in case he twitches. Oh, but one thing – how thoughtless of me to forget!" Henchman bent down beside me so that his face was just a foot from my own. His beery breath washed over me. "There are only nine of us. And these things must be done by the dozen. So who, I wonder, would be the most appropriate person to make up the three extra strokes? Yes – who indeed? Perhaps it should be the Librarian to whom you have caused greatest offence…" He stood up. "Gentlemen? Are we ready?"

I squirmed to left and right, thrashing my head from side-to-side, but it did no good. They had me pinned as tight as a snared rabbit. I was whimpering with the humiliation of it all but, even then, I wasn't sure if it wasn't all a bluff. Perhaps in five seconds they'd let me go, laughing at the terror etched into my face. Honestly – it was a joke; it had to be a joke. This sort of barbarism went out with the War.

And then I heard the sound of running footsteps and the first blow scythed into me. At first it was a dull throb, but the pain suddenly exploded, as if a hot poker had been laid flat across my buttocks. Mewling with pain, I bit down savagely, teeth grinding into the leather belt.

"One!" cried Henchman.

And the others followed. I could almost guess who had struck each blow. A timid pat from Tait; a run and a grunt of pure sadistic pleasure from Hitchen.

After seven, the whole of my bottom was one throbbing mass of pain. I rested my forehead on the cool of the table as the tears pooled around my nose. I even remember the smell of the table polish.

"Eight!" called Henchman, before adding quietly to someone behind me. "Make each blow count."

I felt quick hands unbutton my trousers and tug them to the floor. My pants followed.

Four purposeful strides behind me and then the most thundering pain that I had ever experienced. But it didn't end there – oh, he was the master of his art. At the end of the stroke, the knobbled tip of the cane was drawn against the skin to ensure it broke.

That was Ottley, the monster – and it was he who had the final four strikes, each of them more agonizing than the last. I could feel the blood dripping down my legs. So excruciating that I think I may have gagged on the leather and passed out.

Somebody helped me to my feet. I pulled my trousers up. My tailcoat was thrust into my hand.

The boys poured themselves more beer. Ottley standing Lurch-like by the fireplace with the cane. It glistened with my blood. Henchman by the door to usher me out.

"Thank you for attending the house Colours Test," he said, hands behind his back. "It is with great regret that I have to tell you that you failed the test. We look forward to your attendance here next week. Now – shake hands like a gentleman and express your gratitude."

Well, I may have made a hash of most things that I'd done that evening, but I did at least get one thing right. "I'll get you, my pretties!" I screamed as I stumbled out the door. "And your little dogs too!"

An awful night. A horrendous night; barbaric beyond belief. And yet, and yet… it was from that night, I think, that the first seeds of my interest in politics began to shoot.

Chapter 9

The next morning, I hobbled up the stairs to make tea in the senior boys' kitchen, before shuffling along to BJ's room. I was still wearing the same clothes – even the same pants. I'd slept in them, a few snatched minutes at a time, before waking up with a jolt as the pain razored across my buttocks and the memory of the beating came back to me in all its excruciating detail.

I don't know what other boys might have done. Perhaps run squealing to the Dame, the Housemaster – or even back home to mama and pater.

I think I was still in shock. I hadn't even tended to my wounds. Every step, it was like a blow-torch was being played over my rear.

But more than that – and it is a lesson that many politicians would do well to heed – I did not want to act in the heat of the moment. How many times do you hear of some outrage, and there are the pols instantly drafting new laws, as if it's somehow going to solve the problem. Never does, though: just creates another problem and invariably a bigger one.

So that morning, I was still weighing up my options. And though it may sound odd, that meant continuing with the usual routine while I considered my next move.

I knocked on BJ's door, went in, and put the tray down

before shuffling over to draw the curtains. Still dark outside, the school barely awake, and from over by the bed I could hear the grunting snorts of an animal asleep. I poured a cup of Lapsang – lemon, sugar, no milk, that's how he liked it – into the Royal Doulton teacup and set it by his bedside.

His head was practically under the covers, just his nose and eyelashes peeping out. He heard the chink of the cup. Opened one eye.

"Ahhhh!" he said. The thing about BJ was – and, to this day, he still has this talent – he had the most astonishing accelera-tion. He could go from fast asleep to wide-awake, raring to go, in under five seconds. "Tea! David! Thank you! Good morn-ing!"

He snatched at the tea, pulled himself up against the head-board and took his first noisy sip. That morning, he was wear-ing a white night-cap – almost Scrooge-like, it was – and a plum-coloured nightshirt, open to the midriff.

"Ahhhh!" he said again. With every word, the decibel-level seemed to increase. When he was warmed up, his voice cut straight through walls, could carry to the very far corner of the house.

"How art thou fallen from heaven, O Lucifer, son of the morning!" (An odd greeting, even for BJ; I think he was mem-orising the Bible that week.)

I grunted as I tied back the silk curtains. Another slurp of tea. BJ looking like some Eastern Pasha on his throne. "Let me tell you about last night. A night to savour! Just the …" BJ's voice tailed off in puzzlement. "What the hell's happened to you? You're walking like a spavined old woman!"

I was concentrating, viciously, on trying to untie one of the knots on the swags. I spoke in a small tremulous whisper. "They beat me last night."

"What do you mean they beat you?"

"They gave me a Library Tan."

"What?" he exploded. "They can't bloody thrash you!"

"Well …" My voice was on the verge of cracking. "Well they did." I burst into tears. It was the first of only two occasions that I blubbed at Eton. And just like every other Etonian on earth, it wasn't for the hurt and it wasn't for the humiliation. It was for the kindness. Etonians, Germans and stiff-necked aristos, they're all the same: if you want to see some genuine emotion, if you want tears, goosebumps and lumps in the throat, then just be nice to them when they're on the ropes.

BJ was out of the bed in an instant. Not for him that starchy, stiff-necked phobia of tears that blights so many Eton boys. He was over to me, had his hand round my shoulders. "David!" he said. "David."

I buried my face into his chest and cried for all I was worth; once I'd started I couldn't stop. I can't remember what BJ was doing – some sort of loose hug, I guess. Now that I think of it, we have forged such a close relationship over the years, as our lives have intertwined like two old trees, but we limit ourselves to handshakes and pats on the back. That was the one and only time that we have ever been in a hug. Entirely asexual, too, come to think of it.

At length, my heaving tears stuttered to a halt. I pulled out a hanky and mopped at my face.

BJ poured some fresh tea and passed it to me. "I'd offer you a chair," he said. "Though that might be painful."

I gave him a weak smile.

"So they thrashed you did they, the bastards? How many strokes?"

"Twelve." I sniffed and sipped my tea.

"Twelve! And for an F-tit! I've only ever had six!" He grimaced, a sort of sympathetic scowl with mouth downturned, as if to show that he felt my pain. However, he could only hold it for a few seconds before he was chuckling. "Twelve!" he said. "Twelve? Let's have a look!"

He was irresistible. That is all part of BJ's charm. You know what he's like. People just seem to fall over themselves to do his bidding. He had all that – and quite considerably more – when he was 18. But over the years, he's lost some of his *joie de vivre*. Exuberance and irrepressible optimism have been replaced by a certain amount of calculation. Too many knocks, that's what it is. BJ will always keep bouncing back because that's in his nature. But with each knock-back, I feel that he is prepared to give less of himself. I see now more of the façade and less of the man I once knew.

As I peeled off my tailcoat, BJ busied himself with his new record-player. He put on a piece of music which, even now, holds the very dearest place in my heart: Gluck's *Orpheus and Eurydice*, sung by – to my mind – the greatest British opera singer of all time, Kathleen Ferrier. So many wonderful parts, the *Dance of the Spirits*, the overture to the second act, but if I had to stake my life on a single song, it would be *Che Faro – What is life without you?* Even writing the very title brings a lump to my throat. You'd know the song, I'm sure you would – and, for me, it brings back memories not of BJ, but of something else entirely.

I'd unbuttoned my waistcoat and was shilly-shallying with my fly buttons. Natural prudishness prevented me from dropping my trousers in a senior boy's room; this was Eton, after all.

"Get on with it!" BJ was sat now on the end of the bed, face aglow, like a young child expectantly awaiting his Christmas treat. "Let's have a look!"

I let the trousers drop to the ground and tugged at my pants; a vicious pain shot through my buttocks as the fresh scabs peeled away from my skin. I eased them down to my knees. That was as far over as I could bend.

In the mirror, I could see BJ goggling for a moment before leaning forward, his innate squeamishness conquered by his carnal desire to be shocked. "*Fouquet In Le Touquet!*" he said, exploding with laughter. "Now that's what my Scots grand-mother would call a proper Skelpit Leatherin'!"

"Thank you for your sympathy," I said through gritted teeth, watching in the mirror as he tried to control his mirth. There was a smile for ever playing over his lips. On the one hand, I'm sure, he was revolted by the spectacle of my buttocks, but on the other ... well, it was something new. Something fresh. And even to this day, BJ is still addicted to the thrill of the new experience.

"I wouldn't wonder that you'll have these stripes for life!" he said. "You haven't even had them treated!"

"Not yet."

"Didn't go to the Dame, then? I suppose that was sensible. A Library Tan, you say? Could have the whole lot of them up before the Headman if you wanted. Probably have the ring-leaders thrown out. Don't tell me: Henchman and Ottley?"

He drummed his fingers against his lips, pondering, plotting, working out the ramifications, inspecting the problem from every angle. So many pols these days, they don't appreciate that for every action – every single action – there is a ripple effect. You support one cabinet minister and you have to spurn another. You make a wife of one woman and you leave five oth-ers disappointed. (BJ excepted.) And you get half the Library expelled within two weeks of arriving at Eton, and... well, you wouldn't necessarily be making life easy for yourself.

"First things first!" said BJ, hurling his night-cap to the floor and pulling off his night-gown. He was naked underneath, but for some red cashmere bed-socks. A little paunchy even then, with a roll of white fat plumping out over his hips. He was completely unabashed, just didn't give a damn. Just one of the reasons, I don't doubt, why women found him so attractive.

"We've got to get those stripes sorted!" By now he was deftly tying his white bowtie. Twenty seconds, that's all it took, without a glance in a mirror. A few moments to decide his waistcoat of the day – a Dalmatian effect, very understated for him – and he was tying up some black brogues. "Can't go to the Dame, she'll peach. Can't do it myself, I think I'd throw up. So …" He started running his hands through his hair – you've seen it plenty of times, I'm sure, and the image it always brings to mind is of a wet dog shaking itself after coming out of the water. By the end, he looked like Struwwelpeter; the modern pups pay a fortune for hair like that.

"Stay here!" he said. "Eat biscuits!"

I was getting cold and didn't know what to do. I lay on my front on the sofa and pulled a blanket over me, wincing as it brushed against my backside. Gluck's music washed over me.

BJ burst back into the room. "Good!" he said. "Got you a bacon roll. Swiped some bandages and ointment from Demelza's medicine chest!"

The smell of the bacon roll made me realise I was famished. I hadn't eaten since tea the previous day. BJ was singing along to the music as he rummaged through the mounds of paper at his burry.

A knock at the door. I had my face turned to the wall. A woman's voice. A tinkling feminine voice. And in comes …

Katy.

She must have come up direct from the boys' breakfast, as

she was still wearing her black dress and white ruff shirt.

I tried to smile at her. "Hello."

"You poor thing." She bustled over before letting out a squeal of astonishment as she pulled back the blanket and examined the cuts.

"My God!" she said. "He needs a doctor!"

"Can't do that," said BJ. "Do the best you can."

Ahh me – to think back to the next 30 minutes. Never was there a pain that was so exquisite. The general throb of my backside, the lancing darts of agony as she pulled away some fluff stuck to my skin, and the gentle erotic glide of her finger-tips as she eased the ointment onto my welts. The occasional grunt from BJ as he came over to inspect her handiwork. Katy's little mewls of sympathetic shock and horror, as if she were tending the wounds of a war hero. And throughout it all, Kathleen Ferrier singing about love and death.

As gently as a mother with a new-born babe, Katy applied some bandages. "You're very brave, David," she said, her stomach pressed lightly against the top of my legs. "You haven't made a sound."

Before she left, she kissed me on the cheek.

Fallen in love? I'd almost shot my load.

Chapter 10

As I've said, I still have the scars to this day: four thin white lines that criss-cross my buttocks. They bring back such memories: the humiliation of the beating and the red-raw desire for revenge; Katy, my Katy, and her tender ministrations; the first time that I really connected with BJ, a bond that has been stretched and tested to the limit, but which we continue to share to this day; and lastly, of course, I am reminded of why I first came into politics.

"Run over by a car?" mused BJ after Katy had left. He was walking up and down his room, hands behind his back. "Beaten up by the Townies in Windsor? What about … what about fallen out of a tree and landing right on your coccyx?"

"Why don't I just tell the truth?"

"Peaching?" He stopped mid-stride. "You can't do that!"

He was so right. Peaching, in all its forms, is the very lowest of the low. Not that I have any problem, at all, with peaching in principle. A man must get his revenge any way he can.

But peaching is just so facile! The peacher invariably ends up with far more egg on his face than the peachee, so to speak. It is, as Michael Heseltine learned to his cost, like doing away with a Prime Minister: he who wields the knife can never carry the crown.

No, if you're looking to land someone in it – and this is

especially true in the world of politics where we seem to spend most of our lives trying to do down the next man – there are many more sophisticated ways of doing it. The smile to the face, the handsome clap on the back and the gentle push over the cliff-edge. Better yet, it is the anonymous note to one of the Whips; an old favourite, that one.

But the very thought of peaching – peaching! – to the Dame, the Housemaster, the Headman. Even at 14, it went against every grain of my being; it was so obviously going to backfire.

"Too many people make the error of wanting to have their revenge immediately," said BJ. "Face it, David! You're a pink-faced boy. You've got no ammo. And even if you did have some ammo, you wouldn't know how to use it!"

"So what do I do?"

"Keep your trap shut! Tell nobody! Await your moment!" He was back to pacing across the room; I think he was re-reading the Hornblower books again – Hornblower was for ever pacing the quarterdeck – though it might well have been Flashman. BJ loved both of them, though primarily Flashman because he was such a roistering shagger. "You may not even have to do anything! Sit by the river bank long enough and you'll see the cankered, decaying bodies of your enemies float by."

For at least a week, I could barely sit down. BJ kitted me out with an inflatable pillow which I attached to the inside of my tailcoat. But sitting for long periods was agony; those periods of double maths! My aching head, my aching rear! It was even worse when I went to the lavatory. I'm sure you don't really want to know. After two days, I gave up altogether and took four Imodium to block myself up for a week.

I couldn't run – every step was agony as the scabs moved

against their dressings. And of course I had to keep repeating to every single person I met the story of how I had come to injure myself so dreadfully. In the end, BJ and I opted for falling out of the tree and smashing my backside on the sharp end of a stump. Not that it mattered, because word went round like wildfire. Everyone knew! It was round the house by lunch and, by tea, I guess there wasn't a boy in the school who hadn't heard the tale of the first Library Tan in over two decades.

I believe I've just had a minor revelation. I've often wondered who spilled the beans. It certainly wasn't me. I very much doubt it was Katy. It might, just possibly, have been one of the nine boys who'd flogged me, though it was hardly anything to brag about. But this story was out so fast and spread so quickly that …

That …

There could only have been one possible person behind it: a person intent on using the story not for mere gossip, but for leverage. In other words, a player. It was BJ, had to be. Only taken me 30 years to realise that.

A steady stream of boys – some out for sexual kicks and some just out of honest schoolboy prurience – tripped in to my room, begging to see my backside. But perhaps the most concerned of my visitors was the Dame, Demelza. She was plump bordering on obese, with a helmet of dyed black hair. At least she had no lines – that's one of the perks of having a fuller face. Me? Well, I reckon that I'll stick with pudgy. Only a moron like Nigel Lawson would have lost all that weight when he was a pensioner; I didn't even recognise him after his diet. And when I *did* recognise him, I thought he'd aged 30 years.

"Hear you've had a little accident with one of the other boys, dear," she said.

"Fell out of a tree, yes Ma'am." I remained standing. Even

after three days it was still painful to sit.

"Funny how it's always on the little boy's derrières," she said, trailing cigarette ash onto the carpet. "Who was it this time? Was it that Bouverie – he can be such a brute that boy."

"No, honestly," I said. I couldn't quite make out what she was driving at. "Just me and a tree. Stupid of me. I slipped."

She gazed out of the window, puffing on her cigarette. "Nothing wrong with it, you know. Nothing wrong with it at all. You're not going to find a girl at Eton – so you've got to do the best you can."

"Really – no other boy was involved."

"At least I'm not asking to see your backside!" She laughed at the thought of it. "I know when I'm not wanted. But I'm sure Mr Maguire, he'll most certainly want a look –" Which indeed he did; practically had to fight him off.

The Library Tan had many other consequences. For a kicker, my relationship with Katy the maid reached an intensity and intimacy that I found absolutely electrifying.

I won't quite stretch to saying that Katy's nursing duties made the stripes worthwhile – in fact, why the hell not? I would now, and for the first time, like to put it on record that the pain of that thrashing was more than made up for by having Katy rub ointment onto my bare backside. Every day for a fortnight.

Just the very memory of it sends a quiver of desire up my spine – frankly it's a wonder I didn't turn into a complete masochist. Go on, spank me, whip me, thrash me within an inch of my life – just so long as my Katy can later attend to my bruised buttocks!

After that first time, we worked out a routine. In the mornings, I'd wake BJ up as usual with his tea and would then clean up the worst of the detritus – pizza boxes, newspapers, crisp packets, empty Champagne bottles – then go down for my own breakfast. I'd bolt it as quick as I could, bit of cereal and maybe a yoghurt, and then I would be bustling – BUSTLING – back up the stairs for my morning treat.

As I say, it only lasted a fortnight. But for me – despite all the other shenanigans going on at the time, which I will come to later – it was the most exquisitely gilded chapter of my entire life. And the beauty of it was that, unlike every other dalliance of my heart – Sam honourably excepted – there was no row, no discord, none of the numbing disappointment. As a result, Katy retains an extraordinary position in my heart, a shining beacon of beauty on her own lone pedestal.

Up in BJ's room, I'd quickly make his bed, titivate the flowers, and – crucially – put our record onto the gramophone. Can you wonder that the sound of Kathleen Ferrier's voice has an almost Pavlovian effect on my body? I only have to hear the opening bar of *Che Faro* and this spasm wrings through my body and suddenly I'm pointing like a cocker spaniel.

After a week or so, I'd even bought a scented candle from one of the Windsor tourist shops – I knew that Nanny Irish liked them – so that by the time Katy had come up, BJ's room smelled, as they say, like a tart's boudoir. Bandages, tape, scissors and ointment – how I still adore the smell of TCP! – would be laid out neatly on a side-table.

I'd take off tailcoat, waistcoat, shoes, trousers and pants and then, covered by a towel, would lie face down on the sofa, as demure as can be, for all the world like some fat sot politician awaiting his weekly service.

The drill was that Katy would come up soon after breakfast. A discreet knock on the door and she'd let herself in. It was perhaps a good thing that none of the other boys ever came to visit BJ after breakfast: me seemingly stripped and ready for action on the sofa, candles, low-lights, the oils all prepared on the table…

"Good morning, David," Katy would always say. Like furtive lovers, we always seemed to speak in a whisper.

"Hello, Katy." I'd give her a weak yet noble smile.

She'd hitch up her black-skirt, a little, kneel down beside the sofa and ease back the towel. As delicately as she could, she would peel off the bandages that were taped to each buttock. And, as I recall it, she'd often hum along to Kathleen Ferrier. She always seemed so easy, so relaxed – and I, meanwhile, was like this coiled spring, so tense that when she touched me I could barely breathe.

When the bandages were off, she'd usually say something. "These are looking much better," she might say, with all the formality of a hospital consultant, or, "These scabs are forming nicely." Had I the wit, I would have been touching my toes every morning, with the express purpose of ripping them off. I'd have picked them off with my own fingernails, if only to ensure that Katy continued to see me. But that sort of conniving … well, it was a while yet before I learned to be such a schemer.

Then, ohh! The very thought of it turns me to mush! She would briskly rub her hands together to warm them; squeeze some ointment onto her fingertips; and with the very lightest touch imaginable, would massage the cream into my torn buttocks.

If I ever make it through the Pearly Gates, I hope that at least a portion of my time will be spent with my face hard against a brown leather sofa, enveloped by the scent of Frangipani and TCP, with Kathleen Ferrier warbling in the background as that beautiful houri Katy rubs cream into my backside. What with me drilling my little holes into the pillow beneath me, it was a total sensory overload.

The mingling of the sensations was extraordinary – a mix of this relentless throbbing pain from the four stripes, overladen by the most erotically sensitive massage that I have ever experienced. Not that it was entirely my fault. How was I to know that she was stroking the biggest erogenous zone in my entire body?

The cream duly massaged in, Katy would snip out two perfectly oval bandages. Very meticulous she was. I loved to gaze at her as first she screwed the top back onto the ointment before taking up the scissors. It was like a Communion. I would not say a word for fear of breaking the spell.

Each bandage was laid on a buttock before one more little ritual that still sets my nerve ends a'jangling: the blunt 'RRRRIP' sound as Katy tore off some tape. The bandages would be secured, Kathleen Ferrier would be crooning on about her lost love, and, the last act, Katy would bend down quickly and kiss me on the cheek. Every single morning for two weeks on the trot.

And, on the 15th day, my scabs nearly healed and my lustful fantasies now brought to the simmering boil, I decided for the first time to act. I'd never plucked up the courage to do anything with Caroline at home – and how I regretted that. But this time, at least, I would give it a shot, my spirit steeled by that hoary old adage I'd learned from Nanny Irish – "You know she wants it" – and my pump was well and truly primed.

My backside had just been oiled and the bandages replaced. Katy was bending down to kiss me. Normally, I would lie there, cheek to the sofa as I docilely accepted my kiss. Not this time.

This time, I lifted my head up, leaning on my elbow with my face upturned – and I don't know whether it was by accident or design, but my timing could not have been better. Instead of my cheek, she kissed me full on the lips. So soft. So moist.

This was the thing. You might have expected Katy to draw back, shocked – shocked – at such wanton forwardness from a 14-year-old boy.

But she didn't. She held it for one moment, two moments, and is it my fancy or did those eyes, forest green and so filled with sadness, really shut in ecstasy? I don't know – but every middle-aged man must be allowed his little fantasies. My first kiss. For as long as I live, I will never forget it.

I was just bringing my hand up to caress her cheek when the door banged opened and BJ barged in. Instantly Katy broke away and busied herself with the discarded bandages. I dropped my head to the pillow. No way he could have seen us. Just act normally; he'll be none the wiser.

We were the very picture of ordinariness, just a teenage boy and his nursemaid. Yet BJ – intuition up to the eyeballs – immediately sensed something amiss. Head cocked to the side, he stood there in the middle of the room gauging the wind.

He glanced at Katy before staring intently at me; and in our 30 years together, there has only been one other occasion when I have seen a look like it. We were having a bottle of Rioja in the Red Lion in Westminster; I'd just told him that I was running for the Tory leadership. First of all a flash of rage mixed with the most complete loathing. But only for a moment before he'd mastered himself. His face mellowed to a look of reproach and, ultimately, slight hurt. The unspoken thought lingered in the air that I had stolen something of great value that belonged to him.

Back in the bedroom, BJ righted himself almost immediately, clapping his hands and pacing over to the window. "So! How is the patient?"

"Much better," I said, and Katy, with eyes looking to the carpet, echoed, "Much better."

"Scabs nearly gone, have they? Good, good! Well, I think that your tender ministrations must be at an end, darling Katy. Thank you so very much for the discreet and caring way that you have attended to my room-fag these past two weeks. I am now happy to declare the patient sound in both body and mind! David, you have now officially recovered. Go now! Lift thyself up and walk!"

Katy smiled as she looked down at me. "It's been a pleasure," she said. And you know what that little scene puts me in mind of? My parents standing over me, both of them come to say goodnight after Nanny Irish had tucked me up.

BJ courteously opened the door for Katy. "See you later." She stroked his arm as she walked out; such a tight black skirt, so snug it could have been painted on.

The door closed and BJ stalked back into the room. He stood by the mantelpiece, sniffing at the gardenia in his buttonhole before turning to me. And as I lay there on the sofa, he surveyed me in the same critical manner that a farmer might weigh up a steer; thumbs in his waistcoat pockets, fingers tapping against his midriff.

A sigh, a rueful shake of his head. And, just as quickly, he snapped out of that rare moment of introspection, raising both his eyebrows and nodding to me. He'd paid me my due.

"Randy little stoat, aren't you?" he said, though with a tinge of a smile. "Four years' time, you'll be even worse than I am. Though try that stunt again and you'll have more than just a macerated arse to deal with!"

Chapter 11

As for the rest of the Library, what were they all up to during the two weeks of my recuperation?

Were they so horrified by the flogging that they shunned my company, as if my very presence was reminder enough of the awful sin they'd committed? Did they, perhaps, go easy on me, in the vain hope of trying to expunge their guilt? Or maybe they came to my room one by one, to say in a bluff, manly sort of way, "Sorry old chap, things got a little out of hand, no hard feelings, eh?"

Hah! Forgive my little joke. You probably do not know Etonians quite as well as I do.

They never apologise and never explain – and if you ever think that you're getting an apology out of an Etonian, then just listen to the words carefully, and you will hear that he is not apologising in the slightest, but is merely expressing a measure of sympathy for your hurt feelings. I should know, for as a politician one must become a master of the mealy-mouthed apology.

It would have been fine enough if they'd just avoided me. That's what I'd half-expected: that in their shame they'd send me to Coventry.

But once they'd realised that I wasn't going to squeal, they went to the other extreme altogether. There was no misdemeanour, however trifling, that remained unpunished. There was no fagging errand for which I was not always the primary candidate. And there was no muddy boot or bemerded lavatory that did not somehow have my name on it. The details I will come to later. But I remember how it all snowballed. First Henchman and Ottley were treating me like their personal serf, and then, little by little, Bouverie, Tait, Bitchin' Hitchen and the rest of them joined in until I'd become the whipping boy of choice for the entire Library.

Not that they ever thrashed me again, they never dared, and for that I'm sure I have BJ to thank. For although he spent very little time in the Library, it was clear he'd warned them off.

But there was only so much that BJ could do to protect me. He was a Popper! He loved women! He loved life! He wanted to be out there trawling for more conquests through the fields of Eton and the streets of Windsor; necking champagne in the Cockpit as he nuzzled into some lady's neck; fencing with the senior Classics master over some obscure detail from *The Iliad*.

He did a bit to look after me, but let's just say that I was fairly low on his list of priorities – and fair play to BJ. Why should he have been expected to nursemaid me through my first year at Eton?

The result was that I was pretty much left to sink or swim on my own. Talk about David and Goliath – this was David, aided intermittently by his eccentric fag-master, versus the nine most senior boys in the house.

I've often wondered why those bullies decided to turn my life into a living hell. Perhaps it was for no simpler reason than that they could. But sometimes I wonder if they weren't hoping to drive me away, make my life so unbearable that I'd run pleading back to Nanny Irish and say, "Take me home! Take me away from that beastly school!" That, once and for all, would have erased the thorny memory of the Library Tan.

But I never did go running back to my parents – and that, as any Westminster MP will tell you, is because there isn't a mule in Christendom that was more obdurate and stubborn than myself.

I did at least pass my Colours Test – sailed through, actually. When absolutely necessary, I am more than capable of putting in the work. Most times though, I'd rather not: got better things to do than apply myself to learning stuff by rote. As for those parliamentary briefing papers ... don't even get me started.

I'll bet you imagine that it was from this seething, suppurating, internecine Eton cauldron that I was to evince my first interest in politics. In the past, when I've told friends about my school-days, they have this sort of Eureka! moment, as they trill, "Aha! I see it all! So there you were, a new boy at Eton, hounded on all sides by the Librarians, your life just the most perfect misery, and you were so, so scarred by the injustice of it all that then and there you vowed to do something about it – but not just for yourself, but for all the other little guys who'd been bullied in the world; and so within your first month at Eton you'd decided to go into politics, become an MP, run the whole damn country, and become the ultimate five-star champion for every little guy who'd ever had sand kicked in his face…"

Nice idea, actually. I can see that if I were writing some tear-jerking Barack Obama-style life-story, then it might read very well: the poor little rich boy, struggling away at the blue-bloods' Borstal, bullied by the big boys because of his learning difficulties/indolence – yet in the end he wins through, battle-hardened yet not embittered, and thenceforth, like Superman, pledges to root out injustice wherever he finds it…

And yet the truth of it …

The truth of it was …

That although ultimately Eton did kick-start my interest in politics, it had absolutely damn all to do with injustice and trying to set myself up as a 20th Century Braveheart. (I can just picture that: me strapped to the table in College Hall, about to have my guts eviscerated, as I bawl out that great rebel warcry, "Free Eton!")

In fact, for most of my first year at Eton, I was off in a different direction altogether.

Hitherto, I think I'd generally tried to adhere to school rules. Conditioning, I suppose. Once, at Heatherdown, I'd been caught out of bounds, and this minor matter had been mentioned in my report. Nanny Irish, who was generally the mildest woman you've ever met, had read the report in silence.

"That's not good," she'd said, voice barely above a whisper. One by one she popped her knuckles, each of them sounding like the snap of a dry twig. "Nanny is not … ha-ppy." That's all she said – but all the same she put the very fear of God into me. Nanny Irish was real old school, so she was, but all in due course.

But after the Library Tan, how savagely I swung in the other direction.

My reasoning, as far as I remember it, went like this:

So I'd just been given 12-of-the-best for being cheeky?

So none of the Librarians were ever going to be punished? (Unless I did the job myself – which, of course, I did. Nobody ever thrived in politics without being able to nurse a grievance.)

So the Dame, the Housemaster and all the other beaks were turning a blind eye to this outrage?

And so… if we followed this cheery route to its ineluctable conclusion, then it pretty much meant that the school rules were no longer quite as compulsory at the Headmaster might have liked.

From being the most simpering Little Lord Fauntleroy, I became Eton's staunchest rule-breaker. Rules? *Them's thar for the breaking!*

And didn't I just have the right teacher?

Chapter 12

I've often wondered why it is that politics attracts so many sex-maniacs.

Other big London work-places – law-firms, accountants, advertising crews – have their fair share of extra-curricular sex, don't get me wrong. But generally, in these sort of firms, the work tends to come first: "Let's do the job first, darling, and then afterwards we shall reward each other by having sex." It reveals the wholesome Presbyterian values of delayed gratification that underpin our great capital city today.

And what greater reward can there be than sex? The acclaim of your peers, perhaps? A five-star dinner in the company of good friends? A luxury holiday to the Caribbean? Or, maybe, that electric fizz that pulses through a Prime Minister's body as he takes possession of his new Downing Street home; I'll get back to you on that one.

All nice enough rewards, I'm sure. But sex remains in the same lofty position that it has held since the beginning of recorded time – it is the biggest damn carrot in the business.

What has occurred in Westminster, however, is that sex is no longer just the reward for reaching, say, Cabinet office. It's become the entire currency that makes the place tick: from the Prime Minister to the most humble researcher, from the Cabinet Secretaries to the Master-at-Arms, from the lobbyists to the lickspittle Parly hacks, *everyone* is at it!

And even those high-minded souls who fancy that they're *above* all that sort of tawdry business – that they're too old for it, or just too loved up with their spouses – well, they're hearing about it. All the time, they're getting this drip-feed of stories about the minister bonking the cleaner, the mayor bonking the intern, and the copper with the tea-lady and… after a bit, it starts to do strange things to a man's mind. You start thinking, "It's on offer, it's free, and everyone is helping themselves to this enticing buffet, so maybe … maybe I'll just take myself a little slice of secretary with some researcher on the side." Just ask John Major – fine, upstanding chap, family values and all that, but even *his* head was turned! (And with *Edwina Currie*, for God's sake. The mind boggles!)

Moving swiftly on, for I am a *happily* married man... Sex at Eton: the usual bits and bobs. Bit of fiddling, few blow-jobs, not, as I say, that I ever knew about it on a personal level. But, what with the lack of women and the huge levels of testosterone, Eton did turn every single one of us into the most frenetic masturbators. Despite Maguire's best intentions, Farrer House had a veritable army of onanists, all of them with rod and rag at the ready. Squeak, squeak, squeak went the bedsprings, morning, noon and night. That Bouverie was such a connoisseur of self-abuse that his room came to be dubbed 'The Masturbatorium'. The smell! Like a wild boar having his way with a civet cat.

Now, how to put this delicately? At Heatherdown, I had, ahhh, taken it upon myself to explore the full natural workings of my body. And I had continued these, ahhh, explorations industriously and with vigour after my arrival at Eton. Even had my own room there, the better that I might get to know myself; what a luxury after prep school. The racket in those

Heatherdown dorms; they sounded like they were permanently infested with mice.

During my various explorations at Eton, I didn't really have any fantasies running through my mind. There was Caroline, whom I'd been swimming with a bit during the summer, and whose body seemed to be on the verge of erupting out of her costume; and then there was my green-eyed Katy to add to the list – that bottom, that taut black skirt, ahh me!

After that kiss with Katy, I became more and more aware that I wanted, needed, to find out what a full-grown woman looked like naked. Not that I was of an age to be relieved of my virginity. But before that happy day occurred, I had a very strong desire to do some window-shopping.

Fortunately I knew just the man to provide me with the windows in which I so longed to gaze.

What was it he'd said? "Have your fill of me porno mags – I keeps 'em under me mattress."

One dreary afternoon, I skulked upstairs to BJ's bedroom and there I discovered what I can only describe as some of my most stalwart friends of my teenager years. What times we had together! Just the memory of them makes me smile. And even though I've not seen so much of them of late, I still have the occasional hankering to take them out to play. I daresay their names have changed quite a bit over the years – in fact I don't even know if they exist any more. Yet how those titles bring it all back to me: *Knave, Rustler, Playboy, Fiesta, Mayfair*, and, to my mind, the best of the lot, *Penthouse*; where the women seemed to be this intoxicating combination of the upmarket and the utterly depraved.

That first time, I sat on the edge of BJ's bed in befuddled wonderment as I leafed through *Playboy*. Women, women in all shapes and sizes, some coltish and some more mature, and all of them seemingly happy to let me ogle their nakedness. Every one of them was in this sort of strip-show, starting off fully-dressed, and peeling away item after item until they hadn't got a stitch on, and, oh dearie me, let's have a look round the back just to check you're not wearing a G-string...

It was a *total* revelation – as if after 14 years of living in this bone-dry desert valley, I'd finally climbed one of its peaks, to see ... Such vistas! Such wondrous prospects that I hardly knew even existed. Those first girls – for ever etched now into the hard-drive of my memory banks – why, I can still remember their very names: Esmeralda, a statuesque Amazonian, how I drooled over her, my little eyes popping out on stalks; Angeline, an exotic Oriental; and my favourite of the lot, Chantelle, an all-American cheerleader who looked barely out of short pants.

You cannot imagine my rage, my sheer frustration, as my first session with the *Playmates* was interrupted by a boy call. It was Henchman bellowing like a swineherd at the top of the stairs, "BoooyUppp!"

Just one fleeting moment to adjust my attire and I was out of BJ's room and flying along to the Library. The drill for the fags was that at the first sound of a boy-call, you dropped whatever you were doing, tore out of your room and raced to the Library. Last person in the queue got fagged off, the better to encourage the F-tits to gouge and bite their compadres.

And that particular boy call, as I'd come straight from BJ's room, I was – unusually for me – first in the queue.

Henchman, all haughty elegance in his tails, strutted out of the Library and surveyed the fags. At the rear was Pierre Le Normand picking his nose, the rest of the mob were all twitching and adjusting their waistcoats; while at the front, pleased as could be, was my good self. I jauntily stood there at my ease, one hand on hip, other loosely by my side; it is a pose that today I'm very fond of striking at the dispatch box.

Henchman eyed me larily. "Gentlemen," he said at length. "I think that in a Christian house such as this one, it would be timely to remind you of the words of our Lord Jesus Christ. And did he not say unto his disciples that the last shall be first?" Here he turned to me with a hideous smile. "And that the first shall be last?"

Most of the fags just gawked dumbly, but I knew immediately what he was about. "You can't do that," I said.

"Can't?" he replied. How Henchman towered over me as he stood by the Library door. "Can't? Did the Upstart say I can't do it? I would be very, very careful indeed about using that particular word with me. Have you already forgotten what occurred the last time you told me that I could not do something? I tell you now exactly what I told you just over two weeks ago: not only can I do this, I will do this! Just watch me!"

One by one, he looked at each of the fags before his gaze came back to rest on me. He cupped his hand against his ear. "Something to say? Can I hear you? Speak up, Cameron, speak up!"

Hands behind my back, I stood there and soaked it up. Like a private on parade, I stared at the jagged scar on his neck.

"Quite sure?" he asked. "Absolutely certain? If you're not entirely happy, then you let me know right now!" He beamed at the rest of the fags. They didn't know what to make of it. Like so many sheep, they moved shiftily against the wall.

"Well," said Henchman. "I suppose that if it was good enough for Our Lord Jesus Christ, then we can't really complain, can we? Now, I was looking for somebody to pick up a book from Alden and Blackwell.

"However... however, seeing as it's our very own Upstart, fleetest of all the fags, I wondered if you could pop over to Windsor Castle. My mother was especially after one of their key-rings. Dear Old Mummy. We couldn't deny her that now, could we?"

I should have kept quiet, but out it blurted: "Will you kiss Mummy's ring?"

"Shut your mouth!"

All good training I promise you. You'll hear much worse in under five seconds in Central Office.

Ten minutes later I was traipsing off down the High Street to Windsor Castle. These days, it doesn't seem like any great distance at all, but aged 14 and in your tails, it seemed like you were running the gauntlet, hosed down by every tourist that had a camera. You know the guardsmen who are on parade at Horse Guards, and the way the tourists cuddle in for a picture? Well, that's what it was like for an Eton boy to go through Windsor in tails – only unlike the soldiers at Horse Guards I didn't have a gun to fend them off.

A gang of Japanese tourists even stopped their coach. I started running and a few of them came after me, hunting me down as if I were some exotic new species of whale that just had to be eaten.

Finally I made it to Windsor Castle, bought the naffest key-ring I could find, and on my way back stopped off in Rowland's for a Cornish pasty and chips.

Henchman was in the Library by the time I returned, flicking through *Country Life* – doubtless leering at their 'Girls in Pearls' shot which was the knobs' version of Page Three.

"Your ring," I said. "I hope Mummy likes it. 'Twas the best I could find."

Henchman drummed out his irritation on the side of the

sofa. "Get out! If you say one single word more, I'll send you back off to the Copper Cow." The blood pulsed at his scar as he glared at me.

For a moment I held my ground.

"Go on!" he said, hurling his magazine at me. "Try me! Just one word! Just one word!"

I skulked off to BJ's room to make his tea. He was excavating his way through the mounds of paper on his desk.

"You're late!" he said.

"Sent to Windsor to buy Henchman a key-ring."

"The inconsiderate swine," said BJ. "He's left me waiting fifteen minutes!"

Beans on toast, he wanted, one large can of Heinz and four slices of white buttered toast – swilled down not with Lapsang Oulong, which he considered a morning drink, but a pot of builder's tea.

"Pour yourself a cup while you're at it," he said, continuing to rummage. "*Fouquet in Le Touquet!* I've been looking for that for ages. It's an original Shelley love-letter! Pinched it from the College Library, then forgot all about it!"

He perused it for a while. "Slush," he said. "Could have done better than that when I was thirteen." He turned over the page, continued to read, and then out of nowhere added, "How you enjoying the porn mags?"

"Me?" I said. "I – I – I don't know what you mean –"

In those days, I regret to say that I was rather fearful of expressing my sexuality. All changed now, of course. But 30 years back, I and many other boys felt there was something ever so slightly shameful about the fact we possessed a libido. We may all have been wanking like billy-o, but very few of us would ever have owned up to looking at porn. Disgusting!

"Good healthy stuff, porn," said BJ. "Nothing to be ashamed

about! All perfectly natural."

I gulped as I rubbed my slick hands on my trousers.

"Listen, David," he went on remorselessly. "You fancy girls! You aren't going to see many of them here! There's nothing wrong with reading a porn mag!"

"I don't know what you're talking about," I said primly.

"Oh, I'm most terribly sorry," said BJ, slapping his forehead. "I just thought ... I mean I'd just assumed that like every other F-tit, you were interested in porn."

"No, thank you." Butter would not have melted in my puritanical mouth.

"Not that there's anything wrong with pornography, of course, but if you don't want to look at it, then that's your choice. I completely understand."

"Thank you," I said again, unbending a little after this gross slur to my honour. I finished my tea. "Will there be anything more?"

He was engrossed in his love-letter again. "No that's fine, David. Ta for the tea." I'd just reached the door, was opening it, when he said, "Oh, but actually, there was one very minor thing."

I raised my eyebrows in query.

"Just happened to find one of my porn mags – *Playboy* it was, I think – lying on my bed. Shortly after you came up for lunch. Wouldn't happen to know anything about that, would you? I thought I expressly asked you to desist from spanking your monkey in my room!"

Dohhh! "*Playboy*?" I squawked. My very first outing with Esmeralda Angeline and Chantelle – and already I'd been found out. "Yuk!"

"I thought you'd say that," he said. "No matter. It's not of any great import." BJ hummed for a bit before producing a heavy-duty canvas bag from under his desk. "Men, you know David, are divided into those who approve of porn and those who do not. But, mark my words, even the men who hate it will always love to look. Into which camp do you fall?"

"I –"

"No call for an answer!" He held up his hand. "Now, moving on, I find that I no longer have quite such a taste for *Playboy* and *Fiesta* and the rest of them. Why look at porn, when you can have the real thing?"

He nudged over the bulging canvas bag. "I wondered if you might be able to find a way of disposing of all my old magazines? Bright boy like you – shouldn't be too difficult."

"I – I'll see what I can do." I picked up the bag; could barely lift it with one hand.

"You are too kind," said BJ, though as I left he did add, "And please. No more pulling the pork stick in my bedroom!"

Porn mags – loads of 'em! I scurried back to my room with my booty. There was just time for a quick flick before tea, but I saved the main session for after lights out when I wouldn't be disturbed. Sixty of them, there were – 60! – and before I was done that night, I had been through every one. By the end of it, I was so done in that I was like a limp rag. I had viewed, leered at, and lusted over well nigh 300 women in the altogether. How they would come to fire my fantasies! Always though, I kept turning back to my first love, Chantelle the cheerleader. If only I could get to meet her, I was sure we'd get along. I'd take her walking by the river in Windsor.

The next morning, I put them all under lock and key in my old Heatherdown tuck-box. "Sleepless night?" said BJ when I brought him some tea. He had this wide, disarming smile, eyes on me all the time so he wouldn't miss a thing. "You look like you've seen a ghost! What ever have you been playing at?"

"Couldn't sleep," I said.

"Poor David," he said, his smile just falling short of an outright smirk. "Best get some rest! You look all done in!"

As I left, he crowed after me, "Got rid of all those magazines, did you? Didn't cause you too much trouble, did I?" His jeering laughter trailed after me down the passage. "You couldn't get down those stairs quick enough!"

Things would have been just fine if I'd kept the mags to myself. But that was never my style. I had to share BJ's munificence.

Chapter 13

"Wherever did you get them?" said Pierre Le Normand, eyes like saucers as he leafed through one of the *Fiestas*.

"I have my sources," I replied modestly.

"But – but they're amazing!" said Ricky Martine, bringing the copy of *Penthouse* right up to his nose. "I didn't know you could get breasts that big!"

Toby Edwardes, on the bed next to Ricky, was snuffling to himself. "My God!" he said as he turned a page with trembling fingers. "She's being porked by a builder!"

Ricky looked over his shoulder. "No, she is not being porked by a builder. She is *porking* a builder. Active, not passive."

He wiped the dusting of spittle from his lips. "I didn't even know that was legal!"

Even William M'Thwaitey, usually so quiet, was moved to speech as he sat by the window. "I like this one," he said, chewing at his spectacles. "She's jolly nice!"

Yes, there we sat, all ten of Farrer's F-tits somehow crammed into my tiny little room, four on the bed, two by the window, two on the armchair, me at my desk and even wheezy old Mark Davide squatting on the floor by the door. I felt like a nobleman who, in time of famine, had suddenly produced for his loved ones the most fabulous hamper from Fortnum and Mason.

As you probably know, many of those boys – including William M'Thwaite, Toby Edwardes, Mark Davide, Ricky Martine and Pierre Le Normand – are still my friends to this day. It is, perhaps, a weakness of mine that I only feel truly comfortable in the company of Etonians and members of the Bullingdon Club. Time and again, I've been told that I should mix more; that I should be more inclusive with my kitchen cabinet, have more women, more grammar school lads. I know it, I know it – and *when* I become Prime Minister, I will endeavour to remedy the situation. But that is when I'm Prime Minister. and not before. Just haven't got quite enough time at the moment.

I could not tell the boys where the porn mags had come from, but how I basked in their approval.

"I – I couldn't borrow this tonight, could I?" said Ricky.

I hadn't really banked on this. I'd somehow thought that I might be allowed to show off my porn hoard before returning all the magazines back to my private library. But now the genie was well and truly out of the bottle.

"Oh – do let me take this one, please," squeaked Pierre, lean, scrawny, his adam's apple bobbling in his stringbean throat.

"Can I take two?" said Toby. "Oh please, David! You can't hog them all!"

Things were rapidly getting out of control. "Hold it!" I said, raising my hands for a bit of calm. "Hold it! Just cool it!"

After a bit of jabbering they all quietened down, though most just went back to leafing through their magazines. Such furious concentration etched into the boys' faces; a sight to have gladdened their teachers' hearts.

"If we're going to do this, we're going to do it properly," I said, grabbing my new French vocab book. "If I don't take a note of who's got what, then they're all going to get lost – and then where will be? Okay – Pierre, you're taking the January issue of *Fiesta*?"

"Yes please," he piped. "Do you want any money for it?"

"Well, errr –" Honestly, until that moment the very thought of accepting money from my friends just because they wanted to borrow my sordid magazines had simply never occurred to me.

Pierre looked at me anxiously. "It's no problem, David," he said. "Here's 10p and I'll have it back to you by tomorrow."

"Ahh," I said. The other fags watched as I leaned back in my chair, scratched the back of my neck. "Well, I suppose that would be very kind of you. It'll help with the, er, sort of admin costs, that kind of thing, make sure we keep our supplies up."

"Oh, thank you, David!" said Pierre as he scuttled out of the room. "You're such a brick!"

"Here's 20p," said Toby. "All right if I take these two?"

"Fine!" I said, before looking up and seeing what was in his hot little hands. "No – hang on! Actually I want that *Playboy* back if you don't mind." I certainly wasn't going to have Toby pleasuring himself over my Chantelle; like as not she'd be delivered back to me as spattered as a painter's radio.

So, out they all filed from my room, all jutting trousers and with their porn mags stuffed down their waistcoats – and at the end of it all, I found that I had £2.54. That was more than a week's pocket money! Worth at least three good treats at Rowland's, possibly four if I cut back on the chips.

You had never seen such a happy F-tit in all your life as me strutting along to Rowland's that afternoon. I'd told a couple of the fags that I'd sock them tea, but for some reason they were otherwise engaged.

I had the works – ham, egg and chips with four 'rafts' of fried bread and two cans of Coke. I did not mind at all that I was by myself, for I was quite content to stack up my loose change in front of me and dream my dreams of becoming a porn baron.

Say I made £2 a day, that would be roughly £15 a week, or well over £100 a term! I'd be rolling in so much money that ... that ... I could dine at Rowland's every day of the week! I'd be more than just a porn baron, but a porn emperor! How quickly my dreams snowballed. Perhaps Chantelle the cheerleader might get to hear of how actively I'd been promoting her cause and come visit me; sort of like the PM trekking to the provinces to pat the heads of the party-faithful, now that I think of it.

That night, alone in bed with Chantelle, how I luxuriated in those fantasies. Truly it felt as if at long last I had spied my destiny.

The next day at breakfast, the fags table looked like a pack of whipped dogs – anyone would have thought we were going down with bubonic plague. Gaunt white faces, hollow eyes sunk deep into red sockets, their once lustrous hair now greasy and lifeless, their sickly pallid hands trembling from sheer exhaustion; mere husks of the boys that I had seen the previous night.

BJ made a beeline for me as soon as he came in. Standing over us, hands on hips and wearing a livid harlequin waistcoat, he looked like a cross between a court jester and Henry VIII. "*Fouquet moi!*" he bellowed. "Has David been beasting you?"

I looked up at him, sickly, the knife shaking in my hand as I buttered some toast.

Henchman then came over, coffee in hand, and glowered at us. "What's happened to these damn fags? They look like they're going down with scurvy."

"Possibly," said BJ, as he sauntered off for some eggs and

bacon. "Either that or they've taken the term 'self-abuse' to a whole new level."

Three days it lasted, and perhaps it was well that it came to an end. Our poor racked bodies were falling to bits. It was as if every night, we each of us suffered ourselves to go through this horrendous trial by ordeal. How we hated it, were ashamed of it and of all that it was doing to our slight frames. Yet it was quite impossible to resist. The pity of it. Oh the pity of it! Such a wretched sight we were as would have melted even the flintiest of hearts.

That third night, I tottered back to my room and was tucked up in my bed by 9pm; I longed for sleep. I had barely closed my eyes, when there was Chantelle, kneeling by my bedside, stoking the fires – and I know this is how all the addicts sound, but it's true, it really is – and the next thing, there she was, and I'm wanting her and hating myself and…

Only twice that night, which was good for me.

But it had to come to an end, and in a way I'm thankful that it did, as who knows what might have happened to the fags if it had been allowed to continue. Has anyone ever pleasured themselves to death? Well, I don't know. Be an interesting one in the coroner's court, wouldn't it? 'Cause of death: excessive masturbation.' All I can say, however, is that we ten fags may not have actually succeeded in killing ourselves through self-abuse. But we must have given it a damn good try.

Frankly, I'm surprised we even had three nights. Gossip flies round an Eton boys' house even faster than it rips through Westminster – and that's saying something.

The next day, at about 6-ish, I was at my burry doing some extra work. But it was difficult – Chantelle was there too, lolling in front of me as she draped herself over my radio. I was trying to do some latin, *Amo, Amas, Amat*: I love, you love, she loves. *Amabo, Amabis, Amabit*: I will love, you will love, she will love. *Amabam* … It was just intolerable, how could I possibly concentrate when, there in black and white, Chantelle was leering at me in her suspenders and telling me that she loved me.

I was just on the verge of taking her off to my bed, when there was a knock at my door and in walked m'tutor, Maguire. I hid the *Playboy* in a flash, shoving it under some textbooks.

As courtesy demands, I stood up.

"Good evening Sir." M' tutor often pottered around the house in the evening to have a word with the boys, but there was a weird vibe about him: intuition, you see. Maybe a bit of this magical dust was already rubbing off from BJ.

"Take a seat, David. May I sit here?" He sat in the armchair, cosy as can be, and I was suddenly aware that if he turned his head even three inches, he'd have a direct view of Chantelle's breasts which were peeping out from underneath my Latin Primer.

"I am aware, David, that we did not get off to the best of starts with that fire-alarm incident. But I can see that you are struggling to reform. So I am going to do my best to give you one more chance." He nodded, as if pleased he'd got off to such a flying start.

Hands clasped together, chin on my knuckles, I was the very picture of earnest diligence. I nodded gravely. "Yes Sir."

Maguire licked his little finger and tamped down a rogue eyebrow. "I've been rather concerned, David, about the boys in F-block. They have not really been themselves these past couple of days."

"Oh yes, Sir?" A slight note of alarm in my query.

"At first I thought that they might be going down with some

illness. Then … I could not … I would not have believed my ears, had I not heard it from the House Captain himself!" His eyes were swivelling in their sockets he was so excited. "Pornography, that's what it is!"

I nodded again, sympathetic, concerned even. Funny that I should have mastered that look at such a young age: MPs use it all the time when they're being harangued by a constituent.

"Yes, pornography, David!" He puffed himself up like a turkey-cock, sending a quiver through the jowly wattles around his neck; even brought a bit of colour to his gravedigger face.

"Now – this is not at all easy for me. But … You don't know anything about this … this shocking … this disgusting tide of filth that is wreaking such havoc among the first years?" Christ alive! If Maguire even moved his eyes a single inch, he'd see Chantelle. God, she was looking lovely; the little minx was flirting with me right underneath Maguire's nose!

Time for another earnest look to the eyes. "Pornography, Sir? No Sir!"

"And that is not just on your honour but your Eton honour?" He looked at me gravely.

No problemo, Mr Maguire. "On my *Eton* honour," I recited, "I know nothing of this pornography that you're talking about."

Maguire, sitting there writhing on my bed, seemed to brighten up. "Thank you, David. I just wanted to hear it from your own lips. I did find it very hard to credit. Perhaps at 14 you're too young to even to know what pornography is?"

"Well, I'm not really sure, Sir. Somebody may have mentioned it in Biology, but it sounds absolutely beastly, and also deeply unnatural – " I looked down at Chantelle; just the sweetest girl. She winked at me and teased the tip of her tongue out of her mouth, as if there was nothing she'd like more than...

"I agree," said Maguire. "You're so right – it *is* unnatural. Such wisdom on such a young head."

He started scratching at his chest with relief, like a bald gorilla feeling for fleas. "I was mistaken! I sometimes am, you know David, and on those occasions, I think it is correct to apologise. I am sorry."

"That's quite all right, Sir."

"Well, that's that then." He sniffed as he walked to the door, "Let you get back to your extra work. What is it tonight, David – bit more Latin, I see, very good, very –"

He paused and his jaw dropped open. A pulse of electricity rippled up the back of my neck.

"What?" he raged. "What is that on your desk? Oh, you... little Judas!" He stepped smartly across the room, hurled the Latin primer onto the floor and snatched up my *Playboy*.

"What? What!" He was practically lost for words. The magazine was shaking so hard in his hands that I thought he was going to rip it in half. "And what, then, is *this*?"

"Ahh," I said. "Using it for my Biology practical, Sir."

"Don't be so ridiculous! This – this ..." he trailed off as he leafed through more of Chantelle's pictures, pausing at a particularly tasteful one of her on a hay bale, seemingly about to spank herself with a riding crop. "Where did you get this from?"

Skating on very thin ice now. "Got it from a boy in another house, Sir. He said it might help me with the Biology. Err ..." I gauged the length of the pause exquisitely. "Is this the pornography thing that you mentioned, Sir?"

"Is it indeed! Do you have more of this smut, this filth? Have you been giving it to the other boys? Well have you?"

"No Sir! I wouldn't dream –"

"I don't know whether to believe a word you're saying …"
He stalked over to my bed and wrenched back the mattress.
"What's this then?" he screamed, the spittle fairly flying out of
his mouth. "What's this then, you vile miscreant? A boy in my
own house! Lied to me! Lied to my very face!" Along with the
Playboy, he was now clutching up copies of *Fiesta*, *Knave* and
Parade.

Things were desperate now. "Somebody must have put
them, Sir," I squealed. "Planted! I've been framed!"

"Is there more?" he shouted, face quite contorted with rage
as he stood not six inches away from me. "Tell me honestly,
boy! Is there more of it? Have you got more of this filth?"

"No Sir!" I squeaked, though things were rapidly getting out
of control. "On my honour, Sir! On my Eton honour! I don't
know how they got there, Sir!"

"Unspeakable wretch!" He barged past me and started tugging out the drawers from my burry, before searching through
the wardrobe. For a moment, he stood there panting in the middle of the room, eyes rolling, before he caught sight of my
tuck-box in the corner.

"Aha!" he said. "I knew it! I knew it! Open that box immediately!"

"Lost the key, Sir!"

"Don't believe it for a moment. Empty your pockets!"

I tried to palm my key-ring but I was so cack-handed that he
spotted me.

"Yes!" he said triumphantly. "I'll have that Cameron, if you
please. Give it me now! Ohh … you viper in the nest! You
Jezebel! You monster!" He knelt down by the tuck-box, hands
shaking so much that he could barely get the key in the lock.

The key clicks.

The top of the tuck-box is thrown back.

Ohhh …

This one's going to be difficult.

"Hooo! Hooo! Hooo!" he screamed at the top of his voice. "I cannot believe it! I cannot believe it! You have lied to me! Again and again you have lied to me! And not just on your honour, but that of the school's honour as well. And … Oh no! Oh no!"

He'd found the little notebook with all my meticulous accounts from the previous three days. "Pierre Le Normand!" he shrieked in astonishment. "Thirty pence for two *Fiestas* and a *Penthouse*! This is sordidness such as I have never encountered!" His tongue darting out to lick dry lips, before he continues his scream-fest. "Ricky Martine? Twenty pence for two *Playboys*? You even charged him ten pence for a late return! And no, oh my good God, no!" and at that, he let out a great, keening howl of rage. "M'Thwaite! Dear, sweet, innocent M'Thwaite! You've even turned him too!"

"I –"

"Don't speak another word!" He held up a shaking hand. "To be reading this pornography yourself is bad enough. But then to have used it to pervert the minds of the other boys in your year … it's too horrid to contemplate! All of them! Every one of them! You have corrupted every one of them with this filth! This depravity! Such a perversion of nature! Never in all my years as a Housemaster have I seen anything like it!"

He swept up the magazines, clutching them in front of him as he stood trembling by the door. "A porn dealer," he said. "In my own house! In my own house! I would not have believed it possible!"

"I'm very sorry, Sir." I tried to force out a tear, but nothing would come.

"You will be!" he said. "You will be! You will be on the bill tomorrow to see the Lowermaster, and it will be he who decides the punishment to fit these monstrous crimes. And to think that I was close to believing you."

He opened the door. "Lies!" he screeched. "Lies and more lies! Pornography! Dealing in pornography! Corrupting the other fags! And the worst of it, boy? The worst of it? You have dishonoured the school and brought shame to the name of Eton! Never, never have I seen such wickedness!"

Chapter 14

BJ, when he heard the news the next morning, laughed so hard that I thought he was going to be sick.

"You are an imbecile!" he said, before emitting this high-pitched, "Wheee-Wheee-Wheee" sound, like a young sucking pig. It was one of the strangest laughs I've ever heard.

"You kept them in the tuck box!" Wheee-wheee-wheee. "You rented them out to the other boys!" Wheee-wheee-wheee. "You're going to be for the bloody high-jump!"

I resignedly continued to pick up the bits of pizza and old chips that were lying on the floor. I don't think I've ever provided another human being with such intense amusement.

BJ was lying in bed, Lapsang Oulong untouched by his side. He'd made me go through every detail of what had occurred with Maguire.

"And what did he do then?" he'd ask excitedly. "What did he say next? I want to hear all of it! Don't miss out a single word!"

There were so many wheezed interruptions, BJ holding his hand up to stop me, that it took me more than half-an-hour to tell my sordid little tale.

"That is the funniest thing that I have ever heard!" he said. "Who would have thought that giving you all those porn mags could have turned out so happily?"

My second beating at Eton was quite different from the first.

For a start, it was a very formal affair. And for seconds – and I know this may sound odd – I had been rather looking forward to this strange communion that I was about to have with history.

"Back so soon?" said the Lowerman when I appeared before him two days later.

He stood up and took off his black gown and jacket. "First time the fire-alarm. Now you're a porn dealer. Whatever will be next?"

What indeed? Had he known the answer to that little question, he might have echoed Mr Maguire with a "Hooo-hooo-hooo!"

I stuck exactly to the tale that BJ had cooked up for me: I'd found the porn mags in the lumber-room where we stored all the trunks. The dealing? Well, it just got out of control. "I was wrong, Sir," I pleaded. "I've been bad!" You can't beat a good *Mea Maxima Culpa*.

"Pah!" The Lowerman rolled up his sleeves. Very brawny arms, he had, and with his cropped hair, red braces and hob-nailed boots, he was about as near as you could get to a Regimental Sergeant Major outside the army. "Pah!" he said again as he marched over to the black beating block that stood in the middle of the room.

The block was like a set of three Library steps, etched with age-old graffiti. On one side was a rack with five canes, while on the other were some 'courtesy tissues', as well as swabs and alcohol. He took each of the canes out in turn and gave them a couple of ferocious cuts into the side of a leather armchair. He twirled those canes with all the panache of a maestro violinist wielding his fiddle-stick.

"Six it is, then!" And then – such history! Only ever could

you hear this at Eton. "Will you have the wad or the bullet?"

In one hand he offered up a gnarled leather strop, about the size of a bar of soap, and in the other, an old bullet. Each of them, even the bullet, were covered with tooth-marks, but the strop, still flecked with fresh spittle, was as mauled as a dog-chew. I stared at them, goosebumps singeing up by the back of my neck, for I was all too aware of their remarkable pedigree.

I think even a Leftie like Mandelson would have been able to appreciate the awesome power of the past that was imbued within the wad and the bullet, as sacred to Eton as any relic in the Holy Roman Empire. For these two artefacts, which had been stuffed into the glistening maws of so many thousand boys, had been picked up from two of Britain's most historic battlefields.

The bullet, six slim inches of ecstasy, was from the relief of Ladysmith during the Boer War. I quivered at the thought of how many boys' mouths had slipped round the blunt round tip of this silver bullet, their lips peeled back in a perfect orgasm of agony.

As for the wad, it was said to be as old as Eton itself. My Pater's toothmarks were on it, as well as the toothmarks of my Pater's Pater before him. On that very wad of leather, Walpole had bitten hard to hide his screams; Gladstone had chewed on it; Shelley had champed down on it, many times over. Walpole, Huxley, Orwell, BJ, they all of them had chewed on this griz-zled old piece of shoe leather, said to have been stripped from a French knight at the battle of Crecy – and now it was my turn to take my place alongside the greats.

"The wad please, Sir."

I knelt on the bottom step of the block and could feel the his-tory pulsing off the old oak. Just to think of all those men who had knelt there before me! And now I, also, was cramming the wad into my mouth, tasting its acrid taint, all too aware of how thousand upon thousand Etonians had also savoured its tang over the centuries. Never has such a small piece of shoe leather held so much history. Oh, to analyse its lingering DNA, for it would give you a complete template of the British nobility stretching back more than half a millennium.

"Tails up!" said the Lowerman, and then, just one final piece of the caning quadrille as he barked, "Take it out!", as I hauled out the house flag that BJ had earlier stuffed down the back of my trousers.

I leaned forward over the top step of that scarred beating block and clasped the rung on the far side. I'd been to Communion, but this was far and away the most religious experience of my life.

Two smart steps from behind me and the cane slashed down – and, I promise you, I felt the tears stinging at my eyes. But it wasn't for the hurt, that red poker roar. It was something else altogether. For as I'd bent over the block, I'd been able to stare up at its underbelly. How scored it was with graffiti, with name after name hacked into the wood. And there, right at the top, longer and deeper than all the others, and written as if it was meant to stay there till the end of time, were the two words 'Arthur Wellesley'. Wellington himself, the man who'd won Waterloo on Eton's playing-fields, had had his bottom beaten on that very block.

It was all way too much for me. By the time the Lowerman was done, I was just a complete juddering mess, tears streaming down my cheeks, as I clutched at the courtesy tissues.

The Lowerman stood by the door as I shook his hand.

"Thank you, Sir," I sniveled, as I wiped the tears from my eyes. "I wondered, please, if I might also bite the bullet?"

Shall I tell you, though, my greatest regret of that whole affair?

It was the loss of Chantelle. Maguire had taken away the whole host of magazines, and it was the last I ever saw of her. It was as if our enthralling love affair had been cut short in its very prime. Such high hopes I'd had for her; such dreams. Over the years, I have bought many, many porn magazines – hundreds of them, enough to fill a skip – purely in the hope that I might one day gaze on Chantelle's beauty again.

But I never have.

Chapter 15

A few days later, as I was making BJ his tea, my fag-master was to have the conversation that would ultimately lead to me becoming a Conservative.

Mind you, it also led to quite a few other things, too – not least my very near death. But that afternoon, as I lounged on BJ's sofa with a huge slice of chocolate cake in my hand, I had no inkling of what the mad man had in store for me. I was reading a copy of the *Daily Telegraph*.

It would be a few years yet before I came to love that last great bastion of the English Empire, but I was reading the *Telegraph* because it had a story of some pertinence: a couple of Etonians had been roughed up by gangs of 'Townies' in Windsor. Apparently the two boys had been seized as they'd come out of a tea-room and the louts had thrashed them about a bit. It seemed that there may also have been some sexual mischief-making, but that most interesting matter had been glossed over.

Meanwhile…

BJ had given himself the day off school and was lying in bed memorising poetry. I don't know where the idea came from, but, having already memorised all of Churchill's speeches, he had set himself the task of learning the hundred greatest poems in history. He only had to read them out loud twice and they were completely meshed into his hard-drive. God, it was irritating – especially when you consider that I had to practically sweat blood to learn even 20 words of French vocab.

"I'd like to buy you a present, David," he said. "As a small token of my esteem for all your efforts."

I looked up from the *Telegraph*. "There's really no need."

"No David, I insist!" he said. "You shall have a present and you shall go and buy it for yourself this instant!"

Now, if anything was going to set the alarm bells jangling, it was that. BJ buying me a present as a token of his esteem? Well, I may have only known him a month, but even I wasn't that wet behind the ears.

I took another bite of cake, using the time to think. BJ definitely had an angle, I was certain of that, but as yet it was far too murky for me to discern.

"You want me to go and buy you a present?"

"No, David, I wish you to go and buy *yourself* a present! Better hurry, before the shops close in Windsor. Should be some cash in my wallet – take a fifty."

"Fifty pounds for a present for me?" Oh, these were dark waters indeed that I was travelling o'er.

"Don't mention it," he said, scratching at his chin as he stared at the ceiling. "Just run along to one of the hardware shops and buy yourself a decent crowbar and a good length of sturdy rope –"

"Hang on!" I put down the paper. "I'm buying myself a crowbar and some rope?"

"No boy should be without them!" he said. "Buy yourself some toothy-rotters with the change, if you like."

"What am I going to do with a crowbar?"

"Be off with you, David. All these questions – you're giving me a headache!"

So I dusted the cake crumbs from my shirt, buttoned up my waistcoat, and returned the *Telegraph* to the walnut newspaper rack on the wall.

And – of course – BJ's party-piece. I've seen him do it so many times over the years that when I leave a room now, I almost expect it: he always saves the best for last.

My hand was on the very door handle. I'd all but quit the room.

And… "Oh David, just one more thing."

That was the moment when there was the tiniest click in the tracks of my destiny, so slight that it was barely audible. It was the sound of the points being changed as my little train was about to set off on a different track altogether.

BJ was fussing with his bed-cap. Vivid scarlet it was, and for a moment it seemed that he was Satan himself. "David," he said, "I think you should join the political society. I think it would be good for you."

That was the first time, that I can remember, that I ever heard a mention of the word 'Politics'. It meant absolutely nothing to me. Of course I vaguely knew that it referred to our airy-fairy masters that resided in some Gothic house of horror in London. But as to who they were and what they did, I had not the faintest clue. So they affected our lives in some sort of high-fallutin' way and had it in their powers to change the very course of nations? Well, bully for them!

And my first response to BJ's kind invitation to join the political society? Did I appreciate the honour that had been bestowed on me, a humble F-tit? Did I fall to my knees at this most munificent of blessings?

No – not really. "That's really very, very handsome of you, BJ, thank you so much," I said. "Though I think I'd have more fun taking my nose off with a cheese-grater."

"There's no need to be like that!" BJ said. "It'll be fun! There are lots of laughs to be had!"

How fiendish he looked as he laughed merrily to himself. So must the devil have seemed to Faust when he made his pact.

"And besides – I've been worried about you!" continued BJ. "The other F-tits… for some reason they seem to shun you. I just thought… the political society… it would be the *perfect* place for you to make new friends."

I eyed him warily. "What's the catch?"

"Catch?" he boomed. "Such cynicism in one so young! You'll never have had so much fun in all your life, I promise you! I promise you!" And here he did a passable imitation of Tony the Tiger from the Frosties adverts. "It's gonna be *Grrrr-eat!*"

So many things to ponder as I went to Windsor to buy my own present. I seemed to have traipsed all round the town before I finally found a hardware shop that sold crowbars and rope.

It was difficult to know which was the more perplexing: the purchase of the crowbar, or being press-ganged into the Political Society. I tried to recall the little that I knew about Westminster. Thatcher had got in that summer, I knew that. Was she a Conservative? Might have been – not quite sure. And before Thatcher, it had been that guy Jim Callaghan. Or was it Harold Wilson? That, I guess, was the sum total of my political knowledge.

But for BJ to seriously suggest that the political society was – what had he called it? – "*Fun*"? Well, I can laugh about it now, laugh about it with the best of them. The old Turk got me good and proper on that one. And haven't the chickens just come home to roost?

I returned to BJ's room hefting the crowbar in my hands.

About three foot long it was, and I liked the feel of the tempered steel in my hands. I gave it a swish in the air: felt like you could do some real damage with the thing. "Got my present," I said. "Thanks very much."

"*Mon plaisir, Davide!*" he said, adopting a bizarre French accent. "Now…" He drummed his fingers at his lower-lip in pantomime of a man deep in thought. "Where shall we hide this thing? Aha! I know! I have it! Just lift up one of the floorboards in your room. You can keep the crowbar and the rope in there. If you'd thought to do that with your vast collection of porn, you might have saved yourself that slight *contretemps* with the good Mr Maguire."

I could sense I was on the very edge of an abyss, the fog swirling thick beneath me as I caught a glimpse of the pit.

"Go to!" he said. "Go to! We haven't got all night, you know!"

There wasn't anything else for it but to go downstairs and do my master's bidding. I eased back the carpet and prised up a small board near my bed: easy as a knife through butter.

And that, I suppose, was the start of it.

Chapter 16

Here's something that you may not know about me: I'm a member of the St Moritz Tobogganing Club, done the Cresta Run. Not that I'm embarrassed by it but, like the Bullingdon Club, my shooting and my holidays in Tuscany, it smacks too much of the Tory grandee. So, like so many of the pleasures of my youth, I now have to pretend that St Moritz, the Cresta and Shuttlecock never existed.

But when I do finally quit politics, doubtless ousted in some diabolical coup – just who, I wonder, will wield the dagger-blow? – one of the things I am most looking forward to is returning to St Moritz. For I view my races on the Cresta in the same gilded light with which I now see my run for the Tory leadership: without doubt, one of the most exhilarating things I've ever done.

They dress you up in the oddest clothes, tweeds and helmet and spiky hob-nailed leather boots that must have come from World War II. It's as if you've just joined a rather odd shooting party where there's a high degree of probability you'll get winged.

Cherry brandy beforehand as well as a pep-talk from the Secretary, who carefully explains how over the years the Cresta's runners have managed to break every conceivable bone in their bodies. "Good luck," he then calls with a cheery wave. "You'll need it!"

You start off slow enough, nervily dragging your dagger toes into the ice, aware that ahead of you is that formidable hairpin bend that's known as Shuttlecock. But once you've round Shuttlecock, you have this glorious sensation that the worst is behind you. Suddenly, your feet are up, you pull forward on the sledge, and it is like hammering the gas in a Porsche. Boooom! You're away! Face not three inches from the surface, the acceleration rips through you. At the bottom, knees shaking, not quite believing you've made it in one piece; and all you want is to get back on that sledge and do it all over again.

So very similar to my first year at Eton.

At this stage in my life, the events were like three intertwined strands in a plaited skein of silk: each very different, yet all inextricably linked.

If I had more skill as a writer, I might be able to chop and change my way, seamlessly cutting from one character and one story to the next as I painted the various mile-markers along the route to my becoming a Tory. But that would over-complicate things. Much easier, I feel, to deal with these matters one by one. Soon enough we'll come to Henchman, the Townies and The Black Prince.

First, though, let us immerse ourselves in that wonderfully odd world that I've come to know so well, where in a single day you can be sulky, perverse, vengeful, savage and, I suppose, very occasionally uplifted... I refer, of course, to this glittering cage that I inhabit at Westminster.

Perhaps you think, by the way, that *this* was the moment, *this* was the time when I felt the hook of politics biting into my lower lip. Pah! The very opposite.

That BJ had wanted me to be his skivvy-cum-Secretary had

been obvious right from the start. Like Michael Heseltine, BJ was one of those men who'd had his political career mapped out since he was a teenager. And, but for the minor spanner in the ointment that was my good self, I don't doubt that come the next election, it would be BJ who'd be ousting Gordon Brown from his home in Downing Street. (Can you imagine the makeover that place will need? Sam's having kittens!)

In pursuing his insane dream, BJ set – and achieved – two modest goals for himself at Eton. Firstly, he wanted to master the art of oratory, and he had done this long before I ever got to know him. Even at 17, he could tell the hoariest old joke you've ever heard and still the Eton pups would be stamping the ground for more.

BJ's other goal was to be the head of Eton's Political Society, where – thanks to the sterling efforts of his loyal and devoted Secretary – he could make the contacts that would stand him in such good stead when he was ready to make his assault on Westminster.

"How many more of these bloody things have I got to do?" I whined, eyes practically cross-eyed with tiredness. As for my tongue, it was so swollen that it seemed to fill my entire mouth, as if I had spent the entire afternoon sticking up wallpaper with my own spittle.

"No good ever came from whingeing, David," said BJ, who was just putting the finishing touches to his speech. "Besides, if you weren't doing this, you'd only be wanking in your pit."

"I must have done 400 of these bloody things." I scrawled out another address and licked another stamp. The taste! Even the thought of it still makes me retch.

"*We* have done 342, if you don't mind," he said. "And *we* have approximately another 300 to do. Though I'm not sure about the Liberals, probably a waste of time. But then – who knows! We'll do the Lords! The TUC barons! The publishers! We'll try the lot!"

"You mean *I* will try the lot."

"Being a bit whiny there, if you don't mind my saying so, David," BJ said, leaning back his chair and kicking up his legs onto the pyramid of paper on his burry. "Your lack of optimism has been noted. Perhaps you have forgotten that success is a journey – not a destination?"

"Yeah – and on this particular journey, I've been carrying you all of the way!"

"Tut," he said – and to this day, that single syllable repri-mand remains one of the most powerful put-downs that I know.

BJ scanned his speech one more time, committing it to memory before scrumpling it into a ball and tossing it in the vague direction of the bin.

"Proper little Bob Cratchit over there, aren't you?" he chuckled. "Now we, dear David, are about to embark on the most remarkable venture together. Is there any detail with which you are not entirely happy?"

"No BJ," I said. How weary I was at the unbelievable perk-iness of the man. He was now dancing round the room, arm around some imaginary partner, doubtless dreaming that he'd just won the world ballroom dancing championship. He glided over to the wardrobe, took out an old metal box and prised out a silk top hat, green with age.

"My great-grandfather's, don't you know?" he said. "He wore it at the Siege of Lucknow during the Indian Mutiny. It's even got a hole in the top from a Pandy sniper!"

"Really?" I said.

"Come now, David, you might feign more interest than that, you young pup! You'll never get anywhere in politics without it!"

"Really?"

"Yes! Really!" he bellowed, clapping me round the shoulders. "Don't you look like a proper little gentleman's gentleman?"

In that respect, at least, he did not exaggerate. Earlier that afternoon BJ had fagged me off to the school outfitters, New and Lingwood, to get myself kitted out for the evening. I was now wearing what I can only describe as the full dress uniform of a QE II steward: black bowtie and black dress trousers, white shirt and white gloves, and all of this set off by a white monkey jacket wreathed in gold braid. Give me one of those round pillbox hats and I could have passed myself off as an organ-grinder's monkey.

"Come, David, let us not keep Mr Heath waiting," he said, picking up an ebony cane and some calfskin gloves. "This is going to be an absolute *hoot!*"

Now that – that was probably a stretch.

I know that it ill-behoves us to speak ill of the dead, and that this is especially so when we're speaking of not just an ex-Prime Minister, but an ex-leader of the Tory Party. But Ted Heath! He was the absolute bloody limit! I couldn't stand the man – even when I got to know him as an adult. Is it possible, though, that my opinion of Heath may have been ever so slightly tainted by our first meeting?

What had happened was that the day after I'd become BJ's Political Secretary, he'd had me writing to every member of Maggie Thatcher's cabinet, as well as all the ex-leaders.

And – unbelievably – BJ had hit gold at our very first attempt. He seemed to have Satan's own luck. By an utter miracle, that old curmudgeon himself, Ted Heath, had gone for it. I don't know if any of Thatcher's cabinet even deigned to reply to my letters, but within the week Heath – chuntering spleen and bile from his every pore – had booked himself down to Eton.

After that, there was no stopping BJ. "Look at this!" he'd crowed as he held Heath's hand-written letter aloft. "The old Trot's swallowed it!" That very afternoon, BJ had had me writing out letters – each on headed "Eton Political Society" paper – to every minister in Thatcher's government, and by the end of the week I'd written to every major MP in Westminster.

It's the standard shotgun technique and how well I've come to know it: you pepper away and you pepper away, in the vain hope that eventually you'll hit something. Nobody's got the faintest clue exactly what it is that you're going to hit. But keep at it long enough, and you're *bound* to hit something. Welcome to my world.

As soon as word had got out that Heath was coming down, everyone wanted to get involved – and, take it from me, there are just as many crawlers at Eton as there are at Westminster. Even the Headman wanted to get in on the act, and so it was decided that BJ and a few other committee members were going to be dining with Heath in the Headman's personal suite.

I, of course, was not going to be having supper with this select group.

But BJ had somehow got it into his head that on such an important occasion, he required his own batman. Why I couldn't have worn my tail-coat, God knows, but as it was he'd decided to tog me out in that oversized monkey jacket. My orders, as BJ had repeatedly explained, were that for the duration of the drinks and the meal, I was to stand respectfully just a couple of feet away from BJ's left shoulder. I was to top up BJ's glass. And I was to keep my mouth shut. All very easy, so far. Even for me.

BJ had, however, constructed one dainty scenario for the dinner-table in which I was to play a small yet crucial role. In order to show himself off as a busy Etonian of the world, BJ had decided that a couple of times through the dinner, I would quit the room and then return bearing an urgent-looking message on a silver salver. What the message said was neither here nor there, but the important thing was that I stood by BJ's shoulder, bowed, whispered in his ear, and then flourished the salver.

"Now we're quite clear on this?" said BJ as we strode through the schoolyard. "I don't want any – watch out, you tyke! You nearly trod on my spats!"

"Sorry, BJ." I trotted along beside him over the cobbles.

"Now, I do not want you pulling any faces! I do not want you picking your nose. I do not want you grunting, grimacing, mewling or farting!"

"What?" I squealed with disappointment. "No parping?"

"There'll be plenty enough hot air in that room, as it is."

Upstairs in the Headman's rooms above the Cloisters – what can I remember of them? Stuffed to the gunnels with dusty pictures, leather-bound books, brown furniture – just imagine one of the sets from any of those period dramas, and you're there. The committee were already in, talking edgily among themselves like the sheep they were. Maguire had also somehow got himself an invite and was haranguing the Headman's wife about whatever was his pet subject of the day: porn, masturbation, beating little boys or some other similarly light, frothy subject.

BJ bounded in. "Champagne!" he said, silencing the entire room. "I'd love some!"

Heath rolled in about ten minutes later. What a charmless man he was. Maybe it's just the nature of modern politics, but these days we do expect our politicians to be able to play the game: to chat, put people at their ease, croon over the babies and flirt with the pensioners. That's how it is if you want to be a politician.

But in terms of social maladroitness, Heath was even lower on the scale than Gordon Brown – and that takes some doing, believe you me. There Heath stood in his shabby grey double-breasted suit, not listening to a single name as the boys were introduced to him, before launching into not so much a conversation as a monologue. He hadn't even bothered to look at me, of course, so I just stood by BJ's shoulder letting this tide of words – all delivered in this stentorian monotone – cascade over me.

They were all grouped round him in a circle, Heath blathering centre stage, while the rest of them were like a pack of monkeys picking fleas off each other.

All save BJ, who was like some respectful brigadier, gazing in rapt admiration at the Field Marshal. How he did it, I don't know, but he kept his eyes locked on Heath's. When I came over with more Champagne, he would simply tilt his glass to the side without saying a word.

I daresay that it might have gone very well. It might have just turned out to be yet another of those unutterably tedious evenings that I have spent in the company of a Tory grandee.

But then... but then there'd be no story!

As it was, I started to get most fantastically bored. What with Ted Heath's self-satisfied drone, I could barely stop myself from yawning full in his face. I was hopping around from one foot to the next until BJ glared at me, and so I took it upon myself to go next door to the dining room and get some more Champagne. It wasn't bad stuff, Veuve Clicquot, and, obviously, I took a swig. The bubbles shot up my nose as the fizz lapped over my shirt. Like a snatched kiss, Champagne is all the sweeter for being plundered.

The Headman's wife led the nine of them into the dining room, with Maguire in his usual fashion taking up the rear. He had this sort of prancing, show-pony gait, and was nodding in avuncular fashion to nobody in particular, when he caught sight of me. His face contorted, his jackanapes grin suddenly turning into the most revolting gargoyle – though, looking back, I think that was probably just his normal expression.

For a while I just stood there behind BJ's chair, quietly minding my own business as Heath sprayed food and tedium about the table. He somehow managed to consume at least three slices of roast beef, though never once stopped talking. BJ, sitting next to Heath, didn't need a flunkie by his side – he needed a spatter-deck.

My eyes wandered about the room. There were ten people at the table, but it had been laid for 11 with an empty seat next to BJ. Perhaps I could have deduced something from that.

After a few minutes, I diligently retreated to the drawing room to see if I could root out a salver. Instead, I found two half-empty bottles of Champagne sitting on the mantelpiece – an opportunity too good to be missed. I plucked up a fresh flute, poured myself a glass and then, like Eton's headmasters of yore, I stood warming my bum by the fire and I savoured the moment. God, I love Champagne, though these days it always makes me feel quite intolerably randy, but anyway – back in the headmaster's drawing room, I was mooching about, quietly minding my own business, when this terrific pain shot through my rear.

I must have jumped about a foot off the ground – the one moment contemplating the angelic face of some dead Etonian on the wall, and the next being attacked by a crazy girl with a riding crop.

"What the devil do you think you're doing?" she said in a voice like cut crystal. "Get your hands off that Champagne!"

And as I turned round, I'm damned if she didn't have another cut at me.

"Oi!" I screamed, slopping Champagne over the floor as I skittered round to the other side of the sofa.

And I saw... I saw a girl to take your breath away. It may have been that she seemed to bear such an uncanny resemblance to my *Playboy* Playmate, Chantelle; it may have been the muddy riding gear she was wearing, complete to the tight white britches; it may also have been the way she insouciantly slapped the crop into her gloved hand.

Oh, and there was also the fact that she looked as crazy with anger as I'd ever seen a woman, eyes absolutely flashing with rage, and... well, let's just say that I don't find that unattractive in a girl.

I eyed her for a moment and took a further sip of Champagne. "I," and here I paused very grandly as I wondered how best to describe myself, "I am the personal aide-de-camp of the President of the Eton Political Society." Stick that in your bloody pipe and smoke it!

"Aide-de-Camp, my arse!" she said. "You're just a poxy schoolboy pinching the Headmaster's Champagne!"

"On the contrary," I replied, though my cool, measured tone was slightly undermined by the fact that I was having to skirt the sofa as I tried to keep a healthy distance between the girl's riding crop and my buttocks. "I am drinking the Headmaster's Champagne with the express and personal permission of the Headmaster." I gave a haughty little sniff and tried to look down my nose at her. "And to whom do I have the pleasure of speaking?" Jane Austen, eat your heart out.

She stopped stalking me and stood there. And how I took it all in. She was, I suppose, about three years older than me and dressed in this deeply alluring hunting gear that I had heard tell of before, but had never actually seen close up. Every part of it, from the high stock to the velvet jacket which just revealed the swell of her panting breasts, seemed to have been designed with the express purpose of driving a schoolboy to distraction. What with her long red hair scraped back into a severe pony-tail... then and there I could have fallen at her riding boots and licked them.

"What's with the oversized monkey jacket?" she asked. "Why aren't you wearing tails?"

"It was deemed that, given the grandeur of the occasion, this would be a more appropriate uniform." I brushed a fleck of dust from my sleeve. "I fear, Madam, that we may have got off on the wrong foot."

She rolled her eyes. "Do you have to speak like you've got a hot cucumber stuffed up your backside?"

Just who was this girl, this she-devil, this vixen who was taunting me almost to the point of orgasm? "But I have been forgetting my manners," I said, pouring more Champagne. "May I offer you a glass? Only Veuve Clicquot, I'm afraid, but it's the best that the dear old Headmaster could do."

At that, she took a huge swipe at me, missed, and was just about to start climbing over the sofa to get at me when the Headman's wife bowled out from the dining room.

Instantly, I hid the glass of champagne behind my back; the girl, from being about to strike me, smoothly transformed the movement into a little pat of her hair.

"Patricia!" said the Headman's wife. "Why, there you are! Why are you dallying in here when your dinner's getting cold? And Mr Heath has *so* many interesting things to say."

Just as a good aide-de-camp should, I glided to the dining room door and held it open for Patricia. She glared at me as she walked past and then gave me a thundering crack across the thighs with her crop. For days afterwards, I marvelled at the exquisite memory as I gazed at that intoxicating banana of a bruise.

I looked after the Headman's daughter with big cow eyes as she took her seat next to BJ. What a gent – he stepped back, kissed her hand as he bowed, and then pulled back her chair. Maguire and Heath were the only people who didn't bother to stand up – Heath because he was still burbling on and Maguire because he was seemingly attempting to cram four roast potatoes into his maw: like a snake trying to swallow a small pig.

Anyway – Patricia! What a woman! What a girl! I goggled as she flicked a stray pea across the table before bumpering a huge rummer of claret. I was in love!

But I was forgetting myself – and, more specifically, the highly important job that I was supposed to be performing for BJ. I took out the heavily crested card that he'd had me buy expressly for the purpose. But what to write for my Lord and fag-master? Not that it really mattered what I wrote, but seeing as I was so geed up after my sparring with Patricia, I thought I'd write something to cheer him up. So I helpfully wrote, 'You've never looked so handsome. I think Heath's got a crush on you.'

Tee-hee.

I sauntered into the dining room, elegant as can be. Patricia steadfastly ignored me; how my pulse quickened. I whispered into BJ's ear, "Your flies are undone", before presenting the salver. He gave a slight jerk of the head as he read the note, hissed, "What the hell have you been doing?" and then turned his adoring gaze back to Heath.

With Patricia at the table, I felt like a seven-year-old school-boy who, over and over again, wants to perform the same party-piece at his parents' swanky dinner.

I diddled around in the drawing-room, drank a bit more Champagne. What could I write this time that might draw a reaction from BJ and thus impress Patricia? Inspiration struck: 'He's looking randy – have you seen that pyramid under his napkin?'

I sashayed back into the dining room, quite the dandy this time with one hand on my hip. Patricia was just beautiful, eating her dinner like a trencherman. I bent and whispered into BJ's ear, "Will you require a condom after dinner?"

This glassy rictus smile appeared on his face as he mechanically took the note and read it. If he could, I'm sure he'd have wrung my scrawny neck, but as it was all he could do was smile and stare daggers at me.

And… it was at this stage that I noticed BJ was playing footsie with Patricia while busily fondling her leg. All the while with his attention absolutely riveted on Heath. Unbelievable! Was this man, this bastard, going to cop off with every single woman that I fancied? Was I cursed? Was every women I ever looked at destined to become another BJ play-thing?

I forget the detail at this stage. Patricia – how could she? – now had her hand on BJ's thigh and was working her way up. Even to this day, I've never seen such a fast worker. I don't think he'd said more than two words to her, and yet here they were on the verge of coupling underneath the table.

By now the diners had got onto the cheeseboard. I remember cackling with drunken glee as I penned my final note of the evening. This would stuff him!

Pranced back into the room, barely able to keep one foot in front of the other. I don't know how but I'd ended up on BJ's right shoulder rather than his left, and suddenly found that I was offering the note not to BJ but to Heath. "He wants you, you know it," I slurred before proffering up the salver. Heath took the note, read it once, read it twice to be certain, and then pocketed it before sitting back in his chair with this sillybilly grin on his face.

Frankly, it was the only thing that shut him up all evening – and well it might, since I can't imagine he'd had a better offer all year: 'He's got his todger out and wants you to suck it.'

Such was my introduction to Patricia – and to politics; it could not have been more appropriate.

Chapter 17

All good fun and games: one of the few occasions that I ever managed to land a glove on BJ.

More of BJ and of Patricia later, but first it is necessary to deal with the many and varied malign forces in my life at Eton: the Library. Now I know that I have alluded how, after that first beating, they made my life merry hell.

I'll be more specific.

It occurred the very night after I'd fallen head over heels for the whip-cracking Patricia, when I developed what I think is colloquially known as a 'little boy's problem'.

I remember it well. Still half-drunk after snoring my way through Heath's lecture, I'd tottered back to my room. I'd tugged off my clothes, hurling the white monkey jacket onto the floor, before collapsing into my bed. Fast, fast asleep, I'm dreaming of this kaleidoscopic lavatory. It's a white bowl but it appears to be dappled with every colour of the rainbow. The lavatory is flushed, the water spiralling off into the sewers, and I seem suffused with this lovely warmth, almost like I'm returning to the womb. For a minute, perhaps, I feel this wonderful calm, so soothing… and then, like the abrupt scratch of a record, I'm wide awake, this horrible dampness around my legs, and I realise I've pissed myself. Pissed myself! I hadn't done that since I was six!

Within approximately three seconds, I'd seized on all the horrible ramifications of what had occurred – and it looked *ghastly*. At a school like Eton, where the bullying tends to be verbal rather than physical, this was calamitous. For my entire career at Eton, I'd be labelled a 'Piss-a-bed'!

On the instant, I shot out of bed and opened the window as wide as I could. Rain and a howling gale outside, which was all to the good. I stripped off the sheets, hoping, praying, that it hadn't soaked through to the mattress below. A little bit, perhaps, but it could have been much worse. I heave the mattress off the bed and prop it against the window to try and give it an airing.

Next, I'm scuttling off to the bathroom with my two sheets, wringing them out over and over again with soap and water. Must have taken about an hour in all; I'm shattered, my pyjamas are soaking. I leave the sheets to dry a little; I might just have got away with it. Back to the bedroom and... Eeeuggghh!... it still absolutely reeks!

OK, calm down, what can I do to mask the smell? Air-freshener might help, but what I really needed was something that's completely over-powering – old milk. Tireless as a Duracell bunny, I'm off raiding the Library kitchen for milk, lumpy as I can get it. Bed, blankets on the floor, I'm sprinkling on chunks of the sour milk and the smell is now simply toxic. I'm now scrubbing away at both mattress and blankets with some floor-cleaner that I've found, and that appears to have done the job. It's gone 5am, I curl up onto the floor, wrapped tight in my dressing gown, and pull the rug over me. Almost off to sleep and by Christ, I'd forgotten my piss-stained pyjamas!

Well, it was quite a caper – but in the end I thought I'd got away with it.

As for my evil-smelling mattress and blankets, well, I

sprinted back to the house after chapel and exchanged them for those of my neighbour William M'Thwaite – who, though he may not have been a piss-a-bed, most definitely looked like one.

Phew!

Demelza the Dame was most approving when she came with new sheets. "Getting to know the other boys are you, dear?" she asked. "It's nice you've got a new friend."

I was rather at a loss what to say and watched in sullen silence as she held the sheets up and sniffed them. "Poo-eee!" she said. "That's more than just milk on there, if I'm not very much mistaken."

"Having some cereals in bed, Ma'am. Milk was off. Tried to clear it all up."

"Mind you," she said, chattily. "I wouldn't rule out some of the senior boys. They've got more experience. You can learn ever so much from them." She tossed the soiled sheets into a basket and lit up a cigarette. "With you first-years, I always feel it must be a bit like the blind leading the blind. But if you became friends with a Librarian ..."

"Yes, Ma'am." I nodded mechanically, wishing the ground would swallow me up. "Thank you, Ma'am!"

"Take Cripps! He's a little coarse... but I think you'd get on very well!"

"Thank you, Ma'am."

"No need for thanks, David!" she said, with that homely smile plastered over her fat face. "All I want is for you boys to be happy together."

I could barely close the door quick enough. What was the bloody woman insinuating? It was just repellent! And with Cripps, too – probably the ugliest boy in the school. Ever!

But in the main, I was just relieved to have got away it. My reputation as a hell-raising F-tit would have taken the most monumental pasting if word had got out that I pissed my bed at night.

Undoubtedly it was all the Headmaster's Champagne that had caused it; must try not to get too tiddly again in future. But, just in case, the next evening I took all due precautions: from tea-time onwards I didn't drink a thing.

The next night... there I am, snoring away, and... the same thing happens! Another vision of a rainbow-hued lavatory and this feeling of the most crippling horror as I realised I'd have to go through the same routine again.

It all went well enough, except that by the next morning my room still stank of piss. Now this – this was a disaster. I'd had the window open all night and layered the mattress with Dettol and yet there was no disguising the unmistakable hum.

I was just getting dressed, still mulling over whose mattress I was going to pinch this time, when I heard two Librarians, Tait and Bouverie, walking outside my room.

"Smells like someone's pissed themselves," said Tait.

"Christ it's awful," said Bouverie. "I haven't smelt that since prep school!"

"Who is the piss-a-bed then?"

A knock at my door. I stare aghast, my guilt writ all over my face.

Tait pokes his head into the room; wrinkles his nose in disgust; darts back out; the door slams shut.

"It's him," I hear Tait say.

"How the mighty are fallen," replies Bouverie. "From inseminating his sheets he's now urinating in them."

Like wild-fire: that's how fast it went round the house. *I. Was. Mortified!*

The sniggers of the F-tits, the outright verbal assaults from the Librarians, and even BJ – who was the one person, at least, who I thought might come out batting for my team – insisted on having his fun.

"Here," he chortled as he tossed me a small bag. "Something to help you out at night – a bulldog clip."

If I'd known what was going to happen the next evening, I damn well would have used the clip for that exact purpose.

As the night before, I did not drink anything after tea. I relieved myself at 9pm and again at 11pm just as I was about to go to sleep. It honestly felt like there wasn't a drop of urine left in me.

And yet …

At 3am, there I am waking up in a pool of my own piss. Howl! Howl! Howl! I could have cried with rage. By now, I was very close to setting light to my own bed-linen. But, considering my last foray with the fire-alarm, I once again decided to try and clean up the vile mess myself. Open the window, heft the mattress up, strip off the bedding. I took the sheets and blankets to the bathroom, and its scrub, scrub, scrub again with the soap. I'm practically crying with impotent anger. What on earth is happening to me? What has made me suddenly revert into an incontinent five-year-old?

The sound of a footfall in the passage.

I turn miserably to the door.

And what more pleasant person could I have to catch me at my laundry than M' Tutor, Mr Maguire?

Now, I'm afraid to say that my relationship with Maguire had never really recovered from 'The Great Farrer House Porn Scandal', as it is now known.

Perhaps I ought to give him a knighthood, like Tony Blair did with his old Headmaster. *Honestly* – is that man completely without shame?

But if I fixed it for Maguire to be knighted, then that would well and truly cut his cackle. With a KCMG under his belt, there certainly wouldn't be any tales being told from *that* particular school.

He was in some tweedy suit and brown brogues and had obviously just been out for a boozy dinner with his bum-chums. For a while, he just stood there against the door, arms crossed, taking it all in.

"Hooo-hooo-hooo!" he said, with a broad smile. "The boy who pisses in his bed has been caught out! Three times now you have done it, urinated in your bed just as a sow pisses in its sty, and three times you have sought to put the blame else-where."

"No, Sir!" I said, as I dried my hands on my pyjama top. "I was trying to clean up my own mess. I would never try to put the blame on anyone else!"

"So he says, so he says!" laughed Maguire. "And yet my nose tells me differently. I go into William M'Thwaite's room this morning, and that also reeks of urine! So whatever am I to make of that? Do we have two next-door neighbours who, by coincidence, have turned into piss-a-beds on the very same night? Or could it be –"

He let the sentence hang there as this yawning gulf appeared at my very feet. I had nothing to say.

Maguire walked into the bathroom and started to circle me, all the while lightly clapping his hands. "Or could it be that there is just the one piss-a-bed in the house, but one so malign that he seeks to land his fellow fags in the mire by pinching his neighbour's bed-clothes! Hooo-hooo-hooo!"

He stood there grinning away, head nodding up and down. "But who could that be, I wonder? Could there be a boy so evil, so malicious, who would attempt such a thing? Well, for a long time I wondered. I wondered and I wondered. Was it possible? Could there possibly be such an evil boy in my own house? And you know the conclusion I came to?" He cackled the laugh of a crazy man. "There just might!"

"Sir, it wasn't me," I pleaded. "I'd never do anything like that!"

"Course you wouldn't!" he snapped. "And I don't doubt that next you'll be promising me on your Eton honour that you didn't swap the bed sheets! I must tell you, however, that William M'Thwaite *is* a boy who does have honour, and only this afternoon he assured me, on both his own honour and the honour of the school, that it was not he who had peed his bed."

"But Sir," I said. "It wasn't me!"

"It is regrettable, but for some unaccountable reason I choose to believe William M'Thwaite, over the word of your good self, Master Cameron. Henceforth you are a piss-a-bed! I will have the Dame give you rubberized sheets in the morning –"

"But Sir!"

"And tomorrow evening, I will personally ensure that you are wearing incontinence pads. I wish you goodnight Sir!"

Chapter 18

The sheer and utter humiliation of it! A piss-a-bed! It was a name that was to dog me for the rest of my career at my Eton. And even though I am the leader of the Tory Party, am on the verge of becoming Prime Minister, I will occasionally hear a sly hiss when I'm at the dispatch box: "Who's peed his pants, then?" How it sets my teeth on edge. I can take almost any insult from those Tory backbenchers, but how it cuts me to the quick when they call me a bed-wetter.

I fear that this unpleasant epithet will follow me till the end of the days. In my heart of hearts, I know that even if I turned out to be the greatest Prime Minister since Churchill, I will always ultimately be remembered as the boy who used to wet his bed at Eton.

And this was how it all ended. On the fourth night, I was a picture of the most abject humiliation, sitting in my stinking bedroom doing extra work. It was close to lights out, when there was a knock at the door and in came Cripps. I'd hardly spoken to the boy, certainly never had him in my room. He was corpulent, red-faced with sweat, tombstone teeth and halitosis that would have stunned a mule. He was in pyjamas, dressing gown and slippers, which was perhaps a little unusual for a visit to an F-tit.

"Evening, Davie," he said, padding over to my burry. He

spoke in a bucolic Suffolk burr; God knows what he was doing at Eton. "Sorry to hear about youse mishaps."

By now, he was standing right next to me, bits of straw and the like still adhering to his pyjamas. I looked up at him. "Is it just you, or is it hot in here?"

"Good 'un," he said and let his dressing gown fall open, to reveal his chubby prick hanging out of his pyjamas. "Do you know what that 'un is?"

I stared at it, scratched my head in bemusement. "It looks like a cock – only smaller."

Cripps laughed like the Suffolk yokel he was. "Nice 'un. But I likes to call it Crippsy's love truncheon. Now – I've come 'ere to do youse a favour, Davie –"

"Really," I said at my most disdainful. "Have you washed that thing in a month?"

"I thought I might be able to put an end to that pee-pee problem. I's could let youse into a li-bry secret –" I stared out of the window. "And you knows what they say down on the farm, Davie? One good turn, 'e deserves another."

I pondered his meaning. Suck him off to solve my bed-wetting? Possibly not the best bargain I'd ever been offered. But, reading between the lines, it did very much sound like the Library may have had some hand in my bed-wetting.

I stretched for a pair of scissors. "Get out of here now, Cripps, you unspeakable boor! Get out! Out now! I will not have that, that piece of gristle waved in my face one moment longer! Out! Or I will snip your cock off with my own hand!"

He looked at me, aghast, the bumpkin yokel shrivelling in front of me. If he thought I was going to roll over like just another of his sheep, he was going to have another think coming! "Get thee hence, Satan!" I cried, though possibly that wasn't an entirely appropriate thing to say as I think it actually refers to the Temptation of Christ. And I certainly wasn't tempted by Cripps. Not one little bit.

"Otherwise I'll have that cock off in a trice!" I said. "I will! And I'll stick it down your own throat! You can suck yourself off – see how you like them potatoes!"

Off he trudged, back to his pit, and I was well happy with my repartee – I'd certainly got the better of him and no mistake, even though he was a good four years older than me. And I hadn't had to touch his cock even once. Not once, I promise you!

So I thought and I thought, and realised that if the Library was somehow causing my bed-wetting malaise, they must be spiking my drinks. Either that, or they were doing something to me in my sleep.

That night, I went to bed with a drawing pin pressed into the palm of my hand to keep me awake and a rugby boot on my pillow. I waited and waited, nearly falling asleep, before I jagged the pin into my hand. Midnight, nothing had happened, and then just as I'm drifting off again, I hear a click at the door. Soft light filters into the room and I discern the outline of someone crawling along the floor. He comes to the side of the bed, paws for my hand and dips it into a bucket of lukewarm water. I let him hold my hand there for three seconds, before swinging the rugby boot round as hard as could and clouting him full in the face.

A shriek of pain, the bucket is dropped to the floor; a boy rushes from the room.

The next day, at breakfast, I eagerly scanned the Librarians to discover who had been my tormentor. It might have been any number of them. But, that morning, it was Hitchen who came down to breakfast with a heavily-bandaged eye.

A small victory for the new boys.

Now, I think this might be a timely occasion for me to clear up one very small point.

When I have told this story to friends in the past, they have expressed some mild surprise as to how events turned out during Cripps' night-time visit. A few of them have said that the scene as I depict it does not altogether ring true. My repartee in particular, they say, sounds a little too pat. Some have even gone so far as to suggest that Cripps and I may indeed have indulged in some mutual back-scratching, so to speak.

I would now like to place it on record that this is a *lie!* A gross calumny! An utter distortion of what occurred that evening! I did not – did not – service Cripps, or do anything like that. And as for the claim that I used to visit Cripps' room – third on the right, with a photo of Cheryl Tiegs on the door – throughout the entirety of my first year, I can only say that this is nothing short of scandalous. Outrageous! An inverted pyramid of piffle! I swear it on my honour! On my Eton honour!

Chapter 19

That Tony Blair! At times I feel Blair is the bane of my life! How my gorge rises just at the very thought of him. And what's worse – far worse – is that I'm *still* seen as his heir apparent!

The fact is that Blair is a liar; a blagger; a half-cocked chancer with half his eye on his legacy and half his eye on how much money he can make.

How it irks me to be compared to him. It is so palpably not true that I think it beneath my dignity to comment. Yet I do feel I must protest when people suggest that Blair and I are so alike that we could have been separated at birth; that we're both formless sponges, floating like jellyfish on this vast political ocean, drifting any which way the current sends us.

Blair has not just buggered up Britain, but he's royally buggered things up for every Prime Minister that happens to follow him into Downing Street.

Time was, a few years back, that Sam and I used to enjoy our holidays in Tuscany. Nothing we'd like more than flying off out to Italy for a couple of weeks, renting a villa with friends, boozing, sun-bathing – you know, just a perfectly ordinary summer vacation in Italy.

Not now, though. Now, thanks to all the freebies that were handed out to Blair and his perma-grin wife, Prime Ministers have got no option but to holiday in the British Isles. Stuck on a bloody beach in Cornwall with the grockles, smiling for the paps as we lick our ice-creams on the freezing seashore; pretending there's no place on earth we'd rather be ... when the truth of it is that I'd much rather be in Italy, France, Spain, or anywhere at all rather than having to put up with another Baltic British summer.

Or take bridge. I love playing bridge, been playing ever since I was at Eton. But, oh no – not anymore. Since I've become Tory leader, the bridge has had to be shelved, and instead the only game that I'm allowed to show an interest in is – God help us! – bloody football! One of the perks of being PM is supposedly that I'll get a seat with the nobs at the FA Cup Final – and all so that I can watch two teams about whom I have as much interest as I do in Gordon Brown's haemorrhoids. Well, thanks a bunch, guys, that's really sweet of you, but actually I'd rather be ... I don't know ... suddenly the thought of Brown's haemorrhoids has put me in mind of a particularly vivid simile. Perhaps best not to go there.

Moving swiftly on – and, indeed, the reason I brought up the whole subject of Blair in the first place – I am now no longer able to go shooting. Thanks to Blair's PC-mad world, it would be political suicide for me to been seen out shooting. Pictures of me going pop-pop with my Purdey on the Duke of Buccleuch's estate would be about as disastrous as that Bullingdon picture. (And why Labour never made more political capital out of that particular picture, I have no idea. All they need do at the Election is run that Bullingdon picture on every billboard in the country – along with a caption that might perhaps say, 'Is this the man you want to be Eton's 19th Prime Minister?' – and that would be Gordon and his haemorrhoids back in Downing Street for another five years.)

When I was at Eton, I adored fishing and shooting. It wasn't just killing all the pheasants, the partridge, the snipe, the teal, the woodcock, the geese and the grouse – not to mention the salmon, the trout, the rabbits and the rats. It wasn't just about the dressing up – though at 14 I did *quite* fancy myself in britches and tweed. That said, we were never in the same league as the hunting brigade. After being blooded by Patricia, I still find the sight of a girl in taut white trousers unbelievably erotic.

That winter of 1979, after my first half at Eton, not a day went by when I was not trying to kill one animal or another. Doubtless the psychotherapists would say that I was taking out my Eton angst on the unsuspecting wildlife of Berkshire. And they may have a point. Pets excepted, there was not an animal that moved at Peasemore that I would not try to have a pop at. In those days, I had a little poacher's 4-10, which you could fold in half and hide under your Barbour.

But I actually preferred going out with my Pater's 2.2 air-rifle, complete with telescopic sights. At the time, I'd just read John Buchan's *John McNab* which is essentially in praise of poaching. The story is of some Scottish bluebloods who are so bored they decide to start poaching from their neighbours' estates. Well, what was good enough for McNab was good enough for me, and very soon I had bagged a cat, five guinea fowl and a brace of peacock from the neighbours. Never able to cook them, mind, and ended up stuffing the birds down a fox-hole.

The poaching, though, was never just about the kill. It was about crawling through the undergrowth, getting chased by the game-keepers, and not a few moments of heart-stopping terror as yet another of your nine lives was cast to the wind.

I only mention all this lawlessness, because it reminds me of one last little incident that occurred in Farrer just before we broke up for Christmas.

It was gone lights out and I was nearly asleep, when there was a tap at the door. Somebody came in and instantly switched on the lights. I blinked, a mole coming out of his hole.

BJ, all in black like the Milk Tray man, had a knapsack over his shoulders and an incredibly expensive bottle of Pauillac under his arm. "Evenin' All!"

"BJ!" I said, momentarily flummoxed. "I mean – uhh – hi!"

"Come on then, young David, tonight's your lucky night. Ready to get your chops round my cock?"

I swallowed nervously. By now, BJ had switched on my desk light and was busily opening the window.

"Umm – well, BJ. Err, I don't know that I've had that much experience." I was completely tongue-tied. "Don't you have Katy for this sort of thing?"

"Well, you know what the Turks say?" He unzipped the knapsack and popped the bottle of Pauillac inside. "A woman for duty and a boy for pleasure."

"Yeah – and a melon for ecstasy. Cripps already told me. Well, ahh, what an unexpected pleasure." My mind was awhirl. I mean who would have thought it: BJ wanted me to give him a blowjob! Like – Wow.

BJ had lifted up the carpet and was squatting down to examine the floorboards. "I give up," he said. "Where have you hidden the rope?"

"The rope?" I queried. "I thought… well, you know, Cripps, Bouverie, now you. I mean I thought –"

"It's a joke, you bloody moron!" BJ rolled his eyes theatrically. "I am not about to claim my *droit de seigneur* – though nice to see you so ready to oblige."

"Funny!" I laughed insanely. "Lucky I was so quick on the uptake."

"Yeah, yeah, save all that mush for Cripps," he wafted the backs of both his hands at me, as if trying to get rid of a bad smell. "Where's the rope?"

"The rope?" I said. "Oh yes! The rope! Let me find it for you."

I retrieved it from its hidey-hole underneath the floor-boards.

"Ta. Better have the crowbar while we're at it."

I watched in silence as he tied one end of the rope round the radiator before tossing the rest out of the window.

Without even a word, he slipped the rucksack onto his shoulders and was standing on the window-sill about to abseil down.

"Wait!" I gawked at him. "Will you be long?"

He screwed up his nose as if testing the wind. I can still picture him in silhouette, the black jumpsuit and the white shock of hair against the night window-frame. "Probably not," he said. "Katy's tied up tonight."

"Who are you going to shag then?" I said, wandering over to the window. "And why are using my room as an exit?"

He rolled his eyes, and this rasp of exasperation rumbled up from the back of his throat. "Surprisingly, David, I may not be off to shag anyone at all," he said. "And as for why I'm leaving via your room – well, thanks to *your* fire-alarm debacle, Maguire had put alarms on all the emergency exits."

A little rich, perhaps to talk about *my* fire-alarm debacle. "Where are you going then?"

He laughed at that. "Not for the likes of you, you young pup – besides, you're all flab. Nowhere near fit enough!"

God, he knew how to tempt me. "But if I were?"

"And if you were?" he wrinkled his nose at the thought. "Let me see now – well, there's adventure; adrenalin; drinking; death-defying experiences for deathly bored students. You'd hate it."

"And ... and ..." He'd already disappeared out the window. I felt like the kid calling out "Shane, Shane!" as the hero gunslinger rides off into the sunset. I leaned out of the window. "Do you have a name?"

"We're called ..." He jumped, landing light as a cat before looking up at me. "The Steeplejacks."

Chapter 20

Now – time to fast forward four months. Unlike most senior politicians, I can't be doing with recording everything in minute chronological detail. There may have been a few bits of stuff that occurred during the Lent Half, but for the main action we shall go straight to the summer of 1980, my last half as an F-tit.

I don't think I've missed very much – just more abuse from Henchman, Ottley, and, in their own peculiar way, Bouverie and Cripps.

The one thing that might be worth mentioning is that I'd been working out a lot. After BJ's taunts that I wasn't nearly fit enough, I was doing press-ups and sit-ups every morning, as well as evening chin-ups in the bathroom. What with wanking myself stupid every night, I was soon the fittest fag in Farrer; there wasn't a Librarian who could keep his hands off me. (Just kidding. Even Tory Party leaders are allowed to make the occasional risqué joke, you know.)

You might have thought that Henchman, Ottley et al would have been concentrating on their A-levels. But they still, it seemed, had time enough for Farrer's fittest fag.

A rainy day in May and a Saturday afternoon boy-call. I'd been fiddling around in my room, heard the "BooooyyUppp!" call, and had blithely decided to ignore it. There were plenty of fags scurrying up the stairs to queue up outside the Library; they wouldn't even know I was missing.

Unfortunately they did. Approximately one minute later, Henchman barged into my room without even a "by your leave".

He stood there in the doorway, drumming his long fingers against the wall. "Pulling your pud?" he asked. "Wanted to finish the job off before you answered that fag-call?"

"Fag-call?" I said in amazement. "I'm *terribly* sorry. Had my radio on. Didn't hear it."

Quite an accomplished little liar I was becoming.

"Pah!" he said. "Got a lovely job for you. Better slip on your jacket and tie. I'm sending you off to Windsor."

"I'd really love to help you out." I got up and made to walk past him. "But I'm just off to M' Tutor's rooms. He's asked me over for tea." Even as I said the words, I was cursing myself.

"You have been asked to have tea with M' Tutor?" His lips peeled back to reveal perfect white teeth. "Satan and his imps will be sledging to work before M'Tutor ever asks you for tea!"

"He has," I piped. "He has! He's bought fresh doughnuts specially for me."

"Save your breath! M'Tutor went off to London this morning to have his gnarly teeth fixed. Now – get into half-change, and take this letter to the address on the envelope. I want it delivered to Mike Hunt."

I could whine all I wanted, but there was no getting round the fact that, on pain of being beaten up, I had to deliver this stupid message to Windsor.

I took off my jeans and put on cords, jacket and tie. Just to give the Windsor Townies every chance of duffing up their weekly quota of Etonians, school rules stated that when we went to Windsor, we had to wear either tails or jacket and tie.

I lolled down the high-street, treated myself to an ice-cream in Rowland's, and, in my own good time, took myself down to Windsor.

The address was unusual, an area that I didn't really know. It was a rough looking industrial area by the river and, the nearer I got to it, the less I liked it. It seemed as if Henchman had sent me to a derelict warehouse. The place was completely overgrown, the weeds rampant on the old wharf.

I don't know why I didn't just turn tail and run. Perhaps I was intrigued.

A tatty side-door, paint peeling off at the edges. I could hear music, rock music, echoing from the room inside. I knocked. Knocked again much louder.

A punk, 6'8" in his spiked green hair, all black leather and chains, throws open the door. "What do you want?"

Spikes all over him – in his nose, ears, lip, tongue – and I don't doubt that he had a spike through his prick, too; Maguire would have just loved him.

"Hello," I quavered as I goggled up at this monster. "I was looking… I was looking for Mike Hunt."

Fnnnagghh.

Nowadays, of course, I appreciate that this joke is as old the hills. When I was at Oxford, I even played it on a waitress I quite fancied in Brown's – how we guffawed as she wandered round that packed restaurant calling, "Mike Hunt! Has anyone seen Mike Hunt?"

At Eton, however, the C-word did not form a large part of my vocabulary and I was completely unaware of its comedic potential.

The punk stared at me for a moment and screamed some unprintable word.

I think it might be timely to mention that since I'm hoping this book will become an inspiration for schoolboys throughout the land, I have deliberately not been using the F-word. This, I'm afraid, has meant that several of Henchman's finer conversational sallies have lost some of their original impact. As for the punk, with his language shorn of both the F-word and the C-word, I fear that he has become rather anodyne.

He grabbed me by the lapels and lifted me off the ground so that my face was just a few inches from his. "You ponce!" he screamed through rotting grey teeth. "Come in here!"

The punk then – and I've never seen such ignominious treatment – tucked me under his arm like a farmer carrying a piglet to market.

"Help!" I screamed. "Help! Help!" I was kicking and wriggling, but it felt like I was in the death grip of a man mountain. He grabbed my hair with his free hand and gave a sharp tug. "Shut it! Ponce!"

I was carried to the far end of the far end of the warehouse, but beyond that I could hardly see a thing as my face was buried into the side of his stinking biker jacket. I was dumped in a heap on the concrete.

"Look what I got!" he said. "An Eton ponce!"

I was dragged to my feet by the scruff of my neck. Warily, I looked about me.

There were at least ten of them, all spiky hair, spiky faces, spiky personalities – staring at me like a famished pride of lions that's been presented with a warthog. As for the warehouse, they'd decked it out with some sofas, a couple of standard lamps and a large rug, though there was still plenty of room for the five wrecked cars and the assortment of rusting machinery.

The smallest punk came forward. Don't tell me about it.

Always, always, it's the smallest ones who are the yappiest and the most belligerent – look at Sarkozy. Look at John Bercow!

This punk was only about as tall as me, 5'4", but much older. Leather jeans and a singlet, tattoos rippling over his biceps, studs all over his face; a sea anemone of red hair.

"What," he said, poking me repeatedly in the chest, "is an Eton ponce doing here?" (I can only repeat: some of the punks' more colourful language has, of necessity, been edited.)

If I'd had even an ounce of intuition, I'd have kept my mouth shut. I'd have told them I'd lost my way, something like that. But, as it was, I still hadn't woken up to the fact that Henchman had sent me straight into the lion's den.

"Hello!" I squeaked, voice shrill with nerves. "I was looking for Mike Hunt!"

The midget punk stiffened. I might as well have belched in his face. The silence echoed round that cavernous warehouse.

Suddenly the penny dropped. Mike Hunt? I'd just asked for Mike Hunt? Oh, sweet Jesus!

"Right!" screamed the midget. "Let's kill him!"

"Why?" I screeched, still pinned by the man-mountain's grip on my collar. "I'm sorry! I... I... I just want to go back to me nan on the terraces!"

The midget hawked and spat full in my face. I felt the phlegm slide down my cheek. I didn't dare wipe it away. "Your nan on the terraces!" he screamed. "You're an Eton toff!"

I goggled at him. "Eton?" I said. "That shithole? I effin' 'ate it!"

God, if only I'd spent more time practising my Estuarial English, I could have saved myself one hell of a lot of aggro. If only I'd been allowed to watch more *Coronation Street*. As it was, I could only continue to parrot the most transparently fake Mockney; it was even worse than Dick Van Dyke in *Mary Poppins*.

The man mountain rumbled behind me. "Told you," he said. "He's Eton. Eton all over him."

"Nah!" I screamed, helplessly writhing in the punk's grasp. "I ain't one of 'em! I never been near the 'effin' place! Tossers, the lot of 'em!"

I gawked at the mob of punks lolling on the sofas. They were almost smirking with embarrassment, as if being forced to endure a particularly bad Punch and Judy show.

As for the terrier punk, he was po-going off the ground he was so excited. He had, it seemed, discovered the fatal flaw in my argument.

"Why," he screeched, poking me in the chest with every word he spoke, "are you wearin' an Eton jacket and tie?"

"It's me nan!" I gabbled. "It's 'er birfday innit? I was goin' round for me tea! Ever so worried she'll be that I ain't there! I gotta get there! They'll all be waitin' for me!"

The midget slapped me hard round the face and then frisked me. In my jacket pocket, a rather incriminating copy of the school fixtures.

Another great globule of spit landed on my cheek. "What is this then, Eton ponce?"

"That?" How I squirmed, how I writhed. "Oh that! Got that off one of 'em Eton toffs. On the way to me nan. I mugged 'im! Saw this 'effin' toff, walkin' dahn the street all la-di-da in 'is tail-coat! 'It 'im on the 'ead and pinched all 'is stuff, did'n I?"

The midget slapped me again. "You stole his notebook?"

"Only fing 'e ' ad on 'im!" I said. Boy, I was really having to improvise fast. The story wasn't great, I could see that.

"You're a lying Eton shitbag!" said the midget punk. "Let's spark him up!"

How I pleaded, how I grovelled. "Watch me 'Ampsteads!"

I bawled, desperately racking my brain for more rhyming slang. "Leave off! I gotta see me nan, It would break 'er 'art!"

The man-mountain tumbled me onto the carpet, and three of them held me down as the midget stripped off my clothes. I was left with just my purple boxers. For a while I kicked, screamed and cursed, but I should have saved my breath. "'Tain't fair!" I shouted, "I 'ate Eton!"

A rickety wooden chair was dragged over and they trussed me to it with gaffer-tape – wrists, knees, elbows and ankles. I was petrified. Was the midget going to torture me to death?

"'Elp me!" I screamed. "'Elp! You're 'urtin' me!"

"Gag him!" barked the midget. "His voice is making me sick!"

An oily rag was thrust into my mouth and strapped tight with more gaffer tape. I goggled at them all. Most of the punks were still lounging on the sofas, but the midget was prancing around slapping a fist into a gloved hand. (I don't know why but, for some strange reason, the most bizarre image has come to mind: the priapic Speaker John Bercow capering naked around his official apartments as he pursues his Amazonian wife with a bull-whip.)

One of the punks dragged out a large battery and some leads. The midget continued to pound his hands together. "On with the clips!"

Ahh. This is a very painful memory for me. I find it difficult to go there. But I will do my best to recount things as they occurred.

They attached a crocodile clip to each of my nipples. I knew exactly what was going to come next. I thrashed from side to side, almost upturning the chair, before the man mountain cuffed me around the ears.

"Let her rip!" said the midget. The most searing pain jolted through my chest. Much more instantaneous than the crack of a cane across my buttocks. It felt like my chest was being squeezed by steel bands. My head lurched back and I stared up at the holes in the cavernous roof.

Four, five seconds, I don't know how long it lasted, and, as the current was switched off, I slumped forward in the chair. The midget threw my head back and slapped me.

A bucket of water was tossed over me, and then another surge of electricity arced through my nipples. And yet I wouldn't describe it as excruciating. It was intense and unbearable, without doubt. But the pain was very different from anything I had ever experienced before. And the relief – the sheer relief when it stopped. With a caning, long after it's over, the pain seems to build up minute by minute. But when you're electrocuted, the pain dulls very quickly. After only a few seconds, you're just left with this mild tingle.

The switch was thrown again, I lurched back in the chair, my lips peeled back into a skeletal smile. The pain! It felt like my nipples were being rubbed red-raw with sandpaper. I think I even glimpsed a sinew of smoke coming off my tits. The gagging taste of diesel from the rag.

And then the relief, cascading through me. I licked my dry lips.

What occurred next, I don't know how it happened. I tried to control myself. Utterly impossible. It's embarrassing, revolting even. After the three electric shocks, I'd lost control of my bodily functions. I felt like I wanted to curl up in a hole and die.

I was vaguely aware that the chatter about me had dried up. The sparky man was standing up, shaking his tattooed head in disbelief.

"Jesus, will you look at that," he said. "He's got a bloody boner!"

They all cooed as they came round to look. I could only stare dumbly at my bulging purple briefs. The shame of it. But if you're a guy, you'll know this: teenage boys have no control whatsoever over their hard-ons. The more untimely the moment, the more likely it is that those menaces will rear their ugly heads.

"Come on!" said Sparky. "Let's give him another shot! See what happens next!"

My nipples fizzed, my head arced back, and another surge of blood to where it was least wanted; my heart was tripping so fast it felt like I was going to have a heart attack.

I'm aware of a woman standing in front of me. She slaps me hard across the chest with a pair of leather gauntlets, ripping the crocodile clip from my left nipple. The current stops, the pain eases, and I stare at my saviour.

A woman of the most exquisite beauty – though her face marred by three rings through her nose, a bolt through her lip, and a double stud in her tongue. She squatted down to examine me more closely – and all I could do was gaze at her. She was a Goth, pale white face and the most luminous long white hair – and all of it, I think, entirely natural. A tattoo of a dolphin, leaping the water, on her neck. And, as for the rest of her, she was wearing slashed black from her fingernails to her biker-boots.

"He's an Eton toff!" said the midget punk. "Must be. Sparked him up – look at that boner!"

The woman just glanced down at my midriff, before staring back into my eyes. As I looked into those light blue eyes, I felt the very slight tug of a connection. Perhaps that was just my imagination.

Quite suddenly, she stood up and gave me what I wanted: she slapped me as hard as she could across the chest with her gauntlets. The second crocodile clip was ripped from my nipple. Then, oh sweet ecstasy, she slapped me as hard as she could in the crotch.

Now, a very minor confession to make: it seems that every few months or so, another politician is caught out in another sex-den. There they are, trussed up like chickens as their buttocks are tenderized with a cricket bat. For the most part, the general public don't seem to understand it. They just think it's some completely weird perversion.

But… I think I have a little inkling. I understand it. The pain; the stunning humiliation; the certain belief that this time you're absolutely going to die. And then… the ecstasy of relief that floods through as the pain stops. So when one of my ministers is caught with his trousers down, I will understand it; I will forgive him. He'll still be out of a job, mind, but that's politics.

"Leave him be." That's all she said. I never heard another word from her lips – never knew who she was, or why they listened to her.

She came outside as they made me walk the plank into the Thames, her long blonde hair blowing in the wind. If only I could pinpoint what it was that her eyes were telling me: yearning; compassion; perhaps even desire. Just as I was teetering on the end of the plank, she gave me a kick up the backside with her metal toe-capped boots.

I've had a soft spot for Goths ever since – and indeed dolphins. Why do you think Sam has a porpoise tattooed onto her ankle?

Chapter 21

I swam across the Thames, no problem. The punks might have been hoping that I'd drown, but I was always a good swimmer.

Hauled myself out on the other side and jogged over the fields back to Farrer. I'd lost everything, even my watch. But such relief as I trotted through the front door. A bath, that's what I wanted, and some tea and toast.

And this was the decisive moment in my Eton career – the moment when we truly parted company. Now I was not just breaking the rules because they were in my way. The delight of rule-breaking became an end in its own right.

Why do you think I ran for the Tory leadership, if not to cock a snook at all the people who'd been telling me it just wasn't the done thing? Time and time over, all those stalwart backbenchers patted me on the back and told me I had plenty more to learn before I could have a tilt at the leadership. My chief satisfaction when I went for it? The look on their faces as I forced them to eat crow. "Against all the rules of Tory etiquette for a greenhorn to run for leader," they bleated. Well, you just watch me, Mr Backbencher. You watch me!

I was just scuttling to my room, frozen to the bone, when I saw what looked like a dumpy washer-woman coming towards me.

"Hello, my duck." Demelza the Dame looked me up and

down, nodded. "Purple underpants? Lovely – they bring out the colour in your eyes."

"Thank you," I replied.

"Been off playing with your friend Crippsy again, have you dear? A wonder that he even left you with any pants on! And look! Look how you're bleeding – he's nearly chewed your nipples off!"

She set down the sewing bag that she'd been carrying and lit up a cigarette, inhaling the smoke deep into her belly. "I won't tell if you won't," she winked. "Time was a few years ago when we had a Librarian here who was an absolute terror! He just needed one term with them and those fags were trotting up to his room obedient as sheep-dogs. Yes – those were the days. It was just a wonder to see how he tamed them – Jarman was his name, such a handsome lad, though going a bit to seed even then –"

"Actually – I wasn't with Cripps at all, I –"

"Who was it then, ducks?" she laughed and poked me in the stomach with a chubby finger. "I've seen your eye on that Bouverie when he's wandering through the dining room. Or was it Tait? Everyone's got a little bit of crush on Taity, haven't they, dear? Dark horse that one, I know."

"No, it wasn't Tait or Bouverie either –"

"Not Ottley! He's too big – "

"No! I was in Windsor! Henchman fagged me off to a warehouse in Windsor! I was attacked by punks. They stripped my clothes off. Electrocuted me! Chucked me in the river!"

Demelza let out a whoop of laughter. "Deary me!" She was standing there, one hand on her knees, her entire body convulsing with laughter. "I think somebody's telling porky pies again!"

"Honestly! The Townies nearly lynched me!"

She guffawed, stamping her foot on the ground. "Oh dear, oh deary me! How do you tell them with a such a straight face?"

I was wasting my breath, but I had one more shot. "Honestly – I promise you – Henchman fagged me off to this den of punks in Windsor. They scragged me. Crocodile clips on my nipsies!"

She started pawing for her handkerchief and mopping at the tears on her face. "Deary me!" she said. "I think I'll have to stop you there or they'll be carting me off to the san."

"It's true!"

"All right, all right. Calm down, dear, I'm sure you were only having a little bit of cuddle – but if that's your story and you're sticking to it, then I'll believe you," she said, though she did give a slight eyeball roll to William M'Thwaite who was just prancing past us. "Though thousands wouldn't!"

This set her off again, snuffling into her kerchief as the tears coursed down her cheeks. "Honestly deary, it doesn't matter. I know how hard it is for you all. Here you are, stuck with over 1,200 other boys, and you've got no-one to cuddle up with at night. I don't see anything wrong with it. It's all perfectly natural. Now I know a lot of people think he's just a Suffolk yokel, but Crippsy is actually a very nice boy –"

"But I haven't been with Cripps!"

"Not that I've got anything against Bouverie either, though it would be nice if you could get him to wash more –"

"I'm not doing it with anyone! On my honour!"

She was laughing again. "I've heard all about your honour, my dear, and I know exactly how much it means to you. But it's live and let live here, deary." She nodded to herself. "You know what I think about life – and it's only taken me 60 years to realise this? Get it while it's hot."

"Get it while it's hot?" I queried.

"Wish I'd realised that as a teenager – would have chalked up a sight more boyfriends. Well, one would have been nice. You only really understand it when you're middle-aged." She sighed, stamped out her cigarette butt, and picked up her sewing bag. "Tomorrow, deary, is a gift. We'd like it to happen. We expect it to happen. But there's no guarantee."

It was like soft light filtering through a stained-glass window. I could discern the outline of the most extraordinary picture, but was still unable to make out the detail.

"Tomorrow's a gift?" I echoed.

"Typical!" she said. "You Etonians always want something fancier, don't you? Well, if you want some Horace I can give it you: *Carpe Diem*."

I'd heard it before, but it had never chimed. However, as I heard it this time, standing in that gloomy passage in my purple underpants, the bong that reverberated in my head was the size of Big Ben.

"Seize the day!" I squealed with excitement. It was as if the mysteries of the universe had been revealed to me – for suddenly I had a motto not just for Eton, but for all time. Seize the day!

I now have that motto and its perkier twin, 'Get it while it's hot!' engraved on my cufflinks, ironed onto my running shirts and even etched onto my favourite tie-pin. Some years back, I even went as far as to have a 'Get it while it's hot!' tattoo. It's just above my groin in reverse Gothic script – so each morning I am reminded of it as I'm shaving in the mirror.

Never again would another opportunity pass me by! Never again would I ignore the chance of a kiss! Never again would I sit there festering on the sidelines, when my every instinct was yammering for action.

Seizing the day can be costly – I know that. You can go off at half-cock. Women can be affronted at your brazenness. (Though not nearly as many as you'd think – there's hardly a girl I know who hasn't taken a kiss as a compliment; especially the married ones.) You can exert yourself when perhaps you might be better biding your time.

I know all this. But anything – anything at all – has to be better than that most galling of regrets: the knowledge that you have well and truly missed the boat.

So, it was this little motto, delivered to me by that jolly old Dame, that was the single most important lesson I learned at Eton. It is why, five years ago, I ignored all those hand-wringing MPs who were telling me to sit tight. It is the reason why I am now on the very threshold of 10 Downing Street. In fact, now that I think of it, I'll be damned if I give Maguire a knighthood. It should be my Dame who becomes… Dame Demelza! Be worth it just for the headlines.

"Must be getting on," she said. "Do you know, dear, have you thought of having a turn with Hamill? He's been a bit lonely recently. I know he's a ginger – not to everyone's taste. But he's a very nice boy when you get to know him."

"I don't want to go with Hamill!"

"Calm down, dear!" she said, shaking her head at the sheer callowness of youth. "If you want to stick with your Crippsy, that's fine by me –"

Chapter 22

It was all very well having decided to commit the rest of my life to 'getting it while it was hot'. But if I were to ignore the Dame's helpful suggestion of becoming a rent-boy for the entire Library, what hot things was I supposed to be grabbing from life's buffet table?

That very evening, BJ provided me with the answer.

I was all but asleep, dreaming dark dreams of bleak Windsor warehouses, when he slipped into my room and started levering up the floorboard.

I shot bolt upright in my bed.

"Stand easy," he said. "Just off to see the Steeplejacks."

This was it. This was the moment! I knew it, as soon as I heard. What could possibly be hotter than the Steeplejacks?

"I'm coming too!"

BJ flicked on the sidelight. As usual he was dressed in black, though this time with the added adornment of a bobble hat. Very *Guns of Navarone*.

"Are you buggery!"

I jumped out of bed, opened my ottoman and began pulling my dark blue tracksuit on straight over my pyjamas.

He looked at me with distaste as he spooled the rope out of the window. "And when I next go off to Katy, you'll be wanting to tag along to that one too?"

"Love to!" I said, dancing round as I tugged on my socks. "Katy's a cracker!"

"I've created a bloody monster!" he said as he climbed out of the window. "Do you have any idea what you're getting into?"

"Not the foggiest!"

"You're going to hate it," he said as he dropped to the ground. "And it'll probably kill you!"

"Well, tell mother I died game," I said, though my derring-do image was slightly spoiled by the yelp of pain I let out as I burned my hands sliding down the rope.

"No problemo. I'll personally write your obituary for the *Eton Chronicle*," BJ said, striding off down Judy's Passage. "You can kill yourself, the bastards can throw me out – it won't make any odds to me."

"But… but I might be able to do something really useful," I said. "I might be able to save your bacon!"

"It's possible." He proffered me his hip-flask and the brandy ripped down the back of my throat. "But in all likelihood I'd say you'll just screw things up for the rest of us. Anyway, what do I care? We're off to Westminster!"

The way he said it, it was like Dorothy talking about trekking to the land of Oz. His eyes glimmered with heartfelt yearning. I didn't recognise it then – but I certainly know all about it now. It's the earnest look of the Prospective Parliamentary Candidate, aspiring to set foot in the hallowed halls of Westminster, where he can become "*a force for good*".

Thankfully, they only need a few months in the place and that's more than enough to knock the stuffing out of them. By the by – I may as well get this off my chest now. Whether I become Prime Minister or whether I'm not, I'll likely be leading a party that has had the biggest intake of new MPs in more than a century. There they'll all be, shoving and elbowing each other in the face as they try to clamber up the greasy pole of statehood – it'll be even worse than the Running of the Fags. You'd think I'd just love to behold their energy and bright-eyed enthusiasm, but actually it's incredibly wearing, like being mauled by a pack of beagle puppies. And then you've got to have every one of the new intake over for dinner; whether you fancy them or not.

"Westminster?" I asked. BJ might as well have said we were off to Timbuktu.

"Westminster!" he said again. "Can't you just feel the power in that name! West! Min! Stah! David, I do believe I'm getting rather aroused!"

"We're going to Westminster now?"

"Not now you buffoon! Next week!"

"Why are we going to Westminster?"

"Political Society," he said. "One of the committee members. Absolute shyster, I may add – not that there's anything wrong with that. His dad's the Chief Whip. A few of us have been asked to attend Prime Minister's Question Time." And then the moment that the ticking clock of my destiny became just that little bit louder. "Tag along if you like."

I knew it was important to BJ, so I tried to make it sound as if I were impressed. "Great!"

Can you hear the faint rattle of the Tory drums calling me to battle? Do you have a sense that finally – finally – we are coming to that life-changing moment when I became a Tory? Perhaps it was the moment that I set foot into Westminster Hall; or the moment I laid eyes on Maggie Thatcher making mincemeat of Jim Callaghan; or possibly the sight of all the serried ranks of worker-bee MPs, lolling in a stupor on the Commons' benches as they did their duty for Queen and country.

Forgive me – I am teasing. Westminster did indeed turn out to be yet another small but crucial mile-marker on my dusty journey. But not in quite the way you might imagine.

Meanwhile… after that slight digression: the Steeplejacks. They nearly put paid to my Eton career on the very first night. And if there were no Eton career, there would have been no trip to Westminster, no love affair with the Conservatives and no spruce Tory darling brushing up his duds to walk into Downing Street… how that thought would gladden David Davis' heart.

BJ had taken me into New Schools Yard, and we were by the side of the New School buildings. He cupped his hands together and let out a low owl hoot. There was a brief flash of torchlight from high above and a rope-ladder clattered down the wall.

"I better go first," said BJ. "Don't want you falling and knocking me off."

I watched as he swayed himself up. I can't even really remember how high it was, but, then, it seemed like 15, 20 metres. Still, I'd got exactly what I'd asked for: I was getting it while it was still hot. Piping.

A slight glimmer of light as BJ climbed off the ladder and I followed him up. Very nervous; skinning my fingers on the wall. Thanking my stars that I'd embarked on my little fitness regime.

Higher and higher I climbed, past the schoolrooms until I was right up by the roof. Strong hands grasped me by the shoulders and the next moment I was heaved through a small window and tossed onto the bare wooden floor. Winded, I looked about me – and six pairs of eyes stared back.

These guys were probably the coolest guys I'd ever seen. Forget Pop, forget the Bullingdon, and you can certainly forget White's Club – the Steeplejacks seemed to emanate this aura of understated cool. For the most part they were dressed in trainers, black jeans and black turtle-neck jumpers. I don't wear those black turtle-necks anymore but, to this day, when I see some chiselled guy in a black turtle-neck it still brings a lump to my throat.

I recognised some of the boys, Poppers, Sixth Form Select; these weren't just the nobs, they were the crème de la nobs. And there, lolling in state on a red Chesterfield sofa was the President of Pop himself. How I remember that look, all in black, but with the addition of fingerless black leather gloves and he puffed on a huge Havana cigar. How I long to be so invincibly cool when I'm in Downing Street.

As for the Steeplejacks' lair in the New Schools Attic, they'd made a fine den with sofas, leather armchairs and a sizeable drinks cabinet. Six large candelabras were stood about in the corners, the light flickering from the wind that seeped in under the eves. Tacked onto the rafters were hundreds of photos, yellow with age, of the Steeplejacks of yore conquering Eton's peaks. Pictures that stretched back 70 years – and not of the Poppers or the Tugs, but of Eton's *true* heroes.

"Hi guys!" I said – cheery, personable. You know me.

A long silence that seemed to stretch. One of the boys scratched his ear. Another poured himself some more wine. BJ, standing by the window, actually looked rather embarrassed – the first time I'd ever seen him like that.

The president of Pop, lounging on his Chesterfield, blew a perfect smoke-ring that eddied up into the attic rafters. He studied the glowing end of his cigar. "Why's he here?"

And BJ… I would have done anything for him then. He could have disowned me completely; dismissed me as nothing more than a foolhardy fag who wouldn't take no for an answer. Not a bit of it. "David will be an asset," he said. "New blood."

I nodded vigorously, giving BJ a silent thumbs-up as he offered me a beer.

"Does he know about the ordeal?"

"Shouldn't think so." BJ sniffed as he swilled red wine in a large silver goblet. "He's plucky, is David, but thick as pig-shit." Not the most winning endorsement, but I sort of like it. As epitaphs go, that one might fit quite nicely on my grave-stone.

The rain thrummed down onto the tiles above our heads. The cigar-smoker puffed a few more smoke rings – he'd obviously learned a trick or two from the Lowerman's school of silence. I gawked about me and sipped my beer.

"Let him his finish his drink," said the cigar-man. "Then be off with him. I don't want him back with his pants on."

Pants on? I darted a nervous glance at the others. Was this some kind of *sexual* ordeal?

"Err, guys," I said, flashing my most winning smile. "You know I'm only 14?"

BJ, leaning against the window, stared at me with a wan smile. "Not to worry, David. Finish your beer and off you go."

Run back to my room with my tail between my legs? It just would have been just too shameful.

"Guys, guys!" I said. "I'll do it – whatever you want! I'll do the ordeal! I don't know… what is it?... Do you all want to –"

BJ leant down and clasped me firmly by the elbow. "Come along David, let's be getting along now."

"But I'll do it!" I said, suddenly wanting to become a Steeplejack more than anything else in the world. "Do you want me to join the hookers on the street corner in Windsor? Is that it? The Headman's dog? Do you –"

"David." BJ steered me to the window and pushed me out onto the ladder. A last despairing glimpse of this Xanadu – I wanted it more than I ever wanted Brasenose, White's, the Bullingdon. They just looked so replete; I so wanted some of their glittering stardust to rub off on me.

Why is it, I wonder, that I am so drawn to these exclusive little clubs? For here I am, on the cusp of joining one of the most elite clubs in Britain – the 10 Downing Street Club – and yet always I wonder if it will ever ease the ache that drives me. Is it because I was so relentlessly bullied at Eton – is it that that spurs me? Is it because I feel so worthless inside that I con-stantly need to seek the acclaim of my peers? Or is it, as my psychotherapist suggests, that I am such an amorphous blanc-mange of a man that I need to join these clubs in order to prove my elite status?

BJ followed me down the rope-ladder, shaking his head as he stared at me. "Off you trot," he said. "You're too green. You're too young. Take your time. One day, you might be ready."

You know what? I was to hear those exact same words uttered to me in the Commons tea-room in 2005, when I first expressed an interest in taking over from Michael Howard. "You're too green," chuntered one of the leading lights of the 1922 Committee. "You're too young."

Well, I showed that grizzled Tory MP and, I like to think, I showed BJ too. I was like a young charger that had heard the clarion call for the first time.

"I am ready!" I said. "Whatever it is, I'll do it!"

"You'll lose your Y-fronts."

"Take 'em – they're yours." Exactly the sort of gritty exchange that I used to read in my *Commando* magazines. My heart was thumping with pride. I'd do it! I'd damn well do it! I'd show those, those Steeplejack Johnnies that a 14-year-old boy could lose his pants with the best of them. I'd be the youngest Steeplejack in Eton history – not that I had any ideas, mind, what I'd do when I became a Steeplejack. But I knew, very, very much indeed, that I wanted to be one. Besides, maybe it'd help me pull more girls.

And BJ meanwhile – what was he up to? He was trudging along in silence; rather, I suppose, in the manner of a father trudging through St Moritz as his yapping seven-year-old son pleads to take a turn on the Cresta Run.

"Is it Windsor that we're going to?" I squealed. "Do you want me to streak down the high-street? I'll do it! I will!"

BJ took a pull of brandy, and busied himself with scratching at his hair, which he still does to this day when he's perplexed.

"Does it involve other boys?" I said. "You want to pinch their pants?"

At length, BJ cleared his throat. "See that flag-pole? Just get onto the roof and run your pants up it."

Seemed like a bit of a let-down, actually, after all my rather far-fetched fantasies about prostitutes and streaking. "That's it?" I asked. "Just run my pants up the flag-pole?"

"Yep." BJ belched. "That's all there is. Stick them up there and you will be the youngest-ever Steeplejack. I'll see if I can get a mention of it on your gravestone."

I danced round him like a puppy. "So what's the best way up?"

"We usually go straight up the drain pipe. Give you a bunk up if you like. Like a last tot before you go?"

I took a sip, though I didn't need it. I was an Etonian on a mission – and, as I know now, it's the very worst type of Etonian there is.

Then, for the first time, I was to hear a sentence that is so universally used in Westminster that it might even be our catchphrase: "This conversation never happened."

I stood on BJ's shoulder and scrabbled up the old cast-iron drainpipe like a monkey, hand over hand with my feet braced against the wall. I sometimes used to climb into my rooms at Brasenose like this; never once failed to impress the girls.

It wasn't exactly easy, but I wouldn't have called it much of an ordeal, either. I mean, I'd thought those blades in the Steeplejacks were actually going to serve up something that would put me on my mettle. But that? A little climb onto the top of Upper School? Pah! If BJ didn't look out, I'd beat him back to the Steeplejacks' den! Yes indeed – and *then* we'd see what Mr Smoke Ring was blowing out of his pipe after that!

It seemed no more than two minutes and there I was prancing around on top of Upper School. The flag-pole itself was smack in the middle, almost directly over the School Office. Then a matter of moments and I'd whipped my Y-fronts off – my old purplies I saw and hadn't they brought me luck that night.

I tied them onto the lanyard, ran 'em up the flag-pole, and then – because I am a feckless idiot – I decided to seal the ordeal with my special hallmark. I cut the lanyard and hauled it down. My purple Y-fronts were left jammed in the topmost ring-bolt. With the rope down, they were going to have some slight difficulty in retrieving my pants.

Ooh, what a card I was! I wanted to dance for joy. But, like every other Etonian, I can't dance, so instead I contented myself with running very fast round the roof-top and shrieking at the top of my voice. Let the Watch hear me – I didn't care! They wouldn't see me for dust! I was bubbling over with excitement as I swung myself back onto the drainpipe. I scuttled down so fast! The Steeplejacks wouldn't be able to believe their eyes when they saw me without my underpants!

But the bricks were wet, and in my haste I missed a footing

and managed to plant my foot through a window. Alarm bells drilled out into the night.

What did I care? I jumped the last few feet and, as a couple of dozy Watchmen plodded out from the school office, I was tearing off into the night. What had the cigar-smoker said? Don't let him back with his pants on? I'd show 'em!

My legs had wings as they carried me up that rope-ladder. I'd done it! I'd done it! It was the first really exclusive club that I'd ever joined – and I tell you there is nothing to touch the thrill of getting into your first elite club. That's not to say that I wasn't delighted to have earned, on my own merits, membership of White's and the Bullingdon. But nothing could compare to bundling my way through the Steeplejacks window and knowing that truly The Black Prince had won his spurs.

I bounded onto the rug and hauled down my tracksuit bottoms to reveal my naked rear to the Steeplejacks.

"Ta-daa!" I said.

These silences – I always find them very unnerving. Even now, I still find myself trying to fill the gaps, making pleasantries, just keeping things ticking over smoothly.

I thought that, aged just 14, I might have achieved something rather momentous. BJ had confirmed that if I succeeded in running my pants up the flag-pole, I'd be the youngest Steeplejack in history.

Yet – how to describe this? – I found their reception a little underwhelming. BJ sucking his teeth staring up at the roof; a couple of the Steeplejacks rolling a reefer; and the President of the Pop still puffing his cigar, so languid that he could even have given Barack Obama a few tips.

"No need to bare your backside," he said. "We'd have been more than happy to take your word as a gentleman."

"Well, I did it!" I said, smiling with hands on hips as I stood there by the window. "Even cut the lanyard down! They'll have a devil of a problem trying to get my Y-fronts, I can tell you!"

Puff-puff on the cigar. BJ now mouthing like a goldfish as he stared at the ceiling. Another Steeplejack leafing through a photo-album. The reefer is lit.

"I did it though!" I crowed. "I did it! So can I join your club? Can I call myself a Steeplejack?"

BJ was pummelling his forehead with his fingertips as if he had an acute migraine. I wondered, perhaps, if they were a little in awe of my achievement. To have passed the ordeal in under ten minutes: how could they fail to be impressed?

They ignored me. For quite a long time, actually. Had I done something wrong?

The President of Pop blew one more smoke-ring, as if weighing up a momentous decision.

"Welcome to the Steeplejacks," he said simply – and with those four words, I joined the true Eton elite. This may sound like sour grapes as I never made it into Pop. But just look at the figures – there are around 25 odd poppers a year and only about eight Steeplejacks. Go do the math.

I was so happy, I could have fallen to my knees and wept. BJ looked at me and smiled.

"Congratulations!" and he toasted me with his silver goblet. "Didn't think you had it in you!"

"Neither did I," I said – a bit of bluff modesty never did anyone any harm.

"So you got your pants up the flag-pole?" he asked. "And you cut the lanyard too!"

"They might still be up there by lunch-time!" I replied.

"School pants were they?" he asked, chewing his cheek. "Sort of pants that you might be putting in the school laundry?"

I couldn't fathom where he was going with this one. "Certainly were!" I said breezily, as I helped myself to a beer. I felt I'd earned it. "Wore them all the time. They were my luckies."

"Take the laundry tag off did you?"

"Nah." I swigged the beer straight from the bottle. "Why should I do that…" I trailed off.

The sound of a twig breaking in a still, silent forest.

BJ lifts his eyebrows. A smoke-ring glides into the rafters.

"Oh my God!" I said, scrabbling at the window.

Even as I bolted down the rope-ladder, I could hear BJ and the cigar-man talking in the Steeplejacks' lair.

"Any chance?" asked BJ.

"I think he's screwed."

Chapter 23

Such panic in my heart as I raced back to Upper School – and as I saw the Watch and the two flashing squad cars, I realised that I was completely scuppered.

I had made a small but fatal error. Though on such tiny details do even the criminal masterminds contrive to get themselves caught. In my case, it was all down to a tiny square laundry number, no more than a centimetre long. Very simply, each house at Eton had a laundry letter, and each boy within that house had a number. My unique number – and I still remember it – was H16. That tiny tell-tale detail was now stuck atop the school flag-pole, pointing first to Farrer House and then ineluctably to Farrer's best-loved fag.

I knew that I could have tried bluffing it – "My pants on the flag-pole? Really?! How did they get there?" – but I think I realised that it wouldn't wash.

So either I retrieved my purple Y-fronts or I'd be performing the Walk of Shame. I'd seen it before, when boys were expelled from Eton, and it was not a pretty sight. Even the toughest nuts would start caterwauling as they were escorted into the Headman's study. Then, as the Headman imperturbably looked on, the formal shaming ceremony took place.

The Keeper of the Watch would hack off the buttons from the boy's waistcoat and his tailcoat. The boy's cufflinks would be removed and his tie forcibly ripped off. Then, the final insult, his tails would be snipped off at the waist, leaving him with an old-style bum-freezer. But that wasn't even the worst of it.

The entire school would be called out on parade to form two long lines through the schoolyard and out onto the Long Walk. Four drummers would start rattling their sticks from the chapel steps, the deathly drum-roll echoing about the quad. And the boy, his waistcoat and cuffs flapping in the wind, had to trudge the Walk of Shame. He would walk between the two lines, shunned by masters and boys alike. For as he walked past, we all of us had to turn our backs on him, on pain of a beating.

That, I realised full well, would be my dismal fate the very next day – unless I retrieved my Y-fronts.

The very slight good news, as far as I could I see, was that although a number of men were standing about the flag-pole staring at my underpants, none of them seemed able to get them down.

And the very slight bad news: I didn't know how I was going to get my pants down, either.

There was no way I'd be able to climb the drainpipe again, as there were security officers milling about all over the place. Instead, I nipped along down the High Street and vaulted the fence into the chapel graveyard. For an Etonian, there is no greater honour in this world than to be buried in that graveyard. It is a boon that is seldom offered to old boys. But here and now, I would like to put it on record that if, in 40-odd years' time, Eton sees fit to offer a small plot for the raddled old bones of the school's 19th Prime Minister – well, I would be delighted to be buried there.

I was in the graveyard because Henry VI's chapel was undergoing another of its interminable makeovers and most of

the outside was clad in scaffolding. Just perfect. I was swarm-
ing up the scaffolding like a matelot and was very soon on the
chapel roof. If only I'd had a camera, I'd probably have made
the cover of the Steeplejacks magazine.

For the moment, I could do nothing but watch and wait.
There were still two Watchmen on the Upper School roof. One
had brought up a ladder and was trying to climb the pole, but
he wasn't even close.

I whiled away my time by prising off a roof tile and I used
this to carve my new name into the lead sheeting. When I am
in my dotage, I will amuse myself by thinking of how my children's children, and yea, even generations after, will one day
climb onto that roof, will peel back the lead, and will behold a
name that will still strike the same sort of awe that I felt when
I saw Wellington's name on the Eton beating block. For it will
be the name of Eton's youngest, bravest Steeplejack – and he
will be called: The Black Prince.

I chuckled as I carved out my new nickname. The Black
Prince! Could there ever have been a more fitting sobriquet for
the youngest Steeplejack in Eton history?

The two security guards spent ages messing around by the
flagpole, and I was getting chilled to the bone in the rain. I
dozed for a while in the lea of the chapel roof, and when I woke
up I saw with relief that the security guards had gone. But...
what was this? It was already morning, dawn's rosy fingers
were creeping in the East; a master in tight shorts and singlet
was off down the high-street on his breakfast jog.

This wasn't how it was meant to be. This was never how
The Black Prince was meant to be caught – by a stinking little
laundry mark on his purple Y-fronts. Where would be the history in that? I'd be a laughing stock!

I climbed down the scaffolding onto the Upper School roof

and went over to the flag-pole. High-ish, I reckoned, but still… no point in dawdling.

I started to climb up, hands wrapped round the pole, ankles tight together. It was wet, slippery; for every three feet I went up, I seemed to slide down two. I never looked up, grimly gluing my eyes to the pole just a few inches in front of me. I told myself to just keep on climbing till I reached the top.

I don't know how long I'd been at it, but the wind suddenly caught the pole and it started to vibrate. I then made the fatal mistake of looking down. The drop looked enormous.

I tried to climb up a little further, slid, looked down again, and suddenly I was clinging to the pole like a limpet. I couldn't move up. I couldn't move down. My whole body had gone into spasm. All I could do was grip the pole as it quivered in the wind.

I looked up. The pants were only four feet above me. I stretched but couldn't touch them. I tried to climb, summoned all my energy. Nothing happened. My muscles had locked up. I anxiously peered again beneath me – Christ it was a fall!

Then I started to feel my fingers peeling away from the flag-pole. They were numb with cold. Don't let me go like this – don't let me fall! And then a line came to me from what I now consider to be one of my favourite poems: *If* by Rudyard Kipling. I'd been studying it only that term and had thought it only so-so. But just as I was on the absolute point of letting go, I remembered two lines: 'And so hold on when there is nothing in you, Except the Will which says to them 'Hold on!''

And that's what I did: I held on and hoped the appalling vertigo might pass.

Suddenly, from below, the classic cry that the Watch have been using for centuries. "Rogue boy! Rogue Boy! Stop him!"

The Watch had spotted me from the street. I felt like a fox as he hears the first yelp of the hounds. A surge of adrenalin. As if by instinct, my muscles kicked in. I was climbing again.

I pulled upwards, lunged at the pants – those bloody Y-fronts! – snatched them, and, as the door opened onto the Upper School roof, I was slipping back down the flag-pole.

I landed on the ground – like a cat, I was, like a cat! – just as the Watchman lumbered up to the flag-staff. He snatched at my heels, but I was so fast, so agile, that I easily had the better of him. A dart to the left, a shimmy to the right, and I was tearing up the scaffolding onto the chapel roof.

He was so slow! Had barely made it past the first tier.

A victory dance was in order. I slipped the pants on my head – not quite Batman, I admit, but sometimes you have to improvise – and started declaiming to the fat ape beneath me. "I am the Black Prince!" I called down to him. "Tell the Watch! Tell the Beaks! You shall never take the Black Prince alive!"

I tried to do a bit of a dance but, as that's never been my forte, I started running very fast on the spot instead – sort of leaning forward and swinging my arms out to the side, like one of those Olympic speed-skaters. I thought it might become the Black Prince's trademark dance. Very cool. Very smooth.

Then, without slipping over even once, I swarmed down the scaffolding and leapt over the graveyard fence. There were 15-odd Watchmen milling around waiting for me, but I led them a merry dance over South Meadows before finally snucking back to Farrer just in time for breakfast.

And that was how the legend of the Black Prince was borne. At least that's my story – and I'm still sticking to it.

"It's funny," said BJ, when I was recounting my adventures the next evening. "A rather different story is being told among the Watch and the Beaks."

"A different story?" I squeaked. I'd just bought a large and ornate gold picture frame from one of the Eton antique-shops, and was busy framing my purple Y-fronts. Clubs such as the Steeplejacks must always have their trophies. To outsiders, these little trinkets may seem palpably ridiculous – a pair of purple Y-fronts indeed! But to the club members, from the new-bloods to the seasoned veterans, it is the matchless stories behind these trophies that can fire a man's soul.

"The story that the Watchman is telling differs in a number of salient details," said BJ, goggling at the vast picture frame. "You're not really proposing to donate that to the Steeplejacks?"

"I thought it might add a bit of colour," I said.

"God help us!" He sipped some Bollinger. "No, the story that's doing the rounds is that you started doing some sort of little dance on the Chapel roof. Apparently you slipped on the leaves, gashed your head on the ladder and knocked yourself out."

"That's outrageous!" I'd just come to a particularly tricky bit with the frame: boxers up, or boxers down? Or even boxers back to front?

"Then, with the Watchman nearly upon you, you burst into tears! Were on your knees, had surrendered and were begging him not to hurt you. Your exact words, I believe, were, 'No, no, please no! I give up! Please, please don't hurt me!'"

I was drumming my fingers in irritation. "The bastard's just made it all up! He just couldn't stand being bested by an F-tit!"

"Or indeed a boy with a pair of purple Y-fronts on his head," said BJ. "It is then said that the old soak let his guard down for a second and you kicked him as hard as you could in the Crown Jewels. Not exactly Marquess of Queensbury."

"What a cowardly blow!" I shrieked. "I'd never do anything

like that!"

"And then, leaving the poor man groaning in a puddle of slime on the chapel roof, you made good your escape down the scaffolding."

"Never!" I said. "That's –"

"That's what they're saying! Took him more than an hour to get off the roof top!"

"But – but... How could he say such things! I would never stoop so low! A Steeplejack must do what he can, of course, to try and escape from the Watch. But to kick a man in the gonads ..."

"Not, perhaps, the act of a gentleman?"

"Exactly," I said. "It would not be the act of a gentleman. But for this man to invent such stories... why... it reflects badly on him and it also reflects badly on me. It may even take away some of the lustre from the legend of the Black Prince –"

"Ah yes, David, I wanted to have a brief word with you about your new moniker."

"Good, isn't it?"

"I'm not altogether sure." He helped himself to one of the caviar blinis that I'd prepared for tea. "How is that nasty bang on your head, by the way?"

Instinctively I reached for my scalp. "A little tender. I was bleeding like a stuck pig!"

"You're limping a little, too." He smirked as he sipped some more Bollinger. "Sure you don't need that foot seen to?"

Chapter 24

As I recall my first year at Eton, it seems like a series of skir-mishes in a never-ending war, with no-one ever quite able to land a knock-out blow.

I can think of no better preparation for life as a politician. In Westminster, you tend to have a few allies. These people, it goes without saying, are cordial and good company. But in order for them to be considered 'an ally', they've actually got to be going places. There's no point, say, in allying yourself to some seamy Home Counties backbencher who's done nothing in 20 years, who's going nowhere. Or course you might be able to give him a leg-up; but what, more pertinently, is he going to be able to do for *you*?

Your allies have got to be on the same trajectory as yourself.

Then there are the opposition MPs. Once you've become a player, these contacts can be useful in the long run. But, for the most part, I treat Labour MPs like I might deal with a neigh-bour at a cocktail party. Happy to chat, might even have a quip or two – but generally I haven't got the time to be buttering them up.

It's nothing personal. It's just that they're never really going to be able to do me any good. Although they can't do me that much harm, either. At least you know what they're about: they want you out of your job and make bones about it. They, at least, have the courtesy to look you in the eyes as they try and stab you in the heart.

Lastly, we come to that great mass of MPs with whom we're forced to forge a workable relationship; all those ambitious Turks in your own party, all of them scrabbling around like ferrets in a sack. In this respect, Eton is just like Westminster. You may not like each other – in fact you may well *loathe* each other – but by God you've got to get on. If you both have a good run, you'll be with each other for decades.

We're all pleasant enough to each other's faces. That, apart from sex, is the most basic currency that we have in Westminster. But as you get closer to the top of the tree, there comes a time when you've got to make a call: which of the two shysters who are currently jockeying for position is going to be able to do you the most good in the long run? We can sit on the fence with the best of them. Love sitting on the fence! But when they're electing a new leader, you do eventually have to pick your Prince – and just pray that he comes through. If he does, Cabinet office beckons along with the limos, the glory and all the other little baubles that we seek. If he doesn't… well, just ask all David Davis' loyal supporters how they're getting on in a few months' time. Once the other pigs have got their snouts in the trough, it's mighty difficult to get a look in. As they say in Westminster, "The fat pigs get fatter …"

And, speaking of Westminster… it was in May 1980 that I made my first trip there. A lot of skirmishing going on beforehand, as Henchman tried to have me thrown off the bus for being incorrectly dressed – I was wearing a blue polka dot bowtie, which he claimed was an infringement of school rules. BJ – bless him – saved the day. He actually had a copy of the school rules on him, and though Henchman spent half the trip poring through this booklet, he could find no mention of F-tits being specifically barred from wearing bowties with half-change.

For his pains, I did manage to land one particularly good blow on Henchman. I was one of the last on board the coach. As I'd stuffed my duffel-bag into the hold, I'd located Henchman's executive leather rucksack and added in a little present just from me.

What a consummate political operator BJ was, even on that humdrum trip up to Westminster. Anybody else would have just sat on the back seat and been yarning with their mates. But BJ sought out the son of the Chief Whip, and – even though he found the boy the most tedious bore – spent the entire journey being just as diverting and amusing as he knew how. Now *that's* what I call a player.

So we arrived at Westminster, the Mother of all Parliaments, the place that I hope to bestride for many years yet. My friends, when they ask me now about that first trip, often wonder if I felt destiny's hand on my shoulder as I stared up at that Gothic horror-show for the first time. Not really, no. I was more concerned about jockeying myself into a good position so that I could be there when all the fun started.

I was a couple of boys ahead of Henchman, just another awestruck 14-year-old as I gazed open-mouthed at those high stone walls, marvelling at the sheer history of the place. Security in those days was not nearly as tight as it is now, but visitors' bags were still given a cursory examination.

Light the touch-paper and retire …

I'd just got through and was dawdling a moment as I tied and re-tied my shoe-lace. Henchman, so smooth he seemed like a Tory MP in the waiting. And God, what would I give to have him as one of my backbenchers? Obviously, I would have to find some suitable position for my old house captain – perhaps a long and prosperous career as minister in charge of paper-clips might be in order.

He plumped his leatherette knapsack onto the table. Zippp! Et voila!

The security guard, from being bored out of his mind, was suddenly getting very excited indeed. A knife, he'd found, a 10-inch Sabatier that I'd pinched just that morning from the kitchens. Along with the knife, there was also a length of rope, some duct tape and tissues, and – exquisite touch – some chloroform and white rubber gloves that I'd stolen from the Chemistry Labs the previous day. In effect, all the tools for an aspiring kidnapper.

The security officer goggled at the knife and the rope; Henchman goggled at all the kit as it was laid out piece by piece on the table; and, from my kneeling position, I continued to fiddle with my laces.

Henchman was mouthing, "I didn't... I don't..."

The security guard punches the panic button and suddenly the place is alive with police, dressed like storm troopers and brandishing huge machine-guns. I was bustled over to the side. I craned my head to look, trying not to miss a thing.

Henchman, now handcuffed with his hands behind his back, is spread-eagled on the ground. He's screaming at the top of his head – oh joy! – "I didn't do it! I've never seen them before in my life! I don't know how they got there! They were planted – I've been framed!"

Such music to my ears; that was certainly one in the eye for sending me off to the Windsor punks. Shame I never thought to record his screams because, if I had, it would most definitely have featured in my *Desert Island Discs*.

I'm afraid to say, though, that the next thing I did was a

mistake. My only excuse is that I was a greenhorn; I didn't know any better.

These days, I am considerably more efficient in the dark arts of stabbing a man in the back. But the stabbing is the easy part – it's getting away with it that's the problem. *That* takes years of practice. (Just *en passant* – and I tell this story purely for my own amusement – a couple of years back I was in the most *exquisite* position of being able to console a colleague who'd had a bit of bad press when 'twas I who'd leaked the story in the first place! Lovely.)

Henchman had by now been pulled to his feet and even his immaculate three-piece suit was looking slightly awry after being dragged across the flagstones.

"I've been framed!" he was squawking as four policemen frog-marched him past me. "It wasn't me!"

I was right at the back, up against the wall – and perhaps my smirk alone was enough to give me away, but as it was I did something absolutely idiotic.

Henchman, his head thrashing about like a trussed-up bear, happened to catch my eye. And I winked at him.

"It was him!" he screeched, wriggling so hard he almost managed to break free. "It was him! He did it – look at him laughing! He did it! I know he did!"

Instantly, I wiped the smile from my face and soberly studied my feet, but it was a close run thing as one of the masters in charge came straight over to grill me. "You there, boy, Cameron," he said. Crawley was his name, one of those super-keen beaks straight out of Oxford. "Is that right? Did you plant those… those appalling things on Henchman."

"Of course not, Sir," I said, as I lifted up my big baby-blues. "I don't know how he could say such a thing."

"Really?" said Crawley. "Really?"

"On my honour, Sir – and on my honour as an Eton school-boy."

Well, M'Tutor Maguire might well have been able to set him right on *that* point, but unfortunately for Henchman, Maguire was ensconced with his ménage of boys back in Farrer.

"Oh, well, of course, if you put it like that Cameron," said Crawley. "Though he did seem to be absolutely convinced you had a hand in it –"

"He's my house-captain, Sir." I shrugged as I diffidently toed the ground. "He's had it in for me for a long while – ever since I rebuffed his advances –"

BJ, standing just nearby, very nearly ruined the whole effect by tilting his head and poking his fingers down his throat in dumb mime of a cat vomiting.

"Well, yes, well," Crawley said, turning away. "No need to go into that. I'm sure it was just a, ahh, simple mistake that will soon be rectified."

Another killer blow for the F-tits! Though he'd get me back, he always did, and the next time he and Ottley came within seconds of delivering the knock-out blow that would have done for my Eton career altogether. You were close, my dear Henchman, but I am afraid that you do not get to suck on the cigar.

You can well imagine, then, the golden glow that filled me as I followed the crocodile of Etonians through Westminster. It was certainly true that some of the magic of landing Henchman so deep into *la merde* did rub off onto the walls of Westminster itself. I was so happy that my beautifully conceived plan had worked to the last detail, I'm sure I would have been equally delighted to have been taken round a chicken farm.

Crawley and his guide led us up the stairs past Westminster Hall and into the public lobby. The highlights – such as they were – were duly pointed to out us and then we were off down various committee corridors. I find them just as stifling today as I did when I first laid eyes on them.

Then through a regular warren of oak doors and gloomy little passages, and we emerged blinking into this brilliant light. We had somehow landed ourselves seats in the press gallery, directly above the Speaker's chair – and it was here that for the first time Westminster started to weave its magical spell.

I had a front row seat and I didn't even have to crane over the railings to see this gorgeous tapestry arrayed out before me. Maggie Thatcher, of course, was there, strident in her blue suit and pearls; and opposite her Jim Callaghan, still as patronising as ever, but somehow he could never really pull it off when Thatcher had become PM. And there, over at the back in curmudgeonly splendour, was my old friend Ted Heath. Didn't recognise anyone else at all. But you know what MPs are like: it was your usual sea of dark suits with the very rare splash of colour from one of the women MPs. *Yawnola!*

Eventually, after a bit of political pat-a-cake, Thatcher got to her feet. Let the games commence!

Was this it then, do you think? Was this the moment, as I saw the great Margaret Thatcher in action for the first time, that I saw the light? Did I listen to Thatcher deriding the Shadow Cabinet for being the tossers they palpably were, and suddenly have this Damascene Conversion as I fell to my knees thinking, 'Yes! I want a piece of that!'

Sorry – it wasn't Thatcher, either. I can't remember a single word of what she said, but I remember how her hectoring voice grated; in those days before the elocution lessons had properly smoothed out her vowels, Thatcher had a voice that would have stripped paint.

But it was nevertheless during that stiflingly dull PMQs that

I began, a little, to fall under Westminster's mesmerising spell. It wasn't the power and the glory; it wasn't the ministers and the MPs; and it certainly wasn't Thatcher.

It was the women.

I'd never seen so many of 'em! Not in the same place at the same time! Tall ones, short ones, young ones, pert ones – there were so many of them up in the galleries, it was like they were piling out of the woodwork. I could only feast my eyes as I tried to take in every detail of this, this cornucopia of feminine beauty.

Most people, when they think of Westminster, imagine that it is stuffed up to the gunnels with dry as dust male MPs. And that is largely correct, even today.

But it's on the next levels that the women thrive – as the special advisers, the secretaries, the Girl Fridays and key staff. Remember what I said about sex, right at the start of this book? Remember what I said makes that whole whirling Westminster engine tick over so smoothly?

Let me try and explain why there are so many women in Westminster's sub-strata.

Every male MP has his Achilles Heel – and that, more often than not, is that he'll have a soft spot for women. Now suppose that as an MP you're taking on a new team member. You've got the choice of a man and a woman, both equally well-qualified. The man, well, he's just another young guy in a suit. But the woman, with her curves and fluttering eyelashes… she could be a real asset. For even in the unlikely event that you don't much fancy her yourself, she still might be useful in a covert mission to extract information from the enemy…

And didn't I just get an eyeful of them during my first visit. Women in their 20s, 30s, and, to my feverish imagination, they all seemed gorgeous.

But there was one woman... for of course there *had* to be one woman... with whom I was utterly smitten. She was, I suppose, in her mid-20s, with long golden hair. I want to get her hair exactly right – it was shoulder length and she had taken a tress from each side and one from the top and plaited them together. Her face, just beautiful, framed by two perfect blonde kiss-curls.

She wore a beige suit, dress and jacket, and was sitting just off to the side from the press gallery. Whenever Thatcher spoke, she was making the most copious notes. I don't know what it was about her – her trim, stockinged calves or the way she sucked her pen as Callaghan got to his feet. It could even be simply down to the fact that she was an incredibly beautiful woman. But I was besotted.

My eyes would rove and rove round the press galleries – if only I'd thought to bring some binoculars – but always they would come back to this one woman. I was drinking her in with my eyes; could not get enough of her. From the tilt of her head to the way she turned to whisper to a colleague behind her, I was enchanted. And although I had my crushes on Katy, and Patricia and the blonde Goth with the dolphin tattoo, this woman was so mesmerisingly attractive I could have looked at her for a month and still not absorbed every nuance of her beauty.

You know in art galleries how people will spend hours on end in front of a single masterpiece, just gazing and gazing in a state of such rapt attention that it borders on a trance? Well that was me with this woman in beige, with her skirt riding just up over the knee, and playing with the solitaire diamond about her throat. I was quite, quite captivated.

Question Time came to an end, the Ministers shuffled off from the front benches and, with my tongue all but on the floor,

I watched as the woman in beige swept up her papers, nodded to the man next to her, and briskly walked out of my life. I was so numb, I could hardly speak.

Without a word, I followed BJ and the rest of them off to continue our tour of Westminster. We peeked into that rabbit warren where the lobby correspondents drink and fornicate, and very occasionally write. More committee corridors and suddenly I'm in another big chamber, with a hell of a lot of gold and this time red benches. (Green benches for go, as they say, and red for stop – that's the Lords for you.)

However, it was all lost on me, for all I was thinking of was the memory of all those scores of sexy women in the galleries; and, in particular, my woman in beige.

Then, the so-called high spot of the day: The Chief Whip had fixed it for us to have a ten minute question and answer session with Thatcher herself in one of the Committee Rooms.

BJ was quite beside himself. "I am going," he pronounced grandly, "to shake hands with the Prime Minister!"

This would normally have warranted some repartee on my part, but I'd long checked out from Westminster. I hardly even registered that Henchman had been released from the tender embraces of the Parliamentary police.

We were all ushered into your typical Westminster committee room – all high ceilings, dark oak panelling, sombre green carpet and chairs decked out with the Commons' portcullis logo. Nice view of the Thames, I remember that, and underneath a terrace to one of Westminster's innumerable bars.

I ended up having an aisle seat in about the second row from the front, my mind in a complete day-dream as I gazed out of the window. The door opens, the chatter stops, and as one we all stand up. I'm craning my neck round and can't believe my eyes because there, *there*, coming straight towards me is the woman in the beige suit. With every step she takes, her face, her figure, come into finer detail and I realise she is the most beautiful woman I have ever seen.

Behind her: Thatcher. She could have been naked and I still wouldn't have noticed her.

The beige beauty is all but upon me, when there's a sharp thrust in my back, a kick to the back of my knee, and – oh my God! – I'm suddenly pitching headlong in front of her.

I fell flat on my face – pushed, of course, by Henchman – but I did not mind one jot as the next moment I'm being picked up by the beauty. Her hand – *her hand!* – touches mine, her arm clasps me about the waist as she hauls this idiot boy to his feet. She's dusting me down, helping me, even, with my ridiculous bowtie. I'm so red-faced and covered in confusion that I barely know what I'm saying.

"So sorry," I say. "Thank you so much. Thank you." I may even have held my hands up, palm together, to give her a full salaam.

Thatcher, BJ, Crawley – I have no idea what they were doing after I'd been picked up from the floor. I only had eyes for one person.

If it had been bad in the Commons chamber, I was now on the very verge of falling to my knees and declaring my love. Throughout the whole of Thatcher's spiel – of which I remember not one word – my eyes never once left the beauty's face. There were two tables at the end of the committee room and seated in the first rank were BJ, Thatcher, Crawley and some Tory minion. But just behind Thatcher's left shoulder, seated exactly where a proper aide-de-camp should be, was the beauty.

I was closer to her now, much closer, I would say about four yards from her, and as I drank in her beauty, there was not one single detail that I did not instantly fall in love with. In each ear, a diamond earring to match her necklace; a small gold signet ring on her little finger – but no engagement ring, no wedding ring, still virginally waiting for the hand of just exactly the right Etonian; a cream silk shirt with, racily, not one but *two* buttons undone; and, as I remember, soft brown eyes that coolly surveyed the room. And for one single glorious moment, they held my besotted gaze.

People often ask me about what I made of Thatcher when I saw her for the first time. I remember that steel-trap mane, where not one single hair was allowed out of place; I remember a very harsh voice that would brook no argument; I also remember a complete absence of humour. She sometimes smiled and would even occasionally laugh, but never with her dead fish eyes.

No, all that I really remember of that first meeting with Thatcher was her beautiful aide, who on that day, in that place, seemed as serene and as confident as Britannia herself.

I confess. It wasn't *quite* the woman in beige who made me fall in love with the Tories; and it wasn't *quite* the extraordinary number of groomed, manicured women that roamed around Westminster that made me thirst to work there.

They both of them played an important part. But not quite enough for the engines of my desire to reach such a critical mass that my one and only ambition in this world was to become a Tory MP.

On the coach back to school, how I revelled in the memory of that woman in beige – and, even now, I can recall her face, her figure and her classic Tory mien to the very last detail.

I'd been staring out of the window at nothing; heard BJ flop down next to me.

"Did you see her?" he shouted, clapping his hand on my knee. "Wasn't she magnificent! Breathtaking! I've never seen a woman to touch her!"

I didn't even bother to turn round. "Yeah," I said, with all the indifference of a boy who has bid farewell to his lost love. "Thatcher was great. Thanks for bringing me."

"Thatcher?" he bellowed. "Thatcher! Who gives a stuff about Thatcher?" BJ was so enraged that he started poking me in the chest with his finger. "I'm talking about Xanthe!" he said. "*Fouquet in Le Touquet!* Didn't you even notice the woman who picked you up off the floor? Ye Gods! Talk about pearls before swine. Don't tell you me had your eyes riveted on Thatcher, and you missed the pick of the bunch! Xanthe was sitting directly behind Thatcher herself. You F-tits, honestly. Don't you have eyes in your heads..."

Chapter 25

Girls: how I love them.

Not that I would ever, ever be unfaithful to Sam. But if you can indulge me for one moment, I would like to consider a highly hypothetical situation. In fact, it would probably be safer to say that this *hypothetical* situation was occurring in a *parallel* universe: a parallel universe, say, where I'm still leader of the Tories, still destined to be Prime Minister, but where I happen to be just that little bit more red-blooded.

Now, as you know, there are any number of events that can bring down a Tory leader. Usually it's the traditional knife in the back. But, in this parallel universe, I could well envisage that what will do for me in the end is being caught with a mistress.

I'm probably making a real hash of this, but what I'm trying to describe is how, in this parallel universe, a raunchier, more red-blooded David Cameron might avail himself of ... how to put this politely?... the limitless opportunities to shag himself senseless.

And when, as PM, he sees that everyone in the Cabinet is getting his oats, from Hague to that human gargoyle Gove... well... let's just say that Sam would have to be on the very top of her game if she were to keep him from straying. (While I'm on the subject: Michael Gove – a cross between a Scotsman and a human being? Tell me I'm wrong.)

Anyway… There were so few women at Eton that you had to make the most of what you had. Of course there was Katy, still serving out lunch with that dreamy smile and that very slight caress as she leaned over me to stretch for the plate. "Thank you, Katy," I'd say, and she'd always look at me with those dreamy green eyes and say, "No, no, David – thank *you*."

And Patricia, the Headman's whip-cracking daughter, who I'd see occasionally out and about at the weekends. We once passed each other at Alden and Blackwell, the school book-shop. I was just about to leave when she trotted up the stairs off the street.

She looked quite lovely in a white buttoned top and a ra-ra skirt in shimmering gold which matched her hair. Long brown cavalry boots, I remember them too.

I recognised her instantly; how my buttocks tingled at the memory. I stood to attention, held open the door for her, and as she walked in, I bowed and said, "My lady."

Her eyes flickered briefly over me. I was wearing tails. I didn't think she'd recognised me. But of course she knew perfectly well who I was – how could she forget those stolen minutes we'd shared together in her father's drawing room? A moment later, Patricia said hello to me in her own uniquely challenging way: she kicked me up the arse so hard that I was lifted through the door and ended up in a winded sprawl on the pavement. What a girl! What a woman!

As for the blonde Goth with no name – how I *ached* for her to flash those gauntlets again over my pink nipples; and that vicious swipe to the groin! Even to write those words gives me goosebumps! I did mill around Windsor a bit, in the vain hope that I might see my Goth. But I never dared venture anywhere near her house of sparks and debauchery.

So, although I had a few fantasy girls, there were not nearly enough of them to stoke the fires of my monstrous 14-year-old libido. In consequence, I suppose I became the sort of teenage equivalent of a twitcher – a bird-watcher.

Wherever there were girls at Eton, I would go out to watch them. These girls tended, for the most part, to be the masters' daughters. How many countless afternoons I spent on Windsor Bridge, trying to look soulful as I read from the poems of Shelley or Keats, and all the while waiting for those fine fillies to stroll back home from school. As soon as I caught sight of them, in their short tartan skirts, I would strike some lofty pose, stare into the middle distance, and start reading aloud from *Ode to a Skylark*.

The girls clocked me, they certainly clocked me – how could they not have spotted this dashing Etonian, standing on the middle of the bridge, so smart in his tailcoat, yet so dreamy too, as he declaimed the works of the world's most romantic poets? I can still remember their darting glances, their shy hands in front of their mouths as they tried to stifle their tittering laughter. So wanting to get to know me better, yet none of them ever quite plucking up the courage to chat. Not one.

Perhaps it might have been wiser not to have worn my tailcoat. Though I was only 14, I had the aura of not just a Steeplejack, but that of The Black Prince. I realise now that I cut a very imposing figure. How trying it must have been for all those scores of girls, wanting so much to speak to me, but never having the nerve to do it. Week in, week out, they'd watch me, laughing nervously with each other. And, deep down, underneath their short skirts and their tanned legs and their tight, tight white shirts, I could see that all of them were just a complete bundle of girlish nerves. Really, you had to pity them.

However, fired up by the Dame's life-enhancing mantra – "Get it while it's hot!" – I was not prepared to let the minor detail that I didn't know a single one of them prevent me from, ahh, perusing them in the naked form. So to speak.

I know that this may sound ever so slightly tawdry, but it wasn't, I promise you. Really, you needed to be there to understand it. What I did, first of all, was follow the girls back to their homes. Usually the prettiest ones, of course, with the longest legs and the minxiest demeanours. And to those who accuse me of being a delinquent stalker I can only say: fair enough.

But it was all just a little game – from their sly looks back as I trotted along the road behind, they knew perfectly well what I was about. I'd lurk 30 or 40 yards behind them and they would play with their front-door keys and loll on the balustrades – how they flirted, how they teased!

There was one girl though, 17 and the daughter of one of the English beaks. Wasn't she just the most brazen hussy? It took me weeks to discover that she was called Imogen. I'd noticed her from the very first time she'd walked past me on Windsor Bridge. Somehow, her gay laughter seemed just that little bit louder than that of the other girls' as she'd stared at me.

The first time I followed her from the bridge, I managed to lose her when she turned off the Eton High Street. But, the second time, I was much closer and watched as she turned down a little alley. Just in time, I was there to see her on the front doorstep of a modest semi. And as she opened the door, the little minx looked at me; this melting, come-hither look of a girl on the cusp of a womanhood: interested, intrigued, wanting to know more, yet also a little nervous. Perhaps she had already heard of the reputation of *The Black Prince*.

I quickly followed, tarrying a while behind a lime tree on the other side of the road, before – Oh Jesu Joy of Man's Desiring! – she appeared at her bedroom window on the third floor. She saw me instantly. I gave her a smouldering yet rueful smile. Her hands fluttered to her mouth and, as she shot out of sight, I fancy that I may even have heard a little squeal of rapturous delight.

Winning my spurs with the Steeplejacks, well that was one thing. But now to have all but won over this pert darling: truly I had come of age.

Chapter 26

BJ watched in silence as I hammered two six-inch nails into the rafters of the Steeplejacks' lair.

I stood back to admire my handiwork. "You know what Nanny Irish always used to say, BJ – if a job's worth doing –"

"It's worth doing fast."

"Very funny." I plucked at the collar of the black turtle-neck jumper I'd bought only that morning. The harsh wool chafed at my neck. "But see these nails, BJ? These nails are going to still be in that beam when we're long gone."

"Shame the same can't be said for the ridiculous thing that you are so intent on hanging there." He sniffed and poured himself some more red wine before collapsing onto one of the leather sofas. "David – I'm not so sure this is such a good idea."

"No – it is not a good idea," I replied tartly. "It is a *great* idea! You're talking like an old woman! What you don't seem to understand about elite clubs such as the Steeplejacks is that they thrive on their collective history. It's the history, the stories and all the wonderful characters that have been involved with them that make them so special!"

"I am just about aware of the nature of collective history," he said testily. "I'm just not too sure how a pair of purple Y-fronts – in, I grant you, a most handsome gold frame – will redound through the decades."

"I think they will *redound* very nicely, thank you," I said. "Especially as a full account of how *The Black Prince* came by his spurs is now stuck to the back of the frame."

"Do you have to call yourself The Black Prince?"

"Names are very important." I hung the gilt framed Y-fronts up on the six-inch nails; they fitted so well, you would have thought they were part of the fixtures and fittings. "Especially if you wish to create a legend."

BJ swirled the red wine in his silver goblet, staring from the wine to me, and then back again to his drink. "You're cracked."

What was occurring – and I have seen it happen twice since with BJ, both at Oxford and at Westminster – was that the very nature of our relationship was changing. Now I can't fault BJ for this. There was he, several years my senior, and still blithely imagining that we were stuck in the same fag/fag-master roles that we'd had from the start.

But what he'd failed to appreciate was that I learn fast; very fast. Whereas it takes some people years to learn the ropes, I can reach a state of complete mastery in a mere matter of weeks.

He made the same mistake when we were at Oxford. For a short while, with the Bullingdon, he'd been ahead of me. And yet how quickly I was to catch him up.

But to make the same mistake a *third* time when I arrived at Westminster? *Honestly!*

By 2001, BJ was quite the old hand, bestriding the committee corridors as if he'd been born there. With what wonderful condescension did he first show me, his protégé, about the Houses of Parliament for the first time.

I don't know *why* he was so surprised when one day he realised that I was level-pegging with him as an MP. And the next time he looked, I was away, off, off over the hills and out of sight. He was shocked at just how quickly he had been slip-streamed. But then BJ, like so many others, had made the fatal mistake of underestimating not just my tenacity but also, I believe, my sheer cussedness of character.

I well remember the look of dumbstruck amazement of all those Bufton-Tuftons as they realised that their new leader was this whippersnapper who'd only been in Parliament for four years. "Hasn't got a principled bone in his body!" they cried in their impotent rage. "He's a Blair clone – a bloody light-weight!"

Well haven't I just shown them? Shown them all!

And the first time I was ever to witness that look – first incomprehension, followed swiftly by utter incredulity – was in the Steeplejacks' lair as it slowly began to dawn on BJ that I was no longer a boy. For although I was an F-tit in name, there beat within me the heart of *The Black Prince*.

Other Steeplejacks were swinging themselves up through the window into our lair – first Loram, the President of Pop, followed by two more of his sidekicks, Lagneau and Whitby.

Outstretched on the Chesterfield, I laid a languid hand on the humidor and plucked out a cigar. I trimmed the ends with my sterling silver cigar-cutter before lighting up with an expert flick from my new Zippo.

Loram was stood on the carpet, shaking his head. "What, in God's name, is that?"

"My purple underpants," I said smoothly.

"I can see that," he said. "What are they doing here?"

"I thought that they would…" I paused to savour the taste of my cigar. "They would *redound* to the greater glory of the Steeplejacks."

"Have you taken leave of your senses?" said Loram, shaking his head as he went to the fridge. "It's... they're... BJ, just tell him!"

And BJ did exactly what he did in Westminster when he realised that this upstart, this cocksure upstart, was having a tilt for the leadership. He wriggled and he squirmed, but he was squeezed by the sheer weight of *Force Majeure* – so, although he may not have much liked it, he ultimately had to capitulate.

"I don't know," BJ said slowly. "But I think I like them."

Loram paused with the beer bottle to his lips. "You can't be serious?"

"Ummm." BJ scratched at his hair, trying to give himself a moment to think. Well... in for a penny... "I like them," he said again, this time more authoritatively. "I think they sit very well there. Are we just going to continue tacking up more photos of Steeplejacks on all the Eton roof-tops? Or perhaps we should be moving with the times?" He paused now, the master of his brief. "No – I think they're a triumph. I believe that they will indeed come to *redound* through the course of Steeplejack history."

Loram's beer bottle hung limply at his side. "You are joking me, right?"

"I have never been more serious," said BJ. "I believe –"

I coughed. A very gentle cough and yet how I commanded the room. All eyes turned to me. "Let's just leave the issue of my Y-fronts. Let them stay for now and we can decide on the matter later." I took a long pull on my cigar; my timing that day was exquisite. "There are more important things to discuss."

Loram cocked an eyebrow to the hapless Whitby, who just shrugged his shoulders.

What you need to understand about me is that I do not think it is enough simply to join these elite clubs. Some choose to join the Steeplejacks, the Bullingdon, or even Westminster, and are content to leave it at that. I, however, have always craved not just for membership of these clubs, but to make my mark upon them.

"I believe it is time for the Steeplejacks to move on," I said. "Of course we could just continue to climb every building in Eton, in Windsor. But I think that if we are to aspire to greatness, then we do occasionally have to raise the bar."

Weren't they just a picture? BJ in his rumpled turtle-neck, swirling, swirling the wine in his goblet. Loram and Whitby, both with hands on hips, not quite knowing whether to throw this blagger straight out of the window. And the rest of them, Lagneau, Harkness and Renton, lurking dumbly in the background as they awaited their cue.

"What I am proposing," I said, as I rolled the cigar 'tween my fingertips, "is a rolling adventure that will last for all time. A project that will have danger, excitement and – even – romance, and which will create yet more tales of derring-do that will *redound* through the ages –"

"Well, what is the project?" snapped Loram.

"I propose, gentlemen, that we put ourselves to the task of acquiring photographs of every single one of the masters' daughters that happen to reside in Eton – and preferably without their clothes on!"

"Filthy pervert!"

"Bloody peeping Tom!"

There was a muttering of annoyed voices but I knew that I had them now – had them like nuts in the palm of my hand.

"Think of it!" I said. "Rather than our aimless trudges across the roof-tops, we shall have a higher goal – and such a goal! For the beauty of this project is that it can never be completed. For every girl that leaves, there will be a new one to take her place." And here I pulled my masterstroke, for I began to sing

some lines from the *Eton Boating Song:*
   "Others will fill their places,
   Dressed in the old light blue,
   We'll recollect their faces,
   We'll to the girls be true!
   So Swing, Swing Together,
   With our bodies between their knees!
   And Swing, Swing Together,
   With our bodies between their knees!"

A spellbound silence.

BJ sniffed, wiped a tear from his eye. "By God it's *brilliant!*" he said. "One of the best conceived schemes that I have ever heard. Now that – *that*, Gentlemen, is a project that is worthy of the name." He waved his hand about the Steeplejacks' lair. "I mean just, just look at all these dusty old photos! Who wants to see more pictures of Windsor and Eton by night! But if we were to start collecting photos of the masters' daughters… Without a stitch on! Even a century from now, the Steeplejacks will still be slobbering over them! That, gentlemen, is history, and we now have our chance to seize it."

For a moment Loram wavered – and this was just how it was with the senior Tories five years ago. They cautiously tested the wind, sniffed, sniffed again, and then, realising the lie of the land, they jumped onto my rolling bandwagon just as quickly as they could kick their fat little trotters off the ground.

Loram's head tick-tocked from side to side. A quick look at BJ, to me, before – a vassal to his Prince – he capitulated.

"I daresay…" he paused, before continuing more brightly. "Well, we have the camera! And how many times can a Steeplejack go up onto the Chapel roof, anyway? I think… I think it's just *great!*"

BJ was now drumming his feet on the ground. "A toast!" he

cried. "A toast to the masters' daughters – and a toast, too, to the boy who first conceived of snatching them: The Black Prince!"

And, you know, it quite puts me in mind of when those old Tories finally got to their feet, the cheers echoing about the hall, as I realised for the first time that the great plodder himself, David Davis, was… *toast*.

Chapter 27

It was gone 11pm and I was striding purposefully down the high-street with BJ in my wake. He was carrying our sports bag, which contained all the necessary accoutrements: rope, grappling hooks, knife, crowbar and a state-of-the-art camera with a Big Tom lens so enormous that it would have had even today's Paps going green at the gills.

"You know where we're going?" BJ said breathlessly.

"Of course I know where we're going!" I snapped. "I've spent weeks dogging these girls!"

"I'm impressed," said BJ, as he puffed along. "Slow down a bit, will you? So, who's the first one on the list?"

"Imogen!" I said. "You're going to love her!"

"And how are we going to get the pictures?"

"*I* will be scaling a lime on the other side of the road. *You* can keep watch."

When we arrived outside Imogen's house, I was pleased to see that her bedroom light was still on and the curtains had not been drawn. Perhaps she had somehow sensed, from when last we'd looked at each other, that I would be coming back for seconds.

BJ braced himself like a buttress against the tree and, with the camera slung over my back, I scampered up him.

"Push me up a little higher!" I hissed down. "I can't reach

the branch!"

"I'm trying, I'm trying!"

"Well try harder!"

I could feel him standing on tip-toes. My hands scrabbled for a branch, caught it. My feet flailed against the tree.

"Ah Jesus!" BJ cried as he kicked the bag into the street. "You caught my bloody fingers!"

"Keep your voice down," I shushed. Now that I was up the tree, the last thing I wanted was for BJ to go and blow it for me. "Go and watch the alleyway. Quickly now!"

I climbed until I was all but level with the roof-tops – and, oh you little beauty, there was Imogen, sitting at her desk, doubtless doing a little revision before her A-levels. She was side-on to the window. My breath caught in my throat as I gazed at her lissom profile. She was still fully clothed; even with my luck, it would have been a bit of a stretch for Imogen to have been doing her homework starkers.

I slipped the Big Tom off my back and eased it onto a branch. Through the lens, Imogen was so close she could have been next to me; I could even see a trace of light down her golden cheek. I fired off a couple of frames. But, as I think you can probably guess, I was after bigger game altogether.

At length, she quit her bedroom and I was in a fever of excitement as I waited for her. What would she be wearing when she returned? Jim-jams? Nightie? The minutes ticked by and, as they did so, I dared to get my hopes up. Perhaps… she was having a shower!

Then. She returns to her room. In her dressing gown! Oh please God, please God, that she's got nothing on underneath! What an unbelievable hit that would be for the Steeplejacks first time out of the gun!

My Big Tom is following her every move. Jim-jams on?

Jim-jams off? On such small details hang the course of our destinies.

She stood in front of the mirror brushing her long brown hair, over and over again. But it was worth the long wait, I can tell you, because next she sauntered over to the window. Her gown falls lightly open at the front to reveal…

My trigger finger was stabbing down so hard, so fast, that the film was spinning through the camera. Imogen's gown is open just enough for me to see half a naked breast on each side and her toned belly. She was thoughtlessly wearing jim-jam trousers so I wasn't able to get quite the full frontal that I'd hoped for. But, for a first outing, this was not too bad at all.

Now, just move over a bit darling and I'll get a full shot... Imogen comes closer to the window. Closer. Her face is all but touching the glass. She's staring out. She's looking right at me – she must be! She knows it's me, I'm sure she does! I take off my balaclava and give her a little wave.

Her face first trembles with very slight consternation, before I see her eyes light up with steely resolve.

"Yes!" I said, clenching my fist in triumph.

"What's happening?" BJ called up

"She's coming downstairs to let me in!"

I was humming the *Eton Boating Song* as I slung the Big Tom over my back again. The Steeplejacks wouldn't be able to believe their ears when they heard this. The opening batsman scores a six with his first shot!

I started to climb down the lime, but there was a rather tricky bit near the middle, where my legs were too short to catch the branch beneath me. I paddled the air, before rather inelegantly resorting to hugging the tree-trunk like a bear.

I was slightly aware of some sort of flashing light.

BJ called up to me, voice shrill with panic. "It's the police!"

Their presence could not have been more untimely. There was I on the very cusp of bringing my courtship with Imogen to a fruitful conclusion – and now the Boys in Blue were sticking their unwelcome snouts into business that was of no concern to them.

I clattered down the tree as fast as I could. By the time I'd jumped to the ground, the police car was just drawing up outside Imogen's house.

BJ was waiting by the alleyway. "Come on!" he shrieked.

I raced after him. Not that I was overly concerned. If I couldn't beat a bobby in a straight race, then it was time to give up and go home to Nanny Irish.

However, I hadn't banked on BJ turning his ankle on the pavement.

"You go!" he wheezed, hobbling along the high-street.

"I can't leave you, BJ!" I cried.

"It doesn't matter about me! There's no point in them catching both of us. Go now – save yourself!"

I looked behind us. Two fleet-footed coppers tore out of the alley and sprinted towards us.

"Off you go, BJ!" I said. "Do the best you can, old boy. I'll distract 'em."

So, as BJ gamely hobbled up the high-street, I pulled on my balaclava and, like a spry bantam cock, turned on the two police. They were much bigger than me, but what I lacked in size I more than made up for in guile. I ran straight towards them, jinking, darting, in, out, like a mosquito. To left and right, they flailed all about them. First I circled them. Then I ran right between the two of them. Like two trolls, they could only lunge and snatch at thin air. They never laid a finger on me.

Finally, as I saw BJ disappear into the distance, I stood, hand on hip, before the two advancing bobbies. "You have done well," I said. "But it is now time for the Black Prince to bid you good night!"

With that, I turned on my heel and darted off towards Windsor before circuitously making my way back to the Steeplejacks' lair.

BJ was the only one there, sipping on a Whisky Mac as he nursed his sore ankle.

"What happened to you?" he said.

"What happened to me?" I asked. "What happened to me? I think I did a very good job in drawing the policemen's fire so that you could limp to freedom. That's what happened to me!"

"Really?" said BJ. "I thought you just ran off and left me!"

"Don't be so ridiculous!" I snapped. "But that's an irrelevance. What I want to know, BJ, is how the police ended up there in the first place."

With his foot up on the side of the sofa, BJ continued to squeeze the ice compact against his ankle. "Haven't the foggiest!"

"Well, it was just a little bit of a coincidence, wasn't it?" I asked. "There is Imogen, on the verge of embracing me in her arms, and then, all of a sudden, the police arrive!" I was angry, no doubt about it. I hate it when a well-prepared plan fails to be properly executed. Although my voice was icy calm, the blood simmered in my veins. "Know what I think happened, BJ? Shall I tell you? I think you made such a bloody racket down on the ground when you kicked that bag that somebody called the cops. *That's* what I think happened!"

"Really?"

"Yes, really!" God, I was seething.

BJ hobbled over to the fridge for more ice. A sudden thought came to him. "Though you don't think... you don't think it

might have been the girl who called the police? You know –
she sees this night stalker in a tree taking pictures… perhaps
she was worried?"

"The girl!" I shrieked, outraged that BJ was now trying to
shirk the blame by accusing Imogen. "That is the most ludi-
crous, the most *fanciful* thing I have *ever* heard!"

Chapter 28

I was never caught by the police, not even when I was misbehaving at Oxford. They've never caught me; in fact I doubt they ever will.

But there was one person who very nearly did do for my career at Eton. For a few seconds in the Lowerman's office, my life hung in the balance. I held on by my fingertips.

At Eton, however, just as at Westminster, it is a strategic error to wound and yet be unable to strike the killing blow. And what vengeance I would wreak! A vengeance that even now is still talked about at Eton; and a vengeance not just on Henchman and Ottley, but every member of that damnable Library that had dared to tan me in my first fortnight.

First, though, the small matter of how Ottley came within an ace of getting me sacked from Eton.

For some idiotic reason that summer, I'd decided to be a wet bob. I was a rower. Should have done cricket, tennis, fives, anything else but rowing. They try and claim there's a lot of skill to it but, as far as I can see, rowing is merely an exercise in pain for meatheads.

It was a balmy Saturday afternoon and I had got it into my head to row the four miles up the Thames to Queen's Eyot. It was a long haul and I'd never done it before, but I'd heard that every Etonian should row there at least once and I wanted to tick that box before I turned my attentions to tennis.

Rowing to Queen's Eyot was just *hellish*. They used to put the F-tits in these fixed-seat sculls that skewed your entire rowing action. Your legs didn't come into the stroke at all and instead you were having to manhaul yourself the entire way by dint of your arms.

But I had Pierre Le Normand for company, and every few hundred yards we'd stop for a break and have a chat. Not being a member of the Steeplejacks, Pierre had never had any booze at Eton and so he was dreaming wistfully of the beer that he'd be allowed at Queen's Eyot. There was a small rowers' bar on that little island in the Thames where even the F-tits were allowed a beer.

It was gone 5pm when we pulled up to the wooden landing stage. Queen's Eyot, as I remember, was a little bigger than a football pitch, with trees dotted all about, and in the middle a lawn with a white wooden kiosk. Some 30 boys were supping beer or cider from plastic glasses as they sat on the grass or at the tables. Dappled sunlight came through the trees and a light breeze off the river; though what I chiefly remember is the relief at not having to row. Both my hands were covered in blisters and I still had the trip back.

Pierre and I wandered over to the kiosk, where a gnarly man was serving the drinks. I was parched and ordered four halves for the pair of us.

Normally, I guess, Pierre and I would have sat on the grass, but four boys happened to vacate a table as we walked past and so we bagged it.

That first half of Directors – well, I knocked it back in one. It barely even touched the sides. The second half went the same way. Bliss.

I started licking the sides of the glass to show Pierre it was his turn to get the drinks in. He trotted off. I luxuriated in the sun. A shadow fell across my face.

"You?" he said. "At Queen's Eyot! How did you get here?"

I squinted, could make out this hulking silhouette against the sunlight. "Came here by horse and cart – how do you think I got here?"

"And now you're having a beer?"

"Ottley," I said with a smile, "your observational skills are unsurpassable!"

"You've got a lot of nerve for an F-tit!"

Hadn't I though? My rise and rise in the Steeplejacks had given me such a ring of confidence that I dealt with Poppers and rowers alike with cheery disdain. Just to quote from Kipling's poem again, 'If you can walk with Kings – nor lose the common touch.' Well, I don't think this is a time for false modesty: At Eton, I did indeed learn to mix with kings, yet at the same time could still quite happily chat to the likes of Pierre. Or even Ottley.

"I have got a nerve," I said. "And you would do well to remember that." I drained the last of Pierre's beer. "You've not heard, then, of the Black Prince?"

He gawped at me for a while, lips moving soundlessly as the words formed in his head. "What, that Colleger from Africa?"

"Pah!" I said. "Go drink your beer!"

From what I remember next, though I was only vaguely aware of it, there was some sort of kerfuffle at the kiosk. Pierre had all but got the beers when he was bearded by Ottley and another enormous rower. I never saw it happen, but it was then, undoubtedly, that the dirty work was done.

Pierre brought back another four halves. I drank my pint fast for my sweat-stained shirt was making me cold. And after this, my memory becomes woozy.

I somehow stumbled over to my boat. Howling with laughter as I dropped an oar, retrieved it, and then set off in the wrong direction. Pierre shepherded me back. For a while I was barely dapping the water with my oar. Woke up with a start and a shake as Pierre splashed me. The most appalling headache was kicking in. I set off rowing again at a terrific pace. After five minutes, I was utterly burned out. The oars fell from my hands and I was asleep even before my head hit my knees. I was out for the count.

Pierre was a life-saver. He hitched the two sculls together and towed them back along the riverbank all the way to Rafts in Windsor. I slept the whole of the way. He woke me up with a bucket of river-water in the face.

"Time to get back, you drunken sot!" he said.

"Drunk?" I said blearily. "Spiked me beer! Bash-tard!"

I don't know how Pierre got me back. We tottered along the road together for a bit, but he may even have carried me some of the way on his shoulders. A vague memory of staggering into the house and being put to bed. I fell fast asleep.

The first I knew that something was wrong was when BJ burst into my room. He took in the situation in an instant. "Hide under the bed," he said, pushing me straight out from underneath the blankets. I cursed as I crashed onto the floor. "Don't make a sound!" he hissed.

A moment later, I hear brisk strides coming down the passageway. "Where is he?" barked a voice that I knew all too well. "Where is that boy?"

Maguire tore into my room. From underneath the bed, I could see his feet as he stood in the doorway. He sniffs once, twice.

"Can't see him, Sir," says BJ.

"Perhaps not," says Maguire as he glides into my room. "But he has been here! I can smell him! I can smell the very beer that was upon his breath!"

"Gone now though," says my doughty fag-master.

"So it would seem, so it would seem," said Maguire, as he paused to sniff at my burry. "And yet he was here just recently. I know it! I know it! But what is this? The boy's urine-soaked bed – warm! 'Tis still warm! The miscreant himself was sleeping here not minutes ago. But where, oh where, can the little Judas be hiding himself?"

Without making a sound, I had curled up into a ball under the bed. I had the most thumping hangover and it felt like all the beer was fermenting in my stomach; I was desperate for the lavatory.

"I'll try the bathroom," said BJ as he quit the room.

"Yes, you try the bathroom. Why don't you try the bathroom, you preening peacock!" Maguire said to himself. "But where could the bed-wetter be? How could the porn-dealer have hidden himself with such alacrity? He was here just before we came in! I know it! But to have flown so quickly? Did he jump out of the window? Well, did he?"

Maguire stood in silence by my burry. It felt like a tattoo had started in my stomach. I was biting down savagely on my cheek to try and distract from the heaving pain in my bladder. My legs twisting together; I could barely stop myself from mewling.

And, in the silence, a single solitary parp.

Maguire sniffs. "Hooo-hooo-hooo!" he says. "I think we know now where the Judas boy is hiding!"

As I grimaced in pain, Maguire's bald head ducked beneath the bed. "Hooo-hooo-hooo!" he laughed. "And there is the evil one! Stinking like a brewery, I'll be bound! Well come on out,

Master Cameron – let's have you off the floor, at the very least!" With that he straight lifted my bed up against the wall and I was left cowering at his feet.

"Well, be upstanding, boy, don't dally!" he said, with a clap of his hands. "I believe that it's still normal school etiquette to stand up when your tutor has entered the room!"

"Please, Sir!" I squeaked. "I'd rather not!"

"Oh, but how so, Master Cameron? How so? Is there something wrong with you? Have your legs buckled beneath you from the sheer volume of beer that you drank this afternoon?"

"No Sir!" I said. "It's nothing like that. You couldn't get me a bucket? Please Sir!"

"Order me about like a boot-boy?" he cried "Fagging me off to the bathroom to find you a bedpan! Your own Tutor! I would not have believed it possible, Master Cameron, but your insolence grows greater by the day! And in my own house too. I will not have it, Sir. I will not have it!"

"No!" I said. "I – I'm desperate!"

"Desperate is indeed the correct word for your position in this school at the moment. You will stand up, boy. Stand up this instant! I will not put up with it one moment longer. Up on your feet, you blackguard, and we will see for ourselves quite how desperate you are!"

Twice he kicked me in the chest, queeny little toe-pokes with his dainty brown brogues.

Like a tired young bullock that has been goaded beyond reason, I got to my knees and hauled myself to my feet.

"Ah, Master Cameron!" Maguire beamed at me as he dry-washed his hands together. "Thank you for doing me the courtesy of standing in my presence. And –" A long pause as he digested what was occurring before him. "Ahhhhhhh," he said, the sound of a man replete. "See how he pees himself!"

He watched, fascinated, as first my shorts became wet and then the urine streamed down my leg to form a puddle at my feet. I clutched feebly at my groin, but it did no good; I couldn't turn the tap off. All I could do was stand dismally, staring at my feet as the tide of piss cascaded onto the floor.

Maguire just stood there nodding – nodding and nodding, his eyes absolutely riveted to my crotch. And, even as this sorry spectacle continued, he was talking to himself, "He pees himself by night – he pees himself by day. But oh – what a sorry, sorry picture he makes. His room – methinks it will reek for weeks, now that he has thought fit to relieve himself on his own carpet!"

I don't know how long it went on but eventually I was all peed out, and stood there swaying in front of Maguire – still not quite certain whether I was entirely finished.

"I'm sorry, Sir," I said. "At Queen's Eyot. Somebody spiked my drink!"

"Somebody spiked your drinks, you say." With a little skip, Maguire danced over to the window. "Hooo-hooo-hooo! Whoever would have guessed it! The Cameron monster is drunk and, as sure as night follows day, he claims that someone spiked his drinks! And when I discovered pornography in this very room, he claimed that the magazines had been planted there. And when he set off the fire-alarm, he does it in his sleep. For every accusation that is levelled at him, Master Cameron always has an answer!"

"It's true, Sir," I said feebly. "I only had half a pint of bitter. Somebody spiked it – probably vodka!"

"Master Cameron," Maguire said affably, leaning back on his hands, crossing his ankles. "Perhaps I have clairvoyant qualities! From the very moment that Henchman told me that you were lying in a drunken stupor in your pit, I thought to

myself, 'How will the wretch try and wriggle out of this one?'
And you know the first thought that came to me, even before I
stepped foot into this rancid room? I thought to myself, 'The
Judas will claim his drinks were spiked!'"

"Please, Sir! I think I've got to go again!"

"You'll do no such thing, boy! You'll hear me out! For I
have other predictions to make – and this time about some of
the events that may be occurring tomorrow morning!"

"Please, Sir!" A tide of beery vomit suddenly cascaded out
of my lips and onto the floor. I retched and retched until there
was not a thing left to heave up from my bone-dry belly.

Maguire, still by the window, watched with indifference, the
sight of my vomit provoking not nearly as much interest as
when I'd peed myself.

When I was done, he sniffed and took a large stride over the
vomit. "And for your next trick?" he said with a shake of the
head. "Perhaps you will now proceed to poo your pants? You
befoul your bedroom like an incontinent cow. In 20 years at
Eton, I have never seen the like!"

Chapter 29

The Lowerman, sitting at his desk, had heard me out, listening in silence as I had railed against the bandits who'd spiked my drink.

He played with his pencil, tapping it against one of the canes on his desk. "How much beer did you drink?" he asked at length. "And be careful now – if you lie, you will not see another day at Eton."

Dark times, indeed – like being caught with one of those insidious dagger-blow questions when you're at the dispatch box. I dared not lie; but I dared not tell the truth either.

"I don't know Sir, honestly I don't know," I said, wringing my hands in front of me. "If I did know, I'd tell you. But my mind – it's just a blank. From the moment I arrived at Queen's Eyot to the awful moment when I realised that I'd brought shame to the name of Eton, I cannot remember a thing."

"You can't remember?" he said in a flat monotone, never once looking at me as he stared at the tip of his pencil.

"I have no idea, Sir," I pleaded, knowing that I was on trial for my very life. "It can't have been much."

"On the contrary, Cameron, the bar-keep tells me that you had at least two pints and quite possibly more!"

Christ, that was a close one. "I – I don't know, Sir," I quavered. "I can't deny it, but it just doesn't sound right to me –"

He snatched up the cane and thrashed it down onto his desk. "Your Tutor also claims you managed to bring up a full quart of liquid in your own room!"

"I – I don't know," I cried. "I'm so ashamed of myself."

For the first time, the Lowerman looked at me. "Give me one good reason why you should not be expelled from Eton this very morning." These days I sometimes watch *The Apprentice* and I think I can genuinely say that I know how those young business goons feel as they plead for their lives to Sir Alan Sugar in the boardroom.

"I –" I fiddled with the drawing pin in my hand and then thrust it firmly into my wrist, all the way in. I almost squeaked for pain but it did the business, as the tears were then tumbling down my cheeks. "I have brought shame to the name of Eton," I cried, "and I would that you would let me stay so that I might have the chance to prove myself worthy of this school." (Things just don't change, do they? That's almost *exactly* what the kids say when they're grovelling to Sir Alan. Though they probably don't use *quite* such high-fallutin' language.)

The tears had started to dry up a bit so I stabbed the drawing pin into my other wrist. *Jesus, it hurt!* I let the tears fall down my cheeks and onto the floor; I didn't want to ruin the effect by mopping at them with a grimy hanky.

"I don't know why," said the Lowerman. "But I think this time I believe you. Your tears have moved me very much, Cameron – for I think they show that you are intent on reforming yourself. So… much against your tutor's advice… you will be rusticated from Eton for the period of one week, and, to speed you on your way, I will now give you six of the best."

"Thank you, Sir," I snivelled.

Finally, after all those months of waiting, I got what I'd been longing for, wrapping my lips round that old Eton bullet with all the ardour of a damsel in love. With what delight I bit down onto the bullet's metal as the cane strokes sizzled my buttocks.

"Thank you, Sir," I said later as I shook him warmly by the hand. "Oh, thank you, Sir!"

"You're sitting in the last chance saloon," he said – and in that one moment he was Sir Alan Sugar personified.

Evans the chauffeur was despatched to pick me up and I glumly sat in the back of the Bentley while he slung my bag into the boot.

"Didn't think we'd be seeing you back for three weeks," Evans said chirpily as he eyed me in the mirror.

"Damn your impudence!" I said. "And wipe that gurning smirk of your face!"

Back home, my parents were all grim foreboding. The interview with Pater in his study; it was unpleasant.

Mama, trembling in the passage outside, still a trace of tears on her face at the thought that I might be the first Cameron in history to be forced to tread Eton's Walk of Shame.

But it was Nanny, dear old Nanny Irish, who nearly had me piping my eye. She was the sweetest old thing, she really was. She lived in a modest apartment at the top of the house, had lived there for nigh on 50 years. How I remember her sage wisdom throughout my childhood. She'd nurtured me, cosseted me, chided me – and, possibly even more so than my parents, helped mould me into the man that I am today. But it wasn't just the love and attention that she lavished upon me, for she had also instilled her wholesome, no-nonsense values – values I believe I will treasure for the rest of my days.

I knocked on her door and went in, and there she was, sitting in her favourite armchair by the window, surrounded by toys and tea-caddies and all the other little nick-nacks that I had so loved to play with in my childhood. And as for dear Nanny herself, with her white hair and little round glasses, she seemed as old and ageless as Gagool herself. She smiled that sweet, gentle smile that I had come to know so well over the years.

"You're a wrong 'un and I always knew it!" she said, putting down her knitting and opening her arms in welcome. "Come here and give your old Nanny a kiss!"

I approached nervously – and with some justification. I was just leaning down to kiss her withered cheek when she delivered a colossal round-house blow to my jaw.

I sprang back, massaging my cheek.

She slipped the brass knuckleduster from her hand. "Fuck me that hurt!" she said as she kneaded her gnarled fingers. "Must be losing my timing."

"Yes, Nanny Irish." I gingerly took a seat opposite her on the other side of the bare hearth. I was sitting on the very edge of my chair, legs like steel springs, ready for anything. When the mood took her, she could strike like a cobra.

"So what happened this time, you prinking half-wit?" She clasped a ciggy between thumb and forefinger, her wrinkled lips puckering up like a rusty sheriff's badge as she sucked the smoke deep into her tarry lungs.

I warily eyed the socking great bull-whip that lay next to her on a scarred side-table. Beneath its shimmering black coils was a bowl of bemerded pear-drops on a lace doily. "I – I am here because... because the school authorities thought it might be best for me to have some time on my own."

"Bollocks!" She hawked a huge globule of brown phlegm into the spattered fireplace before picking up her knitting. I believe that it was a mauve shawl she was making for mama. "Have they kicked you out?"

"Err, no Nanny," I said, probing my mouth with my tongue. She'd definitely chipped one of my canines and I think she'd loosened a couple of molars.

"Rustication, eh?" Click-clack, click-clack went the long white knitting needles as she sucked on her false teeth. "What did you do?"

"It was drink," I said. "Somebody spiked –" I watched, terrified, as she lay the knitting down and very lightly grasped the handle of the bull-whip. She brought the whip to her nose and sniffed.

"Leather!" She smiled, the false teeth wandering about her mouth. "Smells good!"

I barely had time to blink before the whip cracked and fizzled past my nose. I leapt out of my seat. She'd missed me by an inch. A thin haze of dust hung in the air from where the whip had thrashed into the yellowing antimacassar. "Stay!" she lisped, before adding more equably, "You were saying?"

"I got drunk," I gabbled. "I had two-and-a-half pints of beer! It was a hot day – it was entirely my own fault!"

"Good boy," she said, flicking the whip back and returning to her knitting. "Nanny must be told the truth."

"Yes, Nanny."

"Ahh," she said, almost whispered. Click-clack, click-clack flew the needles. I didn't like the look of this one little bit. "And next time?"

My hands were dewy with sweat. I wiped them on my trousers. "I – I think they might throw me out."

"Oooh." She spoke so softly now that I could barely hear her. "That would be… bad."

"Yes Nanny." I stared wildly about me, wondering if I might be able to make a dash for the door.

She carried on knitting for a while before her eyes darted

back at me. "Well, can't be helped." She smiled merrily. "Come over and help yourself to a bonbon!"

"Thank you, Nanny." Inexplicably, I let my guard down. I think I'd been at Eton too long; had forgotten just exactly what Nanny Irish was capable of.

I was just by the side-table, my hand poised over the sweet bowl as I searched for the least disgusting pear-drop, when she struck – so quick, so fast, that I didn't even know what had happened until I saw the knitting needle sunk deep into the table and realised she'd skewered my hand.

She'd got me clean in the fleshy part, between thumb and forefinger. "Gaaah!" I shrieked. "Shit!"

A leather boot scythed into my balls and I buckled at the knees.

"How dare you!" she spat. "How dare you use that filthy word!"

"Nanny!" I screamed. "Please! No!"

With one hand still bearing down on the knitting needle, she grabbed me by the nose, burying two fingers deep into my nostrils. "Now you listen to me, you little fucker!" she rasped. "If they kick you out of Eton, then –" and here she paused to give a vicious twist of her forefinger. Blood geysered down my nose. "Then Nanny will not be happy."

She sniffed mildly, before adding. "What did I say?"

"Nanny will not be happy," I whimpered.

"That is correct," she said. "Nanny will not be... ha-ppy."

"Yes, Nanny," I said. "I'm sorry, Nanny."

She released her fingers from my nose and cuffed my ear so hard that I saw stars. "Look where you're bleeding! You're incorrigible! Now get out! Get out!"

I scampered to the door, unsure whether I was still in range of the bull-whip.

"Very good," she said, with her hands now peaceably in her lap. "Now, what do you say?"

"Thank you, Nanny!" I said, wiping the blood from my chin. "You're the best Nanny in the whole wide world."

"And don't you bloody forget it!"

There was a blurred flash of black; the whip cracked and I felt this instantaneous sting where she'd taken off the tip of my nose. Her crazy laughter echoed in my ears as I clattered down the stairs.

Chapter 30

Vengeance! Vengeance will be mine, saith the Lord – and saith David Cameron too.

People sometimes ask me about what I enjoy most in politics. "Where's the fun?" they ask, bright eyes shining with eagerness. "What do you like doing for fun?"

Well, I certainly don't tell *them* what I do for fun. You, however… I don't know why, but I feel a rare moment of candour coming on; so let us try and make the most of it.

There are many 'fun' things that you can do in Parliament – and sex, as you already know, is probably top of the list. Further to that, there is also wining and dining, the occasional freebie to a foreign field, and, if you're high enough up the tree, your own limo. For the top dogs, we also get the most lavish Grace and Favour buildings. Chequers? As Tony Blair liked to say, 'Check It Out!'

But, if you really pressed me on this, I would have to say that pretty near top of the list of my list is… how to put this politely?… righting personal wrongs. This might more colloquially be known as 'doing down the bastards who've tried to stiff me'. And let me tell you that in Westminster there is certainly no shortage of those bastards.

When I was on the way up, this business of revenge had to be done so slyly. You couldn't afford even the slightest whisper of it to get out. The Whips' Office, for instance: leaky as a sieve. It would have been such a schoolboy error to have leaked some tittle-tattle direct to the Whips themselves. Instead, you always had to remember that, as we like to say, 'Deviousness is its own reward' – meaning, of course, that rather than go direct to the Whips with your tasty piece of gossip, you leaked it to the biggest blabber in the tea-rooms.

And now that I am truly at the top of the tree, I am almost aquiver with excitement at the sheer variety of ways at my disposal to do the reptiles a disservice. The key, I've decided, is to promote the bastards – dangle the carrots in front of their noses, make them think that if they put in a few hundred extra hours a month, they might just bag Secretary of State. And then… just as they think that Cabinet rank is within their grasp, 'tis snatched away from them. Perhaps a leaked story to Her Majesty's *Sun* newspaper? Or perhaps I'll even have them into my private office in Number Ten, look them manfully in the eye as I tell them that they're "just not quite ready" for the top job. No! Better yet, I'll tell 'em they can't have the job, because it's going to their worst enemy! Hooo-hooo-hooo!, as old friend Maguire might say.

As with so much of the skulduggery that I have mastered, it was at Eton, of course, that I was to have a crash course in the dark arts of revenge.

Notwithstanding the threats and curses of that demented fruitcake Nanny Irish, I was still determined to make those bastards in the Library pay for putting me through a year of unremitting hell. They had sown the wind – and, now, best batten down the hatches, boys, because Hurricane Davie is on the horizon!

It was gone midnight, and BJ and I were having a snifter in the Steeplejacks' lair – gin, it was, and he was having me snort it up through my nose.

"*Jesus* that hurts!" I screeched as the gin razored out my sinuses. "I like it!"

"Thought you might," he said, twirling a Bollinger bottle in his hand as he topped me up. "I don't see why you can't just content yourself with getting Henchman and Ottley. As for the rest of them – they only gave you a light tanning."

"The Black Prince never forgets a slight," I said, mopping the blood from my nose with a hanky. "I will have them! I will have them all!"

BJ chewed on his lip. "Going to get the whole lot of them? In a single go? What are you going to do – lace the Library beer with emetics? Have them all trotting off to the lavatory as they take their A-levels?"

"Pah!" I gazed at the framed picture of my purple Y-fronts. It was surrounded by a score of photographs of Eton's young lovelies, with a breast peeking out here and a buttock there. The pick of the bunch – and I promise I'm not making this up – was in the shower and didn't have a stitch on! Not a stitch! Mind you, the shower was so steamed up that you could barely tell whether it was the girl or her mother. But anyway...

"Steal some stuff from the Headman's apartments in the Cloisters?" BJ suggested. "Plant it in their rooms?"

I swung my legs off the Chesterfield and leaned forward to address him. "BJ – what you are failing to understand is that I want this to be *big!* I want those boys to know what it's like to be beasted by... *The Black Prince!* What I want, what I need, is for some event, some shindig, when all of the swine will be together. Well?"

BJ tugged at his lip. "Well... Wait!" He crashed his hand into his forehead and said in a voice like thunder. "How could

I have forgotten? They're… they're all off for high-tea next week! Off to the Tudor Hole!"

I can feel my fingertips itching with impatience as they hover over the keyboard, for I now come to what was, without doubt, my favourite memory from my entire five years at Eton.

The Tudor Hole! Just the very mention of its name brings a smile to my lips. Tudor Stores was, like Rowlands, another little Eton shop where boys could stuff their faces on lardy crap to fatten themselves up for market.

At the back of the Tudor Stores was the Hole, a private dining room where a dozen boys could comfortably seat themselves around a large rectangular table. Each year, it was normal for the senior boys in every house to go out for one final meal together; so they could talk about old times and toast each other's prospects.

Most boys in the school would go off to the Christopher or the Cockpit, or one of the decent restaurants in Windsor, but the cheapskate Librarians from Farrer had set their hearts on having high-tea at the Tudor Hole.

It had been deemed necessary for a couple of fags to help out with the feast and BJ had helpfully engineered it so that I was in attendance, the better that I might enjoy the fun.

William M'Thwaite and I, both in tails, were standing close to the door of the Tudor Hole. We were bearing large glasses of probably the most disgusting drink on earth, a Brown Cow – a pint of Coke and a scoop of Vanilla ice-cream.

The Library, smug as anything at having just finished their A-levels, came in to the Hole and I can still picture every man jack of them: Henchman and Ottley, not even deigning to look at me as they whisked their Brown Cows from my tray; Cripps, the Suffolk idiot, licking his lips in what he can only have taken for a come-hither smile; and the Bouverie, still reeking of sperm and sweat as he played his lonely game of pocket billiards. BJ, as usual, was late, all bluff apology as he declined the Brown Cow for a glass of red wine.

You should have seen them tuck in to the crisps, biscuits and cake – though perhaps a little incongruous that they were 17 not seven. M'Thwaite and I took their orders – rafts of fried bread, piled high with eggs, bacon and beans, along with anything else that you could possibly heat up in a deep-fat frier.

Making myself as docile and amenable as I knew how, I topped up the Brown Cows, handed out bread rolls, and modestly went about my business – a-twitch with impatience for the next act. She was not to disappoint me.

A woman, a most striking blonde, entered the room. She was way, way taller than me, and wore an off-the-shoulder dress of shimmering magenta silk that fell almost to the heels of her black stilettoed boots. Mascara, eyelashes, ruby red lipstick and a lot of slap, she'd got the works.

Instant silence – they just goggled, like a pack of starved dogs that had just been presented with a neatly trussed-up doe.

How she commanded the room as she sauntered in, running her fingers through her Marilyn Monroe hair. In turn, she looked straight into the eyes of every Etonian at the table. "Hi boys. I'm Mandy," she said. Very husky voice, as if she gargled gravel every morning. "I've been sent here by a very special friend!"

Bouverie thumped the table. "We don't know anyone that special!" he hooted. How right he was.

A bell rang and M'Thwaite and I had to go next door to pick up plate after plate of lard-saturated bread for the big boys' high-tea.

And when we came back, just as I'd hoped… Mandy was gone!

M'Thwaite nudged me as we waited by the kitchen door. "What happened to her?" he said.

I winked at him. "You don't want to know."

There followed what was one of the most magical hours of my life. M'Thwaite and I would trundle in and out of the Tudor Hole with seconds and thirds of rafts and beans and deep-fried pig; the Library, meanwhile, just sat there gorging themselves like Strasbourg geese. A strange silence had settled over the room, with just the odd sound of pigs at the trough. Occasionally they'd catch each other's eye, a happy smirk, a cock of the eyebrow.

Cripps: altogether too, too obvious. He sat there leaning forward with this dreamy smile on his face, before suddenly his hand twitched and he poured his Brown Cow all down his front. Henchman, imperturbable apart from a trickle of sweat gliding down his white cheek. And Ottley, the animal, letting out a sudden grunt as if he'd been punched in the chest. Those are the ones that I remember best.

Et finalement: le grand dénouement. I'd just scuttled back to the kitchens for some more Coke. By the time I returned to the Tudor Hole, Mandy was emerging from underneath the table. Her hair was slightly askew and it would be fair to say that her make-up now looked just a little the worse for wear. William M'Thwaite, standing next to me, couldn't take his eyes off her. "There she is!" he squealed. "Do you think she's been there all the time?"

Mandy grabbed hold of the side of the table and hauled herself onto her tottering feet. Then she gave a little smile to herself, squared her shoulders and walked to the door.

Oh, but you could have heard a pin drop as, lolling against the door-frame, she smacked her lips and wiped the back of her hand across her mouth. Her ruby red lipstick, smudged before, was now smeared all across her cheek.

"Guys," she said. "You've been great! But just one small question before I go?" And with that, she waved and ripped off her wig – to reveal a bristling grey crew-cut. She gave them a brilliant smile before laughing. Her voice seemed to drop by an octave. "Do tell me – is it an Eton thing? Because those have got to be the smallest cocks I've ever seen!"

Bedlam! Total and utter bedlam! Bouverie and Cripps looking like they'd been coshed over the head; Ottley gaping at his crotch, still not quite sure what had occurred; Tait looking like he'd just soiled himself; and as for Henchman, he was like a white marble statue – I think he'd gone into shock. BJ quietly sat in the corner drinking his red wine and snickering to himself.

"Golly!" squeaked M'Thwaite. "You don't think she was sucking all their willies, do you?"

"You know, I think she possibly might," I said as I led the way out of the Tudor Hole. "And I don't think she was a she, either!"

An hour or so later, I caught up with BJ in his room. He offered me some *foie gras*.

"Brilliant!" he wheezed, and sat there clapping his hands to applaud me. "Worth every penny!"

I nodded my acknowledgement. "So where did you get him?"

"Oh – you know –"

I let it pass at that. As in Westminster, we none of us need to know the details of how all these sordid strings have come to be pulled.

"Just one more thing, BJ," I said. "You didn't by any chance happen to avail yourself of Mandy's charms?"

"Why – why you've got a bloody nerve!" he spluttered. "Why ever … How… I've got Katy for that sort of thing, and jolly good she is too! What a squalid little mind you have that in that devious head of yours."

"How rude of me." I wiped at the crumbs on my lip with a napkin. "I'm most terribly sorry."

"So you should be, you saucy monkey!" The old boy was so outraged, he'd gone quite red in the face.

"It's just that… well, I couldn't help but notice that your flies are still undone…"

Know what the brute did next? Went straight onto the attack: typical politician. "Well if we're going down *that* route," said BJ, "then why did we have to hire Mandy at all? Surprised you didn't get underneath the table and service them all yourself!"

"You're hurting!" I laughed in his face.

"I mean – you must have had at least half of the Library already. Surely you must be trying for the full box set?"

"What!" This time he'd gone too far. Of course, it's perfectly fair to make jokes about people's sexuality and I could take a joke as well as the next boy. But this one – it wasn't even a low blow; it was an outrageous boot to the groin. "That is very hurtful!"

BJ crowed with laughter. "That's *exactly* what Crippsy said when he heard you'd taken up with Taity!"

Chapter 31

And so we come to the final act, that moment in my life when, through the most incredible concatenation of circumstances, I became a diehard Conservative.

What I have endeavoured to do in my little book is show you some of the signposts along the way. On their own, they were each of them fairly insignificant. But added all together, they were like the ingredients of a recipe, all of them combining, intermingling, to create the richest fruitcake imaginable. (Perhaps calling myself a fruitcake is not the *best* available metaphor. Maybe a hot soufflé? A very complex textured blancmange? A plate of deep-fried scampi – how can you resist me?)

I sometimes wonder: was it my destiny? Was I always fated to lead the Tories? Or is it just happenstance – and if one single ingredient had been missing from my life, from that first Library Tan through to that last bizarre session with old Nanny Irish, then perhaps none of it would have gelled together in quite the extraordinary way that it did?

One thing that I do know is that without BJ, none of it would have happened. Eventually, I suppose, I might have become a Tory. But I very much doubt that I would ever have had the chutzpah to run for the Tory leadership after only four years as an MP. It's amazing to think it: but for my relationship with BJ,

I'd probably not even be in Westminster. Most likely, I'd be some smoothy-chops in the City, with more money and less work; maybe I'd even have acquired a mistress by now. Swings and roundabouts – although there are fewer opportunities for extra-curricular shagging in the City, the bankers are not quite such good fodder for the tabloids.

Funny, isn't it, how my little musings always eventually revert back to sex? Sam, are you hearing me out there? Enough of that, though – for we have a story to tell. And what a crackling finale I have for you!

The picture collection of the masters' daughters was going well. Loram and Whitby, once they'd been convinced of the greater glory of our crusade, set to with a will; Whitby once spent almost the entire night hanging from a lamp-post, just so that he could snap an 18-year-old at her morning ablutions.

But, though we had many titillating photos, it has to be said that we still lacked a jewel for our crown – the picture of pictures, the snatch of snatches, that would put all other photos to shame.

There was only one girl, really, who was going to fit the bill: Patricia. Her looks, it went without saying, were without equal. But further to that, she lived in the Headman's apartments in the Cloisters, and even getting a peep into her bedroom was going to provide just the sort of tasty challenge that I relished.

Loram had shown himself up for the half-pint bottler he palpably was: "I just don't think it can be done, Prince," he said to me. "It's too difficult – too dangerous. And if they catch you. Well …"

Well, indeed. It has to be said that although parading myself down the Walk of Shame didn't sound great, I was more worried about Nanny Irish. If they kicked me out of Eton, there was every chance that next stop she'd be sending me to join the

Pope's Castrati choir.

Still, the legend of *The Black Prince* was not quite yet secure. Further to that, I was morally obliged to adhere to The Dame's dictum of 'getting it while it's hot'. And, perhaps overshadowing all else, I didn't half fancy having a peep at Patricia in the nuddy. Phwooagh! Just the thought of her topless in those mud-bespattered britches, having at me with her riding crop... even now, it makes me come over all faint.

Such a tricksy circle to square. On the one hand intent on getting those pictures of Patricia ... on the other, trying to deter the good Nanny Irish from attacking my nether regions with a pair of rusty shears.

I'd just have to make sure I didn't get caught.

The day I'd picked for getting the pictures was a Thursday, a few days before the end of the summer half. I'd picked it because BJ had already informed me that Patricia would be off riding that afternoon. Though how on earth he knew, I have no idea. And when I learned that Maguire was going to be out for the evening, I knew that Lady Luck was going to be with me that night.

It was about 7pm, and I was just pulling on the elite uniform of the Steeplejacks: my black turtle-neck. I had further added to it the personal emblem of *The Black Prince*, a white *Fleur de Lys*, embroidered onto the left breast.

BJ knocked on the door; I think it was probably the last time that he visited me in my room.

"Phew!" he gagged, clutching his nose. "Can't you do anything about that terrible pong?"

"No I cannot!" I said testily. I'd tried everything to get rid of the stench from my Queen's Eyot excesses, but the smell seemed engrimed into the very fabric of the carpet.

He gaped at me as I smoothed the wrinkles from my turtle-neck. "But... but you're not coming tonight? It's the Political Society! It's my last meeting as President! It's going to be the biggest show we've ever had. We've –"

"The Political Society?" I can still remember the complete disdain with which I spat out those words. "Do you have any idea quite how tedious that lot are? They're just a load of self-satisfied dullards who don't ever, ever know when to shut up!"

How prescient was that, eh? And to think that I'd never even met bloody John Bercow!

"Heath was pretty bad, I must admit," said BJ. "But this time it's the Prime Minister!"

"And she's likely to be any better than an ex-Prime Minister?"

"Exactly! This is real power! Just think on it!" He was almost clapping his hands with excitement. "The Prime Minister herself! In person! We've got the Thatch! We've got the Thatcher!"

"Thatcher?" I said. My voice dripped with contempt. "Thatcher-Schmatcher."

"OK – well, forget Thatcher then. What about doing it for me?" He'd started attacking his hair, grabbing a great hunk with his right hand and tugging away as if he were trying to pull it out at the roots. "You'd really be helping me out. I need my batman!"

"Your batman?" I said. "Dress up in that white monkey jacket? Dance attendance at your shoulder? Possibly – just possibly – I've got better things to do with my time."

"It's a noble job!" he exhorted, both hands now yanking away at his blonde mop. "You'd be doing me a favour! We're pals! You're my buddy! It'll be fun!"

I slung the camera and the Big Tom lens over my shoulder. And, I like to think, I acquitted myself very well there.

Sometimes relationships evolve and reach a natural hiatus. When this happens, it's important to end things on the right note – so that even when you're sacking your most trusted Lieutenant, it must be done with a firm handshake and a warm pat to the back. "BJ, it *has* been a lot of fun," I said, stretching out my hand. "I'd like to thank you for everything you've done to help the cause. But it's time to move on. *We* need to move on. I think we need some breathing space."

"Please," he said, clasping my hand. "Just one more time? For me?"

But you know what they say, and this holds good just as much for PMs as it does for F-tits taking formal leave of their fag-masters: always leave the bastards wanting more.

I slid down the rope and for a moment hung there at the window. And if there's nothing left to say – then don't say anything. A smile and a flutter of my fingers and I was gone.

Getting on top of the Cloisters was no cake-walk; although the shadows were long, it wasn't even yet dusk. It meant I had to be much more circumspect when I was prowling around the school. I spent 30 minutes foraging through various bits of undergrowth before I ended up round by the Headman's garden. It was so manicured it looked like one of the gardeners had been at it with a pair of nail scissors.

I worked my way through the herbaceous border and up to the side of the building, where I was pinning my hopes on an old wisteria that stretched right to the roof-tops. I knew it was risky – but it was going to be risky, whichever way I tried to climb up onto the Cloisters' roof. I swung up onto the first branch and, with a song in my heart, swarmed up the side of the building.

Patricia! The Steeplejacks wouldn't be able to believe their cotton-picking eyes! About half way up, I was passing a first-floor window, when I heard the sounds of a general mêlée going on inside: the Headman doubtless having fun with his chums, and good luck to the lot of them.

I climbed up onto the roof and over to the inner side of the Cloisters. As I'd already observed, the topmost walls of the courtyard were castellated, which provided a number of convenient loopholes for me to rest my Big Tom.

I scuttled round to the other side of the Cloisters, so that I was now looking direct in through the Headman's apartments. But where, oh where, was my pretty one? I was worried that Patricia's room might be overlooking the garden, in which case I'd probably have to abseil down and dangle my leering head right next to the window-pane. As it was, though, after just a quick perusal of the rooms on offer, I spotted Patricia's: hunting stuff chucked into a fireplace and a blizzard of multi-coloured rosettes above it. What is it with those rosettes? Is it part of the laws of show-jumping that every single rosette has to go on display?

Of slight concern was that Patricia had a corner room and I couldn't see her bathroom. The best angle was diagonally down across the full length of the courtyard and, if I really pushed it with the Big Tom, I could just about get a glimpse of her bed.

My preparations made, there was now nothing for me to do but wait, and I did that with all the diligence of a big-game hunter. There was almost a touch of fairy-dust about that magical night, as if I had been sprinkled with the most intoxicating euphoria. I marvelled at that purpling sunset – oh, if only Patricia knew the treat that I had in store for her!

I first spotted her when she was trotting along the first floor corridor – white britches, check; black velvet jacket, check; riding crop – yep, the little minx had that with her too! I was in a fever of excitement as I brought my Big Tom up to the ready.

A matter of seconds later and she was into her room – whip and riding hat tossed into the fireplace and she flung her jacket onto the bed. As I stared through the lense, I was quivering with excitement. This was it! This was it! She was going to do it! And then... she disappeared. Must have gone to the bathroom to freshen herself up.

The hussy kept me waiting for ages, and after about five minutes my left arm was trembling. The angle into Patricia's room was so fine that I was having to lean out over the Cloisters while my feet were braced against the stonework. But there was nothing to lean the Big Tom on so I was having to support the whole of that massive lens with my left hand. It was murder. After a while, I could only hold the lens up for a few seconds at a time – and for the rest of it, I had to squint into Patricia's room and pray that I didn't miss my moment.

She'd been gone at least 10 minutes. I tried propping the lens against one of the castellations, but the angle was hopeless and I could only see Patricia's door. So there I was, cursing away to myself as I tried to massage some life back into my left arm, when I observed a little flurry of action in her room. The door had opened; someone else had gone in.

I had that Big Tom up to my beady little eye in a trice, to see... to see... to see BJ. BJ! Advancing across the room and Patricia leaping into his arms. She'd hit him so hard that he'd been knocked to the floor and there they were writhing around in the fireplace amid the crops and the boots, and – oh sweet Jesus! – I hadn't even noticed this before but she was only wearing bra, britches and a riding hat. BJ! The bastard!

These weren't the sort of pictures that I wanted for the Steeplejacks. Not at all! What I'd wanted was just, you know, a photo of Patricia coming out of the shower, her towel falls to the floor, she stoops to pick it up – something tasteful, something timeless. And now this! This! Patricia practically making the beast with two backs with BJ – oh, no, no, no! This was not the sort of photograph that was ever meant to adorn the hallowed walls of the Steeplejacks' lair.

Still, I was making the best of a bad job, my little trigger finger stabbing away as the film trickled through the camera. It was difficult, trying to keep my feet braced, and I nearly managed to upend myself completely. But, with all the fortitude of a veteran paparazzo, I stuck with the job.

By now, the pair of them were standing up, eating each other's faces off as they slammed against a wardrobe. BJ – I just couldn't believe the bastard was doing this to me! – was undressing himself one-handed though I was pleased to see that he was having big problems with his waistcoat buttons. Patricia, meanwhile, was pawing away like a hunter at the start of the Grand National. Metaphorically, that is – don't you just find it's this sort of incidental detail that can really bring a scene to life?

It's difficult to describe the blur of thoughts kaleidoscoping through my mind – a little enthralled, perhaps, at the sight of Patricia; and a part of me, too, was just the professional Steeplejack, meticulously recording what was occurring in her bedroom; but what I chiefly felt was shock that I had been let down quite so badly by my own old friend BJ. It wasn't that I was hurt by the sight of Patricia grappling like a Farrier Sergeant with BJ. It was just, I don't know... I guess I was just a little disappointed. Was it too much – too much? – to ask for him to have kept his grimy hands to himself that evening?

It wasn't just my left arm that was aching now but both legs. I'd got cramp in my feet from where they'd been hooked round the crenellations, and it was so bad that I had to leave my post.

I was stamping on the ground, pummelling my calves as I tried to restore a bit of circulation. I might have been missing the best stuff of the night, but it couldn't be helped.

I was away two minutes – that's all it took. And when I next slipped into my position, feeling that dull throb in my left arm, I saw immediately that the dynamics had changed markedly. They'd moved to the bed but, in order to even get a sighting, I was having to lean out like a limbo dancer.

Can you imagine it? Leaning out over the Cloisters, arms and stomach muscles trembling from fatigue, and suddenly BJ hoves into view with Patricia. They're both topless and, as far as I can make out, he's down to his boxers.

But what's this? What's this? For a moment my mind goes blank: it cannot compute. For there are not two pairs of legs on the bed, but *three!* The bastard had inveigled somebody else into his depraved couplings – just how the hell had he managed that? The lens was so heavy in my hands that the frame was wobbling all over the place. I've got my eyes glued to the camera, but the bedroom hoves in and out of view like a ship at sea. Who the devil has he got in there with him? That's what I want to know, for so far all I'd managed to see were two long legs in stockings entwined round BJ's midriff. Patricia, meanwhile, had climbed on top of him and seemed to be clawing his back.

Who was she? Who could it be? I was cursing for sheer exasperation. And then… and then she suddenly came into view, clear as anything, her face stretching upwards as she yearns for BJ's kiss. It's… it's… Katy!

Oh my sweet Katy, that he has brought you to this! That he has so defiled and abused your frail body that now he has lured you into the bedroom of Patricia, the Headman's daughter. Sweat stinging at my eyes as I take picture after picture. Now they're both underneath him, the minxes, in some hideous BJ-love-sandwich, and all I can do is goggle at them through my swaying lens as all three of them writhe over each other like feasting panthers.

Then: perhaps one of the most squalid, tawdry incidents that I have ever had the misfortune to witness. BJ on his back, cuddling in between the two of those houris, and they're slipping down his plump naked torso, each of them kissing his neck, his nipples, lower and lower they go.

I can't believe you're doing this, Katy, my Katy – you don't have to demean yourself in such an awful manner, and yet, and yet, pretending all the while that you're absolutely *loving* it… BJ, head and shoulders propped up on a satin bolster, is admiring the disgusting floor-show that's taking place on his chest, and… looks out of the window. Looks out of the window, as if staring straight at me and – his face grinning the most ghastly smile, he stretches out his arms to give me a double thumbs-up.

My arms, my legs, my whole body jerks in revulsion. The Big Tom tumbles out of my arms, the weight of the lens snaps at my neck, and the next moment my feet are scrabbling for a purchase on the stonework; I can feel myself cartwheeling backwards into the abyss. A shrill, terrified squeak of terror, my feet are looping over my head and I'm clawing at thin air.

Still seems like quite a long way to becoming a Tory, don't it now?

Chapter 32

Can't stop! No time for further interesting musings about sex, the machinations of Westminster, or even what it was that attracted me to Sam in the first place…

You may not have realised it, but… this story is reaching something of a crescendo!

I was in freefall off the top deck of the Cloisters and I can tell you now that if you hit the deck from that height, the only thing you're going to be needing is a harp.

I was twisting in the air like a cat, saw some windows flash past my face and snatched at the outer sill. The Big Tom lens smacked into my head and a moment later I thumped into the side of the building. It seemed to rattle every bone in my body. But with so much adrenalin scorching through my system I didn't feel a thing.

Hanging from the window-sill by my very fingertips, I took a quick peek at the drop. Perhaps it was the lowering darkness, but it still seemed massive – a leg-breaker at the very least. I lifted some fingers and started working them along the edge of the window, but of course it was shut tight. Think and think fast! Well, seeing as I only had one option, I had to get on with it.

Holding on with just my left hand, I punched my fist through the window. A few seconds to knock away the worst of the jagged shards, and my arm was through, scrabbling to find the handle. A twist and a turn – please God don't say they've double-locked it – but no, they haven't; the sheer relief as the window swings inwards. Once more unto the breach, dear friends, once more, and sucking the air deep into my lungs, I heave upwards and haul myself through the window. A close shave, Davie, I told myself, but I think you might have got away with it.

I was in some sort of corridor on the top floor. A few seconds to catch my breath, sling the camera properly over my back. I closed the window, drew the curtains to try and hide the broken glass, and started to check myself for injuries. Bit of a graze on my face, I could feel that, and my hands looked okay. But there was a deep throb in my forearm and when I pulled back the sleeve to examine it closely, I could see a large shard of glass embedded deep into the flesh. It wasn't painful as yet, but I was going to have to act quickly.

I tore off some strips from the sheeting at the back of the curtain and tied them into a tourniquet, which I slipped onto my arm. My fingers couldn't get a purchase on the glass so I ended up plucking it out with my teeth. As soon as the glass was out, the blood was coming thick and fast. I wrapped the sheeting around the gaping hole, tugging it tight, before rolling down my sleeve.

It would have to suffice – because I'd just heard voices coming from the far end of the corridor. "Rogue Boy! Rogue Boy! Stop him!" The Watch were after me!

Instantly I'm off in the other direction, camera clumping against my back as I tear down the corridor. I become aware of the very slight problem that I don't know where I am. Another bawling voice from ahead of me, some stairs off to the right, and I'm down them like a ferret down a hole. One flight, two flights, and I saw a place I thought as good as any to make my exit. Down a blue corridor – terribly difficult, you know, to run flat out and yet in total silence. I glimpsed into a room, a load of people there, but I'm past them in the twinkling of an eye.

I can't remember the actual sequence now. A door at the end of the corridor, scrabbling for the handle – open it, soundlessly shut it behind me. Can I hear feet drumming on the stairs? Into a room, another room, and, oh you little beauty, this looks very much to me like I'm in the College Library – that was the elite Library, by the way, where they kept all the good stuff. I know you just love these little details.

Into the home stretch, just one more hurdle to go, only just as I'm about to make good my escape, a door opens – only it's the bloody door that I had every intention of bolting out of and that's really cooked my goose. I sheer off to the side, dash down an aisle of dusty old tomes – you know, along with the *Gutenberg Bible* I think they might have a few of Shakespeare's First Folios in there, too – and now I'm leaning against the back of the aisle, panting like a dog as I try to get my breath back.

Breathe deep, breathe easy; relax – calm down. A flicker overhead and from out of the darkness, there is light – they're turning all the lights on. Now this one, I thought… this one's going to be difficult.

I probably had about a minute – tops. First I took off my camera with its lusty Big Tom lens, checked the settings, primed it. I licked my hands to sleek back my hair as best I could. A last check of my turtle-neck: I smoothed out the wrinkles and brushed off the worst of the glass chippings. And then I slung my camera round my neck and jauntily walked out into the full glare of the College Library.

I'd been hoping that, with a little luck on my side, I'd be able to tip-toe straight out. Once I was through that door, I'd be off like a greased pig.

I think I'd walked about ten yards when I had the complete shock of my life: some mad man leapt out from behind a bookcase, grabbed me by the shoulder and triumphantly screamed, "Gotcha!"

I almost peed my pants! Again! And even before I turned to face my captor, this horrid suspicion was flickering through my mind.

"Hooo-hooo-hooo!" 'Twas Mr Maguire, my dear old Tutor, come to College Library to taunt me with his favourite catchphrase, and wearing that night, as I remember, a rumpled brown corduroy suit with an extra bit of polish on his bald pate for luck

"Hooo-hooo-hooo!" he said, smiling this full broad smile – and I could tell from the glint in his eyes that, truly, this was a man whose cup runneth over. "Henchman!" he called. "See here! I have him. I have the boy twixt my fingertips!"

So there we stood, me hangdog in the middle of the Library, Maguire in front of me nodding and nodding his head. Henchman appeared from one of the aisles.

"See, my dear Henchman, see!" said Maguire, as he began to stalk about me. "I have him! And this time he will not escape me!" With that, he started to shuffle about me like a lilting Flamenco dancer, his feet stamping and his hands clapping cha-cha-cha in the air as his scrawny body limboed from side to side. "And tomorrow," Cha-cha-cha! "We shall be seeing," Cha-cha-cha! "The back!" Cha-cha-cha! "Of young!" Cha-cha-cha! "Master!" Cha-cha-cha! "Cameron!" (Cha-cha-cha.)

Mad – quite mad. That's what happens if you've been at Eton too long. Spend more than 30 years there and they could probably cart you straight off to the funny farm without even having to take in the retirement home. [Hi Nick! How am I doing?]

Henchman walked up, surveying me with cool insolence. "Very good, Sir. Thought I'd lost him on the Blue Corridor."

"But justice was triumphant, just as it always will be! And the beauty of it, Henchman? The sheer monumental beauty of it is that this time – *this time!* – there shall be no wriggling off the hook! He can lie through his glittering teeth, but it will make no odds! How may I expel him – let me count the ways!"

All I could do was stand there and soak it up. I tried to get a word in edgeways – "Please, Sir" – but Maguire had worked up a rare old head of steam.

"Here he is, in the College Library after lock-up! And without permission. He is not wearing any recognised school uniform. He has a large camera round his neck, doubtless with which he has taken innumerable lewd pictures. He has a graze on his face and I do not doubt that it was he who was banging around on the roof of the Cloisters before smashing a window." And here, Maguire's voice, rose up to that of a piping tenor. "We have him, my dear Henchman! We have him by the very nose!"

Henchman, well pleased with himself, had now stuck his thumbs into the armpits of his waistcoat, and was smoothly drumming his long fingers onto his chest.

"Oh please, Sir!" I said. "Please may I say one thing?"

Maguire raised an eyebrow. "Say it!" he hissed. "Say it! Your confession, if you please, Master Cameron!"

"It was just… I'd got something important to say to Henchman …"

"Yes, boy?" said Maguire. "To declare your guilt?"

"What I wanted to ask Henchman was… however did you come by that revolting scar on your neck? I'd heard that it was a duelling scar, though it does seem much too ugly for that…"

Henchman went white and that livid six-inch scar – like something off Frankenstein's monster, it was – pulsed scarlet. If he'd had the chance, he'd have clubbed me on the spot. "Why you –"

He was physically restrained by Maguire – and that, I'm afraid, was the last time I ever heard Henchman speak on the matter of his scar. However… seeing as it's such a great story, I'll give you all the gory details. Henchman, it was said, came by the scar when he was playing the Wall Game, a killingly dull rugby-style game that is played next to a wall. The previous year Henchman had got stuck at the bottom of a scrum by the wall. Bodies pile on top of him; and somehow his head gets trapped in a hole in the wall. The scrum moves, Henchman's torso moves with it; but his head remains stuck in the hole in the wall. Unfortunately it only broke his neck – because my life would have been a sight more pleasant if it had killed him.

Where were we?

Oh yes! Maguire, triumphant! Hooo-hooo-hooo!

"Calm down, dear Henchman," said Maguire. "There is no need for violence. For tomorrow, we shall be waving this boy farewell, *adieu, auf wiedersehen*, goodbye –"

"Please, Sir," I said. "It's not like that –"

"Hush now!" rapped Maguire. "The only service that you can now do yourself is to make full and frank confession. What was it that you were doing on the Cloisters? Was it…" A light bulb exploded in his head. "I have it!" he shrieked. "It was Patricia! The Headman's daughter! You were up on the Cloisters' roof taking pictures of her as she changed for dinner. Oh, but are you not the perfect wretch. Confess! Now! I wish to hear it from your own lips!"

I was reeling, had fallen to my knees, hands clutched out in front of me. "Please, Sir!" I called. Heartfelt, it was. Suddenly, an image had popped into my mind of old Nanny Irish and her bull-whip. "Please, Sir! It wasn't like that!"

"He lies and lies again!" screeched Maguire, as he gave me a dainty little poke on the backside. "Every time you open your mouth, another lie pops out! But now you will tell the truth. Confess! Confess all to Father Tam and you will be shriven of all your many sins!"

Ohh – how tempting it seemed, just to say those three simple words – "I did it!" – if only to put an end to Maguire's insane shouting. And, after all, what did it matter anyway if I were thrown out of Eton? I mean I was probably going to lose my nuts, but at that moment it just seemed that everything was against me. I could genuinely see no way out.

I was on the very cusp of giving Maguire the words that he so longed to hear; they had all but formed on my lips. And then, like a magical whisper from far across the sea, I heard BJ's soft voice as he muttered to me those three sacred words: "Deny, Deny, Deny."

"No, it wasn't me," I pleaded in a small plaintive voice. "I'm innocent."

"Liar!" spat Maguire. "Confess! Now!"

"'Twas not me," was all I could whisper, for I could feel my energy ebbing into the floor; I had nothing left to give. "'Twas not me."

"Confess! Confess to Father Tam!" Maguire shrieking at the very top of his voice as he stood over me.

I was on the very point of collapse, could take no more of the mad-man. But: "'Twas not me."

From far off, I could hear a muttering by the Library door. The muttering grew to a grumbling, the noise came closer and closer, and there I was on my knees, couldn't make out what it is I was seeing, but suddenly ...

Maguire and Henchman were both moved aside. In their stead stood the most wondrous sight that I have ever beheld in all my life – for in that single moment, I truly believed that the Holy Trinity and the Virgin Mary had come down from heaven to visit me.

Tears sprang to my eyes at what I can only describe as the first, the only, numinous experience of my life. In that one moment, I felt that I had been touched by the very hand of God. For there, standing above me, was Margaret Thatcher herself, a dignified yet concerned smile on her face. And surrounding her – oh, who indeed can ever fathom the mysterious workings of the Lord? – was the most sacred Trinity that I have ever laid eyes on. To the left was Patricia, regal and haughty in her black velvet jacket; to the right was my Katy, lip-lickingly lecherous in black dress and white ruffle shirt; and in the centre was the untouchable, unknowable one herself – my besuited Xanthe.

I gazed on those beauties with such adoration in my heart, for it seemed that they had been sent from very heaven itself to save me.

Maguire was babbling in the background. "On the rooftops!" he screeched. "Taking saucy pictures! Expelled by tomorrow!"

Then who should step forward looking like Christ incarnate in a tailcoat, but BJ. He lifted me to my feet and plucked a shard of glass from my collar. "It's quite all right, Sir," he said. He spoke with all the cool detachment of Hercule Poirot as he comes to his moment of truth.

"David is with me. He is the official photographer for the Eton Political Society. We believed that having the Prime Minister at Eton was... worthy of record."

"But... but!" wailed Maguire. "What's he doing out of

school uniform? Why's he wearing this, this revolting black turtle-neck?"

"Ah that, yes, I can explain all," said BJ, though I could see that beneath the veneer, his mind was working feverishly. "I suggested this might be the correct uniform for our official photographer. It is very of the moment – neither David Bailey nor Lord Lichfield are ever seen without a turtle-neck."

"All right then!" screeched Maguire, "All right then! Now tell me! Why, why was this boy malingering in the College Library after hours? Why?"

"What a very good point, Sir," said BJ, turning to beam at Mrs Thatcher. "We thought that the College Library might be a fitting setting for the Prime Minister's official portrait!"

"Gaaaah!" screeched Maguire. "I'm melting! I'm melting!" (Actually, he didn't quite come out with that last bit, but he did happen to sound exactly like the mad old witch from the *Wizard of Oz* and, at such a dramatic point in my story, I do think that I may be allowed some poetic licence.)

And that, dear reader, is how I lived to tell my tale at Eton; how I became a leading luminary in the school's Political Society; and how, in one fell swoop, I became the most loyal and devoted Tory that ever walked this earth.

Some people, when they hear my tale, think that it was Thatcher herself that I fell in love with, but what utter tosh! Although Thatcher and the Conservatives would undoubtedly come to be the beneficiaries of my new-born political zeal, it had nothing at all to do with the PM. Rather it was those three shining angels behind her and, as I look back on them now, they stand like triple beacons in the night. For whenever I am all at sea, unmasted and unmanned, I only have to stare off into the horizon and there they still stand in front of me – my Patricia; my Katy; and my cool, smouldering Xanthe.

Perhaps – and I just know you were dying to ask – *that* is what first attracted me to Samantha. She is this ineffable mix of my three beacons – the regal, the lascivious and the ever-unfathomable.

But of course I'm not quite yet done! You've hung in so long that I feel you deserve a little encore; I have prepared one specially.

It's time that I gave Margaret Thatcher her due, for she did play a small but crucial role in my evolution as a politician.

In the College Library, after Maguire and Henchman had been sent packing, I set about my business as the official photographer of the Eton Political Society. And with that huge Big Tom lens, it was an absolute nightmare. It was the only lens I had, so the only way I could carry it off was to stick Thatcher on a chair and hose her down from the full length of a cricket pitch. "Very *avant garde*," observed BJ.

It all passed without incident, BJ clucking about the PM and Xanthe lingering in the background. Do you know, I never once heard her speak? Not once. I suppose it's probably for the best. Patricia and Katy had slunk off somewhere between bookcases, doubtless thirsting to increase their knowledge of all things Sapphic. As for Thatcher, she was just sitting on the chair and giving me the flintiest eye I'd ever seen. Put a bull-whip in her hand and she'd have given Nanny Irish a run for her money.

Finally we were done; the pictures were probably going to be blurry as hell, but what did I care?

BJ waved me over. "Well done, David!" he said. "As usual, you have *excelled* yourself!"

I bowed to Thatcher and made a suitably grovelling obeisance.

"Thank you, Prime Minister," I said. "You have made this the happiest day of my life."

BJ rolled his eyes at that, but the PM, in her usual blue tailored suit, just stared at me.

"I know you," she said. Her face, body, completely motionless. She reeked of power. "You came to the House of Commons. I've never seen a boy so absorbed by politics."

"Thank you, Ma'am," I said meekly. "It is my passion."

Those basilisk eyes never once left my face. "Do you want to be an MP?"

"Well, I –" My answer hung in the air.

A little smile played on her lips. "Good luck," she said. "Though in 20 years' time you may find your Eton education hanging about your neck like a millstone."

"They don't like Eton?"

"Hate it," she said in that rather strangulated voice of hers. "You must do something to tone it down. Your name, for instance? Why not…" And here, I can still remember that delicious quiver as the wheel of my destiny began to turn. "Why not… Dave?"

BJ sniffed and nodded sharply at me – though for all his concern, Thatcher might as well have suggested I call myself Beelzebub.

Thatcher drummed her fingers lightly on the chair and toddled off to admire some of the fusty manuscripts.

"Well, you heard the old broad," BJ said, as he slipped his arm through mine. "She gets terribly baity if you ignore her advice."

"Dave?" I turned the new name over in my mind. "I quite like it. I believe it has the touch of the common people." Arm-in-arm, we strolled sedately together through the College Library. And at that moment in the movie of my life, I think it might be appropriate to switch on the arc lamps and overlay the soundtrack with the choirs of angels – for it is now time for me to look reverentially up into the Messianic face of the great Thatch herself, as I utter the immortal words, "Call me... Call me Dave!"

Acknowledgements

My thanks to Margot, my wife, to Tim Bremner and to Robert Lagneau. I'd also like to thank William Loram, who first conceived this little project. Lastly, my thanks to two Old Etonians – Richard Sweet K.S. and Alex Renton – who reminded me of some of the more succulent details of Eton life.

Though for the sake of veracity, I should perhaps add that Renton is not technically an Old Etonian: he was expelled from Eton in 1980 for running off to Paris with the prettiest boy in the school.

Renton, I well know, has been dogged by memories of not just being thrashed by Michael McCrum, but also being paraded on Eton's legendary Walk of Shame. I can only hope that this mention in the Acknowledgements helps, in some very small way, to ease his shame.